Poison & Power

GOLDENHEART MYSTERIES BOOK 1

M. PATRICK DUGGAN

I0619435

Copyright © 2020 M. Patrick Duggan
All rights reserved.
ISBN: 9780578706351

Edited by Monique Snyman
Cover Design by Mikki Noble – Paracoze Designs

MPATRICKDUGGAN.NET
If you enjoy reading this novel, please go to the author's website and sign up for the mailing list

"This is an evening of wonders, indeed!"
--Jane Austen, *Pride and Prejudice*

CONTENTS

CHAPTER 1: PICNIC.

"I am not keen on that sky," Bea said. Her golden ringlets of hair danced around in the breeze. "What if it rains? What if we chose the wrong outfits?" She looked suspiciously at the sky as if the clouds were wild animals about to pounce.

"It is but a whiff of cumulus," Georgia answered, smiling at her old friend. "Be confident. Your dress is quite lovely, your bonnet is well-chosen, and you look spectacular in the lilac hues of the season. You are wearing precisely the correct number of buckles and bows. Trust yourself."

Bea was usually a cool head in any room and possessed the quickest wit. Still, Georgia could not recall a time when her friend had appeared so agitated. They were both trained in the way of the Cymbre Order for Finishing. The school was legendary, but very few ever completed their rigorous studies. One outcome of a solid finishing was the ability to appear serene and carefree, no matter the situation. The primary impact was, of course, the ability to read, reason, and remember. The Three Rs were rote for any young lady of the right family and station. Georgia could see Bea's situation weighing on her.

"Are we losing an R?" Georgia asked.

"We lost the reason some time ago."

Georgia opted for a new tactic. "Enjoy the hike. Along the way, see if Ollie or Manx is appropriate and appealing. They both have charming qualities."

"By that, you mean they have nearly identical qualities as they are twins. But it is easy for you to say relax, methinks," Bea countered. "You are not required to find a suitable husband on an unreasonable deadline."

Georgia was in an unusual station for a lady. While she was just as single as Bea, she held specific titles, expectations, and land, which placed her beyond all standard expectations.

"Stay on topic. You still have a year," Georgia chided. "That is hardly unreasonable."

"I have already lost a whole morning hiking up this horrid mountain," Bea muttered. "And those boys are paying absolutely no attention to me. They do seem taken with you, though."

"Well, I am quite glamorous," Georgia said.

"You are tall and never appear to tire out," Bea said, smirking.

There was some truth to that. Georgia had immense stamina did not tend to tire quickly and was unusually fit for a lady. Everyone in her family shared that trait. Old Nan used to jest that the Goldenhearts never lacked energy but also had no common sense.

"What do you suppose they think of me?" Bea asked.

"I imagine they think you are bitter and tired," Georgia said, drolly taking the bait.

Ever since school, Bea and Georgia had tried to make the other laugh by saying outrageous things in polite company. The trick was to make sure the polite company never caught on. The first to laugh was the loser.

Bea chuckled. "And I am not at all ladylike."

"Best days are behind you."

"Cajoling and wheedling."

Georgia laughed. "Don't forget demanding, and you don't smile enough. How will a sour little thing like you ever find a husband?"

"Thankfully, my family is so well-connected," Bea said.

Bea was the fifth daughter of the 7th Baronet of Irvingdale. Despite having a respected name, noble blood, enviable social contacts, and a modest estate, there was no great wealth. She had four older sisters, all successfully married off, but no brothers. Her late father attempted to provide dowries for all of his daughters. Still, even the best-laid plans were subject to the vagaries of reality. The family used what capital it had on the previous marriages, including land and title. For her part, Bea could offer a few family heirlooms, a very modest monthly stipend from a distant aunt, and the option to live in a tiny cottage at the far end of her family estate. She had already moved into the cottage but still took her meals in the main house. As the youngest of such a high-born family, by tradition, Bea had a few options—find a husband, live out her days in the cottage as a spinster and be a burden to her family, go into service as a lady-in-waiting, or become a Cymbre teacher. Bea's brothers-in-law were against spinsterhood. They hadn't gone to the trouble of marrying into the family simply to see it decline. Lord Wickham, who inherited her father's title, was quite adamant if she couldn't find a husband, she would have to go away. She could become a Cymbre teacher if she gave up her name, or serve one of the great families as a lady-in-waiting. Bea wanted to marry, though.

"I cannot become a Cymbre teacher," Bea whispered, looking small and frightened.

"Of course you can," Georgia said. "Honestly, how bad would that be? Cymbre teachers can have many things other women cannot: livelihood and property. Independence."

Bea made a rude noise. "I care not for having things if

it means being alone for the rest of my days. Give me a darling estate and a loyal husband of a suitable family. I would be content to run his house, and spawn a brood of beautiful children."

"Bake his bread and clean the nappies?"

"I would supervise."

"Go shopping with his credit." Georgia grinned.

"I would never say such a thing aloud. It is better to imply." Bea laughed. Then she went quiet again.

"You could always marry down a bit."

"Isn't that why we are here?" Bea stared at the sky again.

Georgia was determined to see her oldest and dearest friend as happy as possible.

Unlike Bea, Georgia had just come into her inheritance, which turned out to be more impressive than expected. She received a lofty title and a small fortune. No longer was she Miss Georgia Goldenheart, ward of her beloved late Uncle Raymond—who had passed away the previous winter. As the sole heir, Georgia now lived in a sprawling manor house in the old city called Wending Way and had enough income to keep her in comfort for the rest of her days. She also held the impressive peer title of Duchess Goldenheart and owned a magical sword passed down through twenty generations.

She didn't know any other duchesses, so it was challenging to say if magical swords were the norm.

"Lady Georgia, you are depriving yourself of the view," Ollie Hampton said, marching up the trail behind them.

Like his twin brother, Ollie was a broad-shouldered fellow with dark hair, blue eyes, somewhat pale skin, and a quick smile. Even if he wasn't of noble or even gentle birth, he was from a family of note. Combine that with his countenance, and he would be an excellent prospect for anyone.

Georgia wondered how either of the twins had gone this long without a serious female suitor. With a broad gesture, he took in the city below and the great Mountain of the Tree above. Following Ollie was his brother Manx, their father, Mr. Hampton, and finally, the house servant Mr. Bailey, who carried picnic supplies.

Ollie's observation about them not appreciating the view was accurate. Georgia and Bea had been talking while facing the steep side of the hill, and neither had looked around.

Georgia turned to smile and gazed out through the cedars above the sprawling city of Oradale. Just below the path where she walked, enormous houses with dark slate roofs ringed the mountainside. These houses were the estates of the newly wealthy. Each home was impressive, but without land and some so close to their neighbors, one could see in the windows. The community was called Broom Lane, after the main roadway nearby. The residents were mostly wealthy merchants who wanted a bit of luxury without getting too far out of the city.

Beyond Broom Lane, the city leveled out into two residential districts—West Plumsbury and East Nova. West Plumsbury was the more upscale area to live if one was a commoner. From this height, Georgia could only see the rooftops, and they all looked the same. Further south was Commerce Lane, where Georgia's solicitor had an office. Beyond that was the Canal District, Rosewild, and Hartwood, where many of the great families had homes on the water, and the king lived in his palace. Georgia herself lived in that area between Canal and Rosewild. Her home was one of the oldest and most beautiful in the area. Looking over the mountainside, she couldn't see much at that distance.

Bea stood next to her, taking in the view. "I can't remember—where is Irvingdale House in all of this city?" she asked.

Georgia pointed west, and just slightly north to the banks of the Findalon River. "Over there," she said. "It's hard to see through the mist, but I think I can make out the top of the steeple of that little church on the edge of your family's estate."

Bea strained her eyes. "All I see are more clouds," she whispered.

Mr. Hampton wheezed. "How much further is this death-march?" His face was full of sweat. He wasn't a heavy man, and certainly not old enough for this kind of pace to be a problem, yet Mr. Hampton looked, well, weak. He was gaunt, pale, and trembling as if any exertion would be too much. That said, Mr. Hampton was the one to impress.

Georgia's plan was simple: use her plucky wit to get the old codger to like Bea enough to approve a match to either one of his identical sons. His family was wealthy beyond measure—they owned most of the warehouses on the docks. The Hamptons were swimming in filthy lucre and respected in the lowest tier of qualified gentry for someone like Bea. Sadly, they weren't a family of titles. They were what Uncle Raymond would have indelicately referred to as 'new money.' An alliance with Bea's family, even by proxy of a fifth daughter, would lend them access to respectability. With Bea's connections, they could buy titles and more.

"Not much farther, Father," Manx said, paying more attention to Bea than his brother. Not that she would have noticed.

Bea felt that Ollie, being the older of the two by approximately 12 minutes, was more likely to inherit the family fortune.

Georgia wasn't so sure. She suspected the old man would split things between his sons if both showed an aptitude in the business. They were twins, after all, and 'new money' people like the Hamptons embraced the idea of meritocracy.

"We are almost there, and you will see it was not such a trek. In fact, we are only a few hundred yards from our gate."

The gate in question was a backway to House Hampton, sprawling just below the trees.

Georgia glanced down at the house. Uncle Raymond would have called it an eyesore, especially since the Hamptons expanded on the original lot to include the three adjacent properties. She thought it a rather lovely sight, though, and could imagine Bea taking over as mistress of the place one day.

Mr. Hampton shook his head and kept walking.

"What are you ladies discussing?" Ollie asked. "Not the weather, I should hope. It looks to be a fine day."

"Merely the trivial talk of women," Georgia said.

"Somehow, I doubt there is anything trivial about your discourse, Lady Georgia."

"May I ask you a question, Duchess?" Mr. Hampton enquired between wheezes.

"Yes, of course, sir," Georgia said. She trailed back in the line to match her step to that of the older man.

"I am not a Sir, but that is kind of you to honor me with the label. You recently, this may sound indelicate—"

"I am sure it will be fine."

Hampton shrugged. "You arrived at the house with some odd luggage."

"Are you referring to the magical Goldenheart sword?"

"Indeed. I do not believe magic is real, but I am a fervent proponent of tradition, my lady. I know you have the ducal title of Goldenheart," he said, "which is in the most enshrined documents of the Three Realms."

Georgia tilted her head in acknowledgment. "It is an odd thing, yes. I spent most of my youth in the Cymbre School and expected to live a very different life. You see, my cousin William was supposed to inherit the entire Goldenheart estate, but he was taken by the blood flu on a trade mission to the Far West two years earlier. The peers register searched for other Goldenhearts, of course, but I am the last. You are wondering how a lady inherited the title of Knight-Protector?"

"I would never question tradition, no matter how obscure," Hampton said. "If you had not explained the trials of your late family, I would certainly find it odd."

Georgia smiled. "Mr. Hampton, we are in complete agreement. If you had said to me I would someday be the keeper of the sacred Golden Blade of the Three Realms and named Defender against Dragons, I would have gaped in dismay or laughed. It is entirely puzzling."

Mr. Hampton nodded, satisfied with her answer, and was hopefully reassured she wasn't some wild harridan—or worse, a modern woman with opinions and ideas.

"So, you accepted your duty."

"We do what we must," Georgia said. "Honestly, I am still not fully informed of the importance of my station. I suspect that I might be the first lady to occupy the chair. If so, I can only hope to fill it with dignity and grace, and do my family no disservice." She hoped he would leave it at that.

He did—sort of.

"My lady," he said, "may I ask a blunt question?"

Georgia tried not to twitch. "Yes, of course."

"Forgive me. I am a humble businessman. I am a successful one, yes, but at the core still of the common variety. When I tell you, we are delighted and honored to have you, a great lady of the Realms, as our guest, well…"

"You are wondering why I am here?"

Mr. Hampton knew full well how she got there. Her solicitor, Mr. Stackhouse, was also solicitor to the Hamptons. Stackhouse told her about Ollie and Manx Hampton, and how they were each unmarried. Naturally, neither was suitable for Georgia to consider, but Bea was another matter. Stackhouse was also solicitor to one of Bea's brothers-in-law, so he was keen to help Bea find a suitable match. As it happened, Stackhouse was invited to the party that night, but he would be out of town. Instead, he arranged to have Georgia go in his place with Bea as her guest. The Hamptons had no qualms with the change.

No one of the Hamptons' station would refuse her, no matter how unusual the situation.

Mr. Hampton sighed.

Georgia leaned in. "Mr. Hampton, I am here on behalf of my friend, Miss Beatrice Irvingdale."

"What is it you hope for?"

"Hopefully, your good family will find her as charming as I do."

Mr. Hampton slowly nodded. Nothing more needed to be said. He looked toward his sons, both unmarried and on the verge of turning thirty. While they had held off from marriage, their prospects had started to become limited. Well, as limited as it could be for men.

Georgia watched as he turned his attention to Bea, and she could almost see the gears turning in his head. Bea was an Irvingdale, an old baronial family. They were descended from two even older houses—the Irvings of the realm of Findor, and the Dales of the realm of Volusia. Those families merged as a small part of the Pact of the Three Realms, hundreds of years ago. Their union was one piece of an elaborate series of noble house pairings that eventually unified three kingdoms. Even though the Irvingdales had fallen in stature over the centuries, they were still a prominent family. All they needed, near as Georgia could tell, was the one thing the Hamptons had: money.

Georgia had worked the whole scheme out with Mr. Stackhouse, so she knew where the law stood. The Hamptons, currently, would never be noble. They had an exceptional reputation, but they had gone about as far as they could. Aligning them with the Irvingdales could change things for both families. In exchange for specific investment from Mr. Hampton and Bea as a bride—Lord Wickham, the current baronet of Irvingdale, could sponsor her new husband for a peerage award. The lucky fellow could become a Knight of the House. With such a title, the groom could win a seat in the Low House of Government.

After a time of distinguished service combined with liberal donations to charity, Bea's husband could get a formal declaration of Gentry status. Mr. Hampton would have to foot the bill for everything, but eventually, his grandchildren would be welcome in Society.

In the meantime, Georgia was reasonably sure the Hamptons would be profiting in other ways. With Irvingdale prestige in his pocket, Mr. Hampton could broker all sorts of business ventures with people well above his station. According to Mr. Stackhouse, he could even funnel profits back into the Irvingdales—and help them regain ground at court. The Irvingdales, armed with cold hard cash, could seat themselves in the High House of Lords. Hamptons in the Low House and Irvingdales in the High meant both families rise.

He looked back at Georgia. "I see."

There. Done. Georgia had introduced the deal. If Hampton had questions, Mr. Stackhouse could lay out the whole plan in excruciating detail.

"Father, we are at the picnic site," Manx announced, pointing to a small clearing with a pleasant view of both the city and the brilliant blue sky.

Mr. Bailey began to unpack their supplies. Manx and Ollie surveyed their position for errant rocks. After kicking a few aside, they looked satisfied. Upon their approval, Mr. Bailey quietly and efficiently spread out three soft Harrateen blankets. He made no sound as he went, carefully arranging the area for maximum comfort.

Off to one side, Bea sidled up to Georgia. "How is it going with your grand plan? Are you winning over the elder Hampton with your charm and wit?" she whispered.

"The man appears neither charmed nor offended. I think we should accept that Mr. Hampton will base his decisions on a combination of factors. He might wish to see if either of his sons finds you appealing. Either way, I suspect he will hold out until he talks to Mr. Stackhouse," Georgia whispered back. "Let us reserve judgment until after the party, but you will need to be particularly radiant, Bea. I recommend you focus your attention on Manx. Ollie has gotten enough of your gaze to last him the afternoon."

"Oh, how dull," Bea said, looking deflated. "Manx is so… well, he's not as dashing and attractive as Ollie, now is he?"

"Were it not for their different scarves, I wouldn't know how to tell them apart. They have the same voice, same manner, and each appears to be precisely as fit as the other. I'm not sure how you make the distinction. For that matter, how do we know they hadn't switched those scarves at least twice on this walk when we weren't looking?"

"Ollie is just a hair taller," Bea said, smirking. "Manx is slightly unkind, but in a fairly attractive way."

"You are brilliant and absurd."

Bea laughed, looking like her old self for once. "And that's why you love me, Georgia."

"Forever and ever, dearest."

"You can also tell them apart by their rings," Bea said. "Ollie wears a silver signet ring with a white pearl, while Manx prefers gold with black opal." She pointed discreetly at Manx, and Georgia realized he was indeed wearing an elegant gold band with a black stone. Georgia made a mental note, just in case she ever got them confused. "I heard Mr. Hampton talking about your magic sword. I take it he disapproves?"

"He's very old-fashioned when it comes to the fairer sex," Georgia said. "I suspect he doesn't much like the idea of women with swords."

Bea shook her head in mock disapproval. "Imagine how shocked he would be to learn you know how to use one?"

Georgia smiled. "I never understood why Uncle Raymond insisted I take those lessons. It makes sense now. As for Mr. Hampton, I was able to introduce the idea of you paired with one of his sons, without being vulgar. Mr. Stackhouse will take it up with him when he returns from his trip. In the meantime, you have a chance to impress these gentlemen."

Georgia turned back just as Mr. Bailey was finishing the picnic setup. The men waited to one side, allowing her to pick where to sit, which was an informal way to handle the protocol. After she took her spot, Hampton's sons effortlessly positioned themselves to face both her and their father. Bea placed herself just behind Georgia so she could talk to the boys, but also avoid the protocol problem. Mr. Hampton awkwardly settled to one side. By not facing Georgia directly, he was technically proving Uncle Raymond right about 'new money.' Georgia let it go, though. Because she was a duchess, they waited for her to begin the conversation now that they were sitting. Georgia began by saying, "The weather is lovely, and this picnic is most enjoyable." After that, the party ate cucumber and mustard sandwiches of the blandest possible variety.

"Do you enjoy your work, Manx?" Bea asked. Ah yes, the old, 'get them talking about work' tactic. Georgia approved. Bea was particularly skilled at appearing quite prim, precise, and able to eat as if hunger didn't exist in her world. She smiled at Manx to draw him out.

Sadly, it didn't go that way.

"Lady Georgia, what is your opinion on the situation in the upper northlands? I just read the most terrible article about packs of winter wolves attacking people on the mountain roads. Some of them are said to be the size of ponies," Ollie asked, interrupting. "Now that you are Protector of the Realms, you must have something to say on the subject?"

Oh, dear.

Things changed as another figure came down the lane from higher up the mountain.

"I say. Who is that odd fellow?" Manx asked, twitching.

A young man with a broad smile, spectacles, and a bowl hat approached. He wore a smart waistcoat, vest, long-sleeve shirt, and trousers, which would have seemed quite reasonable, except his entire ensemble was in various shades of blue. Even his button-sided boots were blue leather. In his hand was an elegant walking cane with a lovely silver handle. The shaft was polished beechwood and intricately carved with a pattern of stars. Georgia gazed at his lapel, where a gold pin made to look like a daisy with some sort of rune etching glinted in the sunlight. The young man stopped, as a songbird flew over and began to chirp. He listened and then said, "I'm sorry, I do not know where she got off to. You should probably keep an eye on the nest until she returns. I mean, that would be the responsible thing to do."

The songbird chirped flatly and flew off. The young man smiled, then turned back and spotted the picnic party. "Good day," he said.

"Good day," Mr. Hampton greeted him back.

Georgia stood up, which forced the boys to their feet. "Good day. Are you perchance Mr. Blue?"

"I am occasionally called that, yes. At your service, Duchess Goldenheart," Mr. Blue said, bowing.

"My word, you know this man, Lady Georgia?" Mr. Hampton asked, blinking rapidly.

"I do indeed, Mr. Hampton," she answered. "Or at the very least, I know of him. Mr. Blue is a wizard."

"A wizard?" Bea asked. "I had no idea we still had wizards."

"Of course we do," Mr. Hampton said gruffly. "There are at least three guilds of them down in the city. I've never had time for magic and tricks myself. Men of business need to be more practical."

"I've never heard anything so absurd," Manx said.

"It is absurd," Ollie agreed. But where Manx meant it in a wrong way, Ollie was thrilled. "Mr. Blue, I am Ollie Hampton. It is a pleasure to meet you."

"The pleasure is entirely mine," Mr. Blue said, shaking Ollie's hand. "Apologies if I have interrupted your picnic."

"Well, you have certainly added the pepper to our afternoon."

"I thought wizards were all little old men with pointy hats and wands. You seem quite young. Are you perhaps someone's assistant?" Manx asked, his eyes rolling.

Mr. Blue laughed, ignoring the tone. "Yes, I am the youngest to lead my order."

"The Order of the Blue," Mr. Hampton said, snapping his finger. "I remember now. You people are the ones who inspected the foreign crates when the Realms were at war with the Hildor Islands. You all take the surname of Blue as an homage to your guild or something, or it's the law—I can't remember now."

"We did, we do, and it is the law, correct," Mr. Blue said. "The Hildori were fond of laying explosive traps on the docks."

"How awful," Bea said.

"It was a difficult time," Mr. Hampton admitted, "and bad for business all around."

"And for the soldiers who perished taking the Hildor Islands, I suspect," Georgia mused.

"As I recall, the Hildor Island War was more than a decade ago," Bea said. "Surely it was before your time, Mr. Blue?"

"My predecessor was the wizard who managed that affair, yes," Mr. Blue said.

"Well, all of this is very exciting," Ollie said. "I must admit, I am greatly amused. What brings you up the mountain today, Mr. Blue?"

"Ah, that would be me," Georgia admitted. "As you know, I am here for two reasons: the first is to attend your lovely party this evening. I've been looking forward to it for a month. The second reason is related to my new title 'Defender of the Realms against Dragons.' Mr. Blue is assigned to be my guide tomorrow morning. Am I correct, sir?"

Mr. Blue nodded. "Yes, Lady Georgia. The Council of Guilds and the Royal Office of The Three Princes both requested I take the ritual walk with you to the top of the mountain. Once we do that, you can begin your life as an official protector of the Three Realms. Afterward, I will be available whenever you need advice or instruction on your new duties."

"Lady Georgia has interesting days ahead," Ollie said.

"If you consider ribbon-cutting ceremonies at hospitals interesting, then yes, it does sound like it." Manx smirked.

"Well, I think it sounds amazing." Ollie turned back to Mr. Blue. "What are your plans this evening, sir?"

"I am a guest of the Barnwell family, just down the lane. I suppose I have no other plans until we walk up the mountain tomorrow."

"Oh, the Barnwells are a respected family. That's perfect," Ollie said.

"Respected, despite putting up a conjurer in their guest room," Manx muttered under his breath.

"They are our neighbors," Ollie said. "Mr. Blue, we live in Hampton House, just beyond the lane. Tonight, my brother and I celebrate our thirtieth year, and I would personally be delighted if you could attend. Perhaps, if I may be as bold as to ask, you could surprise us with some magic. Maybe we could have a séance? I do love a good séance."

Manx and Mr. Hampton both groaned, but not so audibly as to be rude.

"You honor me, Mr. Hampton. I happily accept your kind invitation," Mr. Blue said. "I look forward to surprising you with a trick or a séance."

"Then it is settled," Ollie announced.

"Well, this has all been fine," Mr. Hampton said. "But now the lunch hour has passed, and we should get back to the comfort of home. There is, after all, your party tonight, I have letters to read, and I'm sure Miss Beatrice needs to take a tonic or some such."

CHAPTER 2: PARTY.

Georgia gave her gown one last look in the mirror. Her dress was a very modern soft cotton-silk blend in two shades of lilac with a few accents of pale yellow at the short puffy sleeves. The skirt gathered gently in a high waist that ensured more comfortable movement. She turned to inspect the diamond back design of yellow buttons. Her posture was perfect, naturally, so the effect was appropriate. She nodded her approval to her ladies' maid, Millie.

Georgia's hairstyle that evening also felt modern. She opted for an up-do, more fitting her station, and selected a delicate gold tiara—an heirloom from her mother's family—to wear. The tiara was a bit more opulent than the occasion called for, but it would also draw some attention to her. Perhaps it would even remind Mr. Hampton what kind of associations Bea would bring into a marriage.

Like all the Goldenhearts who'd come before Georgia,

she had long, raven hair, clear skin, and a tinge of amber glinting in her eyes. Georgia's eyes were almost green, though—a trait she'd inherited from her mother—and looked unlike Uncle Raymond's, which had appeared nearly orange in a particular light.

She missed him terribly.

How many times had Georgia sat in his library reading as he fiddled with maps and books? All the while, she never once thought about the day he would be gone. Georgia never dreamed she would be the one who would eventually pore over maps and books. Maybe it's because she always assumed her cousin, William, would take over next. Georgia had the title now, though, and she was alone. Well, sort of alone. She had good friends, of course. But there was no family left. Uncle Raymond had forbidden her to marry until after William was married, settled, and had at least two children. Uncle Raymond and William were both dead. Nobody could truly share her burden.

Millie corrected the position of her skirt while Georgia examined necklaces. "Let's go with the peach pearl locket," she said.

Georgia was finally ready for the party.

She still had to wait for Bea, but with Millie's assistance, her friend wouldn't take too long.

"Thank you, Millie," Georgia said. "You can dress Miss Beatrice now. I will put my gloves on just before we go down."

"Yes, my lady," Millie said, curtsying.

"Sorry to keep you running, Millie," Georgia said.

"Yes, my lady." Millie hurried down the hall.

While she waited, Georgia took a seat at the window and poured herself a cup of tea. She picked up her copy of the *Youthful Ladies Journal*. The first article was entitled, 'The triumphant return of lilac.' Georgia skipped over it and instead read an alarming story about cat-fishing and kidnapping.

Behind her, the magical sword of the Goldenhearts hummed to itself.

She stood up and crossed the room, making her way to where the blade sat on the bed. For years, the sword rested on the fireplace mantle in Uncle Raymond's library. The sword was inconspicuous there and looked like nothing more than a family heirloom. She unsheathed the blade and held it up to the light. The hilt consisted of an old-style pommel, grip, and guard—all made from ancient Lunish steel. The grip was wrapped in black shagreen leather but intricately inlaid with eight-pointed stars. The pommel also had an eight-pointed star inside the sun, with a tiny rune in a language Georgia didn't know. The guard was shaped like bird wings, while the blade was straight and extended almost three-feet. The weapon was sharp and carried a faint otherworldly glow. Tiny, indecipherable runes were etched on the blade near the hilt. She felt like she should know what the runes meant, but couldn't figure them out. Before holding the blade the first time, she didn't believe magic existed, but one touch of the hilt and Georgia was convinced that magic was real. The sword shimmered as it hummed, and a faint song reverberated throughout the room. She moved it expertly, feeling how light the blade was in her hand.

Careful of her knee position and with her elbow relaxed, Georgia slid into the lunging pose. As a child, she had taken fencing lessons, movement, and the practice of defense. Uncle Raymond had insisted she practice with William. William—the thought of him almost broke her stance. Memories of better times raced in to take the place of that tragedy, but they were too late. She remembered precisely the day at the Cymbre School, two years ago, when Uncle Raymond arrived to tell her William had died suddenly on an overseas errand.

"William succumbed to a deadly sickness, but he passed quickly and without pain—or so I am told," Uncle Raymond had said. At that moment, he looked older, exhausted.

Uncle Raymond was her great-uncle—her grandfather's brother. He'd raised her after her parents died in a fire while they were on holiday a few months after Georgia was born. He was a duke and the knight-protector of the Three Realms from Dragons. Since Dragons aren't real, Georgia never took the title seriously and had no idea the title was hereditary until William died. At the memorial service for her cousin, Uncle Raymond brought out the magic sword. He told her the blade was the only souvenir to return from her cousin's trip.

Georgia moved to a raised position, keeping her wrist straight enough so that the force of impact would be free to travel back through her arm. Jamming a wrist while sword-fighting was a common mistake. If the wrist wasn't straight, particularly in a hanging guard defensive move, one could experience unnecessary pain.

Taking the hilt with two hands, she pivoted so the point would drive first.

Georgia leaned her shoulder forward tentatively. The pose would ensure the strike remain at a proper stabbing distance. If a foe drew close, it was essential to maintain space. She took a slight step backward, imagining an opponent more aggressive than disciplined.

"Because you never know when you will be at a cocktail party and break into a sword fight," she whispered.

The sword hummed as if laughing.

Uncle Raymond's words after William's funeral echoed in her head, "You will need finishing as soon as possible. It is vital, for you are the last of our kind." She was sent back to school and spent the next year and a half immersed in study. When she received her full diploma with honors, Georgia was allowed to return to Wending Way—only to find her uncle on his deathbed. The next few months were a lingering haze of grief.

"I don't know what to make of you," she said, talking

to the sword. The faint tune it sang changed to something charming. Georgia smiled. "You are right. Nothing happens instantly. We have time to get used to one another." Gently, she returned the blade to its holder.

Bea strolled into her bedroom wearing a gorgeous linen and taffeta gown. The upper body was eggplant purple, pinned to a striped taffeta in lilac and orchid. As she walked, her blond curls bobbed around her head frantically. Behind her, Millie pursued, still tying the back of her skirt.

"Really, Bea, you're dragging my poor maid behind you," Georgia said.

"Sorry, Georgia, I got bored and thought we'd chat while your girl does her work," Bea said, pouring herself some tea.

"Have you seen this terrifying article in the *Youthful Ladies Journal*?" Georgia asked. "Apparently there's an outbreak of people making up false names and writing secret admirer love letters to one another as pranks."

"Golly," Bea said. "What would the point be?"

"It's a scheme: conmen grifting proper ladies," Georgia said almost in a whisper. Someone of her station should never use the term 'conman'.

Millie looked startled by Georgia's casual use of such vulgar words.

Bea was unfazed, though. Possibly because of her Cymbre training or maybe she thought Georgia was purposely trying to make her laugh again.

"The Royal Office is considering a formal ban on the practice, as there's been a spike in lonely spinsters throwing themselves off the West Bridge," Georgia said.

"That is dreadful." Bea shook her head. She smirked and said, "They should double the watch on the river. Mr. Hampton would call that bad for commerce." Clever. Of course, both Georgia and Bea watched as Millie's eyes widened before she tried to hide her reaction.

Georgia squinted at Bea as if to say, 'okay, stop now.'

"And he would be right to say so. I suppose we're just about ready," Georgia said.

Bea was going to say more, but she shook her head. Enough fun. "I need to put on some blush," Bea said, checking her face in the vanity. "Not too much. I wouldn't want to appear to be fully alive, after all."

"Millie, have a peek downstairs and see if the Hamptons have gone down for the party yet. If they have, we'll follow right after."

"Yes, my lady." Millie curtseyed and left to recon the party. She returned a moment later. "Masters Ollie and Manx are having drinks in the game room with some of the neighbors."

"Good work. Was a man in blue there? He would have a walking stick."

Millie nodded. "Yes, my lady. The wizard is there."

"We'll be right down. Millie, you can take the rest of the night off. I'm sure I can manage from here."

"Are you sure, my lady? I can wait for you."

"Nonsense," Georgia said. "We've dragged you all over the house. Surely the staff is having a fun little party of their own in the basement. You should join them."

"They are no doubt in some dank hole out of sight and mind," Bea commented.

"I should probably wear boots then," Millie said, smiling, and then blushed. "Oh, I'm sorry. I didn't mean—"

"You're allowed to say something funny once a year, Millie," Georgia said. "Go. Enjoy the evening. If I need anything, I can always find you."

"Yes, my lady."

Georgia turned back to Bea. "I'm going to ruin a perfectly good ladies' maid, aren't I?"

"I'm surprised you haven't already." Bea fiddled with her makeup and then looked up. "Georgia?"

"Yes, dear?"

"What if this is all just a big chase for nothing. Maybe I

should go back and get a teaching degree."

"Don't be silly. You have a year to think about it. Your horrid brother-in-law, Wickham, said you have time. He won't force you out of the cottage. For that matter, he can't force you to do anything. I bet your allowance would be enough for you to stay as long as you want."

"Stay as long as I want to live alone in a tiny cottage at the edge of the family estate," Bea sighed.

"I know, it's all frightening," Georgia said. "You come from a certain kind of family with precise expectations. I understand completely."

Bea's face creased with a wry smile. "Do you, Georgia? I mean, I'm so grateful for what you are doing here tonight, and you must know I love you, dear friend, more than almost anyone in the world, but how could you understand this?"

The question, if asked by almost anyone else, would have sounded bitter or even like an accusation. Bea, however, wasn't like that. They had been friends since they were five-years-old, and Bea had always been direct and frank with Georgia.

Georgia tilted her head and said, "Obviously, my life is different. I never had sisters ahead of me to care for first. I did have a cousin who had to marry before I could, however. I never fully understood why until he was gone, but that fact was always there."

"I'm not sure I ever understood that part of your life either," Bea admitted.

Georgia shrugged. "It's all about the law. I must preserve the five-thousand-year-old Goldenheart name, no matter what. In earlier times, when there were more of us, a Goldenheart lady could marry into another family without concern. Alas, when the line whittled down to only William and me as potential heirs, it meant I had to stand by until he was insured a succession. His failure to do that meant I would have to keep my name, even if I marry. Any husband I have would take my name."

"When you explain your circumstances like that, it almost makes sense. That's not terrible, is it? I mean, many fine gentlemen would take their wife's name if it meant becoming a duke, surely."

"Ah, that's the rub," Georgia said. "My husband will never be a duke, merely my consort. I would stay knight-protector. I would have the titles. He would have my name and whatever possessions I choose to give."

Bea nodded slowly. "He would have to come from a high-born family to even be considered by you. It would go against everything he would expect in life."

"Precisely."

"I take it back," Bea said, finishing up at the vanity and standing. She smoothed out her gown, fluffed her beautiful ringlets of hair, and said, "You don't need to understand my situation. Your problems are infinitely worse."

Georgia laughed.

They made their way to the game room, where the men were wrapping up cigars and wine punch. Georgia wasn't a fan of the combination but had to accept it had become customary at these types of affairs. Ollie and Manx were in full tails and ties and looked very elegant.

"Ah, the ladies have arrived," Ollie said through a cloud of smoke. "Welcome. Care for a drink? I've made up this delightful borage with the help of our local staff downstairs." He passed a glass to Bea, who smiled and sipped. Georgia could see it was one of those lemon, red wine, and seltzer abominations. Bea was likely gagging, but she would never let on. For her part, Georgia accepted her glass and held it politely.

"When you say you made it with their help," she started to say.

"I mean they made it, and I watched them, yes," Ollie said with a laugh. "I did stir it a few minutes ago, Lady Georgia. Surely, that effort is worth note."

"Perfectly worthy of note," she agreed, grinning.

Oh, dear. How was she supposed to get this fellow to look at Bea while being a shameless flirt?

"Mr. Blue was telling us about the dark days before the Three Realms came together. His guild of wizards were quite the dealmakers back then," Manx said.

Mr. Blue had switched to appropriate formal attire, which still included an awful lot of blue. The daisy-shaped pin on his evening lapel was also present, as was the elegant cane in his hand.

"Good evening, Duchess Goldenheart," he said, bowing slightly. "Miss Beatrice."

"Good evening, Mr. Blue. It's a pleasure to see you again," Bea said, discreetly hiding her drink on a nearby side table. "You like quite fine, this evening. I see you still have your walking stick."

"A wizard never leaves his staff at home."

"Ah, more guests," Ollie said as other people entered.

A striking woman in a hat made entirely from flowers shimmied in. Her headpiece was so encompassing one couldn't even see her hair, and the gown was a dazzling pale yellow with lilac bows at her shoulders. She tossed her luxurious fur onto a chair. The whole ensemble was bold but not so shocking as to throw off the party.

"Heavens, that's Mrs. Miranda Smythe," Bea breathed.

"She is someone of importance?" Mr. Blue asked.

Mrs. Smythe accepted her vile borage cocktail with a smile and downed it in one gulp.

"She is, indeed," Bea said, "although she's also a bit of a walking scandal. You see, her husband died suddenly last year; taken by that horrid blood flu."

"Tragic," Mr. Blue said.

"He was well-respected and from a military family, handsome and incredibly rich. In his youth, he invested in spices from the south and made a bundle," Bea said. "He left Miranda with a fortune, but then his extended family tried to take it back. She fought them in the courts and won."

"Oh, bravo to her," Georgia said.

"Precisely," Bea said. "The tale should end there, but Mrs. Smythe went on to show up at parties in wild gowns and without an escort. It was almost as if she came alive the moment her husband died. People were shocked."

Mr. Blue smiled. "She stood up for herself and is now stronger than ever."

"Agreed," Georgia said.

"There's more," Bea said, digging in. "The current rumor has it Mrs. Smythe became a writer under a pseudonym."

"What?" Georgia gasped.

Bea nodded. "People are saying she might be writing for the *Weekly Men's Journal* under the pseudonym *Mr. Adina.*"

"Mr. Adina," Georgia breathed. "That is an anagram for Miranda. I think I want to be her friend." She headed over to introduce herself.

"Take me with you," Bea said. "I love her."

"Hello, Mrs. Smythe. I am Lady Georgia Goldenheart," Georgia said quite simply. The great thing about being a duchess was one could be almost rudely direct at parties without causing a scene.

Mrs. Smythe smiled brilliantly and curtseyed. "It is a pleasure to meet you, Duchess Goldenheart," she said. "I must say, I was quite surprised to learn you would be at this affair tonight. In fact, you are the reason I am here."

"Really?" Georgia said. "Why is that?"

Mrs. Smythe laughed. "If I may be so bold as to say, I simply wanted to meet you."

Georgia smiled. "May I introduce you to my dear friend, Lady Beatrice Irvingdale."

Bea gave a slight nod in Mrs. Smythe's direction, but the gleam in her eyes showed her excitement at meeting such an infamous character.

"The pleasure is mine," Mrs. Smythe said with a polite nod.

"Oh, I promise its mine," Bea said.

Mrs. Smythe laughed.

"And this is Mr. Blue," Georgia said.

"A wizard?" Mrs. Smythe raised an elegant eyebrow. "What a marvelous evening this has become."

"Lovely to meet you," Mr. Blue said.

"Smythe is an interesting name," Georgia said, making conversation. "Are you related to Lord Reginald Smythe? What am I saying? Smythe is your married name. Forgive me."

"It's funny you should mention it, as my maiden name was Smith. Come to think of it; when I changed names, I had a terrible time and kept misspelling Smythe whenever signing anything. The urge to put a letter 'i' instead of 'y' in there was intense," she explained. "My late husband, Robert—who, yes, was distantly related to Lord Reginald, used to laugh about it. I was always one minute from mortified, but the sweet man would always say, 'It cannot be helped. We are practically cousins. Perhaps I should go by Smith myself.'" The woman smiled, but a well of sadness seemed to open at the memory. Perhaps it was best to move on to a more cheery topic.

Ollie stepped around Georgia, and called out, "Everyone, we're going to lose a bit of the formality, at least until father comes down. These dear friends are Sir Alexander Madison and his lovely wife, Lady Emily."

A tall, thin, older gentleman, Sir Alexander wore impeccable black tie and tails. He smiled and nodded to everyone who passed. At his side was his wife, Lady Emily, who was reserved in a deep purple gown and no flashy bows.

Georgia knew their name from somewhere but couldn't remember where.

"Mr. Hampton's former business partner," Mr. Blue said as if sensing her confusion.

"Right," Bea said, cutting in. "The Madisons sold their share of the dock warehouses to the Hamptons at a rather tidy profit."

"Goodness, Bea," Georgia said. "How would you know a thing like that?" The story with Mrs. Smythe being a scandalous widow and a possible writer made sense. Bea loved the drama. But knowing about proper business relationships? That's new.

Bea shrugged. "I heard it from my brother-in-law, Lord John Wickham. He often tells me about the business world. Wickham has perfectly appalling table manners, despite his revered family, but he knows his way around commerce."

"How clever."

"It's clever and potentially useful for you, Miss Beatrice," Mr. Blue said, "Or am I mistaken in my evaluation?"

Bea smiled. "Mr. Blue, such a comment borders on rudeness."

"Apologies, I meant it as a compliment."

"In that case, I am delighted and you might be right," Bea smiled.

Another guest arrived—a young fellow dressed in tie and tails.

"Ah, Tommy," Ollie said, shaking his hand. The act seemed to startle Tommy, though. "Everyone, this is Mr. Tom Turner. We went to school together."

"Ah, how nice," Bea said.

"Interesting," Mrs. Smythe said.

"How so?" Georgia asked.

"Tom Turner was only recently released from prison."

"Oh my word," Bea breathed. "How do you know this?"

Mrs. Smythe shrugged. "He was arrested last year under mysterious circumstances. One of the papers had an article, I think. Forgive me. I'm going to go over and boldly introduce myself." She glided over to Mr. Turner.

"People are amazing," Mr. Blue said as their group watched Mrs. Smythe's interaction with Mr. Turner and

Ollie. He turned his attention to Georgia and winked.

"More guests," Bea said as another couple strolled in.

Ollie took the lead again, saying, "Everyone, this is Mr. and Mrs. Duckworth. They live down the street." The Duckworths were a doughy pair. He looked a bit wrinkly, and his tails had a faint stain on the shoulder. Mrs. Duckworth was less wrinkly, and thankfully stain-free. But her gown was a dowdy old green thing better-suited to the previous decade. Still, they looked like they were pleasant people.

Georgia watched as Mr. Duckworth sucked down his borage cocktail at double-speed and then replaced it before Mrs. Duckworth noticed his pace. She caught him on the third glass and shook her head.

More guests trailed in—older gentlemen of business with their wives.

Ollie left the punch bowl with one of the house footmen so he could more efficiently mingle. "Father will be down soon. He's just about ready, I'm sure."

Once all of the guests arrived, Mr. Hampton promptly appeared in the doorway, like the most respectable of lords. Georgia had to admire the gambit. On the one hand, Hampton wasn't gentry, despite his wealth. Instead, he played the part of one beyond his station in a way that didn't embarrass.

"Yes. An impressive switch and bait," Mr. Blue said as if he had read her thoughts.

Mr. Hampton stood at the center of the room next to Sir Alexander, holding a glass of the vile punch. "May I have your attention?" The milling conversation around the room halted. "I propose a toast to my sons, Ollie and Manx. You're good boys, and you'll be good men. Happy birthday, boys."

"Refreshingly simple," Bea said.

"Happy birthday!" the room proclaimed and downed their drinks.

It was at that precise moment when Sir Alexander Madison keeled over.

CHAPTER 3: NIGHTCAP.

Lady Emily Madison stood in shock while people rushed to and fro. "Alexander," she cried, dropping to her husband's side. One of the side tables went over in the mayhem. Hidden glasses of undrunk punch fell across the floor.

Georgia hurried to the man's side, not sure how she could help. "Bea," she said. "You took some medical back in school, right?"

Bea hurried closer. "Medical? Oh, yes. I remember something about checking for a pulse." She turned Sir Alexander on his side and pressed her fingers to his neck. She shook her head, and pulled her hand away from the corpse. "Oh, Georgia, he's dead."

"Everyone, take a step back," Mr. Blue said. "Let's have a look. Someone, alert the constabulary."

"I say, the constabulary?" Manx asked. "Why would they be involved?"

"A man in apparent good health dropped dead at your party," Mr. Blue said bluntly. "I think they might find it of interest."

"Good heavens." Ollie blanched. "I'll send a footman to the local house. It's just down the hill." He signaled to his staff.

"Also, I would recommend no one leave the party prematurely," Mr. Blue said. "The constable will want to speak with each of us."

"Why?" Ollie asked, blinking rapidly.

"Someone may have seen something or noted Sir Alexander behaving oddly before he fell."

"I suppose. But again, why would that matter?"

"Bea, why don't you take Lady Emily to the other drawing-room? She looks like she may need to sit. She's making the other wives skittish," Georgia said. Bea nodded and stood. She gently helped the shocked Lady Emily to her feet and ushered her away.

Mr. Blue inspected the body. "Look at that." He pointed at Sir Alexander's hand. "See the whitish lines on his fingernails? They look almost like little cracks."

"Yes," Georgia said. "What does it mean?"

"Nothing good. Also, along the side of his neck are swelling bumps resembling warts that'd risen rather suddenly. Note the bruising. That would only happen in a rapid reaction," Mr. Blue said efficiently. "He may have been poisoned."

"Poisoned?" Ollie asked. "Are you quite certain?"

"No, I am certain of nothing," Mr. Blue admitted. "Curious."

"What? What is curious?" Georgia asked.

"It looks like arsenic… but that would be odd," Mr. Blue said. "Arsenic doesn't kill this fast unless delivered in very high dosage. Sir Alexander would have been uncomfortable for a while, I think, before succumbing. There would have been some time before it set in. He would have known something was happening."

"But instead, he was mingling," Georgia mused. She hadn't been paying much attention to the Madisons, but she remembered Lady Emily laughing about something only moments earlier. Surely, she wouldn't have been laughing if her husband was showing strange behavior.

"We should wait for the constable. Clear everyone out

of this room but touch nothing. Do not let the servants clean until the authorities have time to look it over," Mr. Blue instructed Ollie.

"Are you quite certain?" Ollie asked. "I mean, it is a bit of a mess now. What will the constables think of us?"

"I'm sure they will form their opinions when they see the body on your floor," Mr. Blue said, his voice taking a sharp tone.

Ollie stepped back. "Forgive me," he said. "Of course, you are right."

Georgia was about to start ushering guests out when she noted Mrs. Duckworth was sipping punch, no doubt, to calm her nerves. The sight left Georgia cold. She stared at the punch bowl and then looked back. "You might want to put that down, Mrs. Duckworth," she told the woman quietly.

Half an hour later, the constables rolled up. The Hampton servants left the game room untouched, as per Mr. Blue's instructions.

"Good evening. I am Chief Inspector Morris," the lead constable announced. Morris was an older man with weary eyes and fading red hair. His demeanor suggested he was someone who never has time to get dressed correctly.

"I say," Mr. Hampton said. "Sir Alexander is dead in the other room, and we're all waiting for you to let us go."

"If it is murder, we'll need them to stay a bit longer," Morris said. "It is the protocol."

Mr. Hampton, clearly exhausted, threw his hands up. "I will be in my study. Carry on."

Morris noticed Mr. Blue and perked up. "Mr. Blue of the Order of the Blue," he said in awe. "You were here when the fellow died, sir?"

Mr. Blue nodded. "Allow me to introduce Lady Georgia Goldenheart, Duchess of the House of Goldenheart, and Knight-Protector of the Three Realms from Dragons."

Chief Inspector Morse blinked rapidly and then bowed.

"Good evening, your ladyship. My word, I had no idea such a title even existed."

"Until a few months ago, I didn't either, Inspector," she said. "But apparently it's been in my family for several thousand years."

Mr. Blue stepped in. "I have made notes for you, Inspector, if you'd like to see them?"

"I certainly would, sir," Morris said.

Mr. Blue nodded to Georgia and led them back into the game room to lay out the scene. Sir Alexander was where they had left him.

"I was not facing the victim directly when he fell," Mr. Blue said. "I did see several people react, though. Most did not seem to understand what was happening."

"That makes sense. Most people were enjoying the party."

"Agreed. Not conclusive of innocence, but perhaps indicative. Upon inspection of the body, we found white lines on the fingernails and warty bruised bumps protruding from the neck, which might suggest arsenic," Mr. Blue surmised.

Morris nodded. "Right. Arsenic." He seemed happy enough to have Mr. Blue there to do his job.

Mr. Blue stepped carefully across the room. "This is where the side table went over. Three glasses appear to have come from it. Sir Alexander was also holding a glass when he fell, and possibly one of them belonged to him."

"Ah, so if there's arsenic in one of these glasses, we'll have a murder weapon," Morris said, jotting notes. "Since you are already here, may I ask you to take the glasses back to your guild for testing?"

"Yes, of course," Mr. Blue said. "I have another appointment tomorrow, but I expect to be back at my office on the day following. I will deliver them to our chemist."

"Thank you, sir," Morris said. "I await your results."

"Very good. Now, there is more," Mr. Blue said,

stepping over to another part of the room. He leaned over and pointed at the ground. "Here we have crushed glass. It may be one of the other guests who dropped their cup in a rush and stepped on it by accident."

"Sure, that makes sense," Georgia said. She remembered a few people moving around the room after Sir Alexander fell, most of them in panic.

"It does, up to a point," Mr. Blue said. "The problem is just how finely crushed the glass is. Whoever stepped on it would have had to exert significant pressure to reduce it so completely. Once again, in the panic of the moment, it is always possible."

"But it should be noted for later," Morris said, doing just that.

"There is also an odd scratch. The other rooms in the house are quite fastidious, but we see a triangular mark just here," Mr. Blue said, pointing out a panel on the wall. "It may be this mark was here all along, but again, a remarkable force was used to make it. As you can see, it is deep."

Morris jotted down the evidence.

"As long as we are here, we might question the witnesses?" Mr. Blue asked the Inspector.

Morris nodded quickly. "Oh, by all means. Perhaps you'd like to take a pop at them with your wizardly ears, sir?"

"Ah, good thinking, Inspector," Mr. Blue said.

Georgia was a little surprised at how the constables treated the wizard like he was, well, a wizard.

"Lady Georgia, perhaps you would care to observe? I have a feeling you'll get the hang of it quickly," Mr. Blue said.

"I would be honored," she said.

"Excellent. We will start with who was nearest to the victim when he died," Mr. Blue said. "I believe that was Mr. Manx Hampton, correct?"

"Manx and Lady Emily Madison," Georgia said.

"We may need to give the widow a few minutes to herself," Mr. Blue said. "These situations often require a degree of delicacy."

❖

Manx was in a state of shock, as was to be expected. His eyes were wide open and darting everywhere. "I must say, I wasn't paying the old chap much attention before he went down," Manx admitted. "Now I feel like a fool saying so because I was standing right beside him. We only invited him to be polite."

"How do you mean?" Mr. Blue asked.

"The birthday bash was all Father's idea. He wanted to use the occasion to introduce Ollie and me to his business friends. We know all of them anyway because we run the warehouses. Father is barely involved these days. But he wanted to do it properly. You know, to ensure a smooth transition when we take over," Manx said. "Sir Alexander is... er, he's been retired for the last year, so he wasn't much use for anything. But then I got to thinking it might look better if he was there. And now he's dead. I killed him."

"Would that be a confession?" Chief Inspector Morris asked, looking like he caught a lucky break.

"What? Oh. No, I'm sorry, I didn't mean literally," Manx said, blinking. "I simply meant if I hadn't invited him, maybe he would have perished quietly in his own home and not inconvenienced anyone."

"Interesting," Mr. Blue said. "So, would you say Sir Alexander was not well-liked?"

"Why would you say that? Everyone loved the man. What are you implying?"

"You were not going to invite him originally."

"Only because Father didn't see much use for him now that he's out of the business," Manx answered.

"Sir Alexander required an exorbitant buy-out from the mutual business. Is that not right?" Mr. Blue asked. His tone was not precisely accusatory but still struck home.

Manx gazed at Mr. Blue for a long moment. Finally, he stammered, "Oh. Oh, no. Sir Alexander deserved every copper he got. He taught Father everything about the business world. If it hadn't been for him, Father would still be selling fish cakes and used buttons on the pier."

Ten minutes later, they were waiting for the next witness to enter the side study.

"Manx Hampton is obviously innocent. The lad was sincere." Inspector Morris seemed convinced.

Mr. Blue nodded. "Yes, he was sincere in one way—he spoke of his Father with truth—and he spoke with some affection for Sir Alexander."

"Well, there you have it," said Morris.

Mr. Blue shook his head. "We need a stronger motive than business."

"Are we certain of the murder weapon?" Georgia asked. "I mean, it does seem to be poisoning from his drink. I just—Mr. Blue, you were skeptical of that somehow?"

"My lady, I wouldn't worry about these details," Chief Inspector Morris said.

Georgia debated whether or not to say something of his dismissal, but her Cymbre training kicked in and she decided to keep quiet.

"Lady Georgia was specifically invited to this discussion in order for us to hear her thoughts. She is very observant. The question of the poison is well-put," Mr. Blue said.

"Oh?" Chief Inspector Morris said, his voice going slightly higher the way one speaks to a child, but he didn't apologize. "How do you mean?"

"If it was arsenic, as it appears to be, the effect seems unlikely to have hit Sir Alexander so rapidly," Mr. Blue said. "The amount of it necessary to kill so quickly would have been substantial and he would have sensed something wrong with his drink. For the sake of discussion, I am assuming it came from the drink."

"You don't think he was poisoned then?"

Mr. Blue shrugged. "I do not know what to think yet. There are no facts."

Chief Inspector Morris nodded and then looked around the room. "We should have all of the glasses taken to your chemist," he said. "I will order them shipped over rather than make you carry them back yourself."

Mr. Turner was the next witness to be interviewed, and he was quite jumpy. Granted, Mr. Turner was a released felon, and Chief Inspector Morris seemed familiar with the man.

"You conveniently showed up tonight," Morris said as Mr. Turner took his seat. "What sort of trouble are you up to now, Turner?"

"You two know one another," Mr. Blue asked.

"Mr. Turner's family lives down the road within the domain of my constabulary," Morris said in a curt tone. "My office arrested him last year, ahem, for reasons I cannot divulge."

Mr. Turner winced. "You are barred from discussing the case, Chief Inspector," he said, looking like he might burst into tears at any moment.

"Why are you here?" Morris asked.

"I came to the party with an invitation," Mr. Turner answered. "I went to school with Ollie and Manx Hampton. Ollie invited me in person. We have been friends for nearly twenty years, as you well know."

"Okay, I think we understand that part," Mr. Blue said before the Chief Inspector could respond. "Mr. Turner, you were standing some five feet from Sir Alexander for a good portion of the evening. Were you not?"

Mr. Turner tamped down his growing agitation. "Yes," he said. "I was talking to— Oh, dear, what was her name? I was talking to the widow."

"Mrs. Smythe," Georgia offered.

Mr. Turner appeared to be pretending not to know Mrs. Smythe, but Georgia noticed the faint smile on his lips when she said the woman's name. He had a little secret.

"Right. Mrs. Smythe. I was talking to her. She seems like a lovely person," he said. "Terrific hat."

Georgia shook her head slowly.

"Did you see anything unusual with Sir Alexander? Perhaps something that would catch your attention?" Chief Inspector Morris barked.

"Well, I saw him fall over and die. That certainly caught my attention."

"That's it," Morris said. "I'm taking you to the station."

"Why, whatever for?" Mr. Turner shot back. "Perhaps you don't like my attitude, Inspector? I wasn't aware that it was a crime. Oh wait, perhaps it is?" He tilted his head and sneered at the constable.

Chief Inspector Morris' face grew red, but he did not respond.

"This is getting us nowhere," Mr. Blue snapped. "Mr. Turner, if you could think back, I would be grateful."

"Very well, I came in, and Ollie Hampton was there. When I saw him at the club last week, he was excited about the birthday party and delighted to see I was no longer locked away. He invited me, and I accepted. That is the polite thing to do, after all. When tonight arrived, I almost didn't come."

"You were ashamed," Morris said.

"It was something like that," Mr. Turner admitted. "I didn't want to embarrass Ollie. Honestly, I should have known better. He's always been a kind soul and was genuinely happy for me. His brother is another matter, of course."

"You don't like Manx. Why?" Georgia asked.

Mr. Turner looked at her. "Manx Hampton is the darkness to Ollie's light. No one should like him."

"You'll say anything, won't you?" Morris asked.

"Only if it is the truth," Mr. Turner answered. He looked at Georgia and then Mr. Blue. "I didn't notice anything unusual at the party. I was keeping my head down and talking to a kind lady. Beyond that, I was just as surprised as everyone else and had no inkling of what was happening."

Morris appeared to be somewhat satisfied by Mr. Turner's summary, but said, "Don't leave town. We may need to question you again."

"I can't leave town," Mr. Turner said. "I have been disinherited and must find suitable employment. I don't suppose you have any job openings at the constabulary, Chief Inspector?"

Morris turned a deep shade of scarlet, which earned him a chuckle from Mr. Turner who left the room.

"He's got a mouth on him," Mr.Blue said, his voice thick with amusement.

Morris shook his head. "That boy will be the death of me."

"I assume, based on your demeanor, he is some family relation?" Mr. Blue asked.

What?

"My nephew," Chief Inspector Morris grumbled. "And no, I cannot talk about what happened or why he went to prison."

Ollie Hampton's eyes were red and swollen when he sat down, and he could barely talk at first. Mr. Blue fetched him a glass of water, and Georgia watched quietly as the young man drank it all in one long gulp.

When Ollie set the glass down, he said, "Okay, I'm ready."

"I'm sorry to ask, but did you see Sir Alexander behaving strangely at any time before he collapsed?" Mr. Blue asked.

"Strangely? How do you mean?"

"Did he appear dizzy, fatigued, or in pain?"

Ollie shook his head. "Alexander was exactly as he always is—happy and slightly reserved."

Chief Inspector Morris wrote that down.

"Did you speak to him much tonight?" Mr. Blue asked. "Did he sound at all different?"

"I didn't say too much to him. Father was a bit put out over something, so I stayed close to him. Manx went over to the Madisons to keep them company. Ever since he retired, Father has had very little use for Alexander." Ollie tilted his head in thought.

Ollie didn't call him 'Sir', but his tone didn't convey any disrespect.

"Did Sir Alexander have any enemies?" Mr. Blue asked. "Old business rivals who may have come to the party tonight, for example? Or even old rivals who didn't come?"

"No," he said, sounding deep in thought. "No old rivals were here tonight. The daughter of a former business acquaintance was invited, but she didn't show up. Father says they ruffled a few feathers, years ago when they consolidated all of the dry docks with the loading docks on the eastern side of the port. They evicted their closest competitors from everything they held and may have pulled a few tricks on the ones they couldn't eject."

"A few tricks?" Inspector Morris parroted.

"Business tactics," Ollie said. "Some of them might have been questionable."

"How so?" Georgia asked.

Ollie turned his attention to her. He still seemed distraught but somehow he held it together. "Well, for example, one of their competitors, Sir Aubrey Algernon, owned a warehouse adjacent to their docks. They owned everything around his warehouse and offered to buy it from him. He refused to sell, though. Father opted to build a literal wall at the edge of their property around the warehouse so that Sir Aubrey couldn't come in or out by the road. It was entirely locked off. The whole point of that kind of warehouse is so you can begin transport inland. The ships come in, deliver their goods, and then you prepare for distribution over land. There are, of course, other ways to use a warehouse. Sir Aubrey could have repurposed the place into a shipping hub, but he would have needed to rebuild the docks in front. It would have cost a fortune. Eventually, he sold them the warehouse and moved on. I seem to recall there were some bad feelings at the time."

"How long ago was this?" Mr. Blue asked.

"It was about five years ago," Ollie said. "But it does get a bit worse."

"How so?"

"Sir Aubrey passed away last year. He was about to bring a lawsuit against Father and Alexander, but the case was dropped when he died. His only living heir is his daughter, Lady Johanna Price. She's married to Sir John Price, who owns the Price Bakery chain."

Georgia had enjoyed more than one of Price Bakeries' delicious apple fritters over the years. "Sir John didn't want to take up his father-in-law's suit then?" she asked.

"Apparently he did not," Ollie said. "From what I heard, he decided it was beyond his reach. There is a rumor that Lady Johanna was quite upset, though. Still, she obviously couldn't go around her husband and continue the lawsuit. We also invited her to the party tonight. Manx thought it would be a nice way to bury the hatchet, but I guess she had other plans."

No, she could not go around her husband, nor could she simply pop in for a party at Hampton House. What if all of this meant taking more drastic steps to avenge her father?

Ollie's eyes welled up again, and he needed a moment to collect himself. Mr. Blue gave him a crisp periwinkle-colored handkerchief, and they all looked away while the young man wept and blew his nose.

"I'm sorry," he said. "I know I should be made of sterner stuff, but Alexander was like a second father to me. I'm losing too many people."

"Oh?" Georgia asked. "Ollie, I'm sorry."

"Forgive me, Lady Georgia," he said, falling apart again. Tears rolled freely down his cheeks. Instead of looking away, he turned to face them and continued despite his emotions.

Mr. Blue looked him in the eye and nodded as if to say 'let it out.'

Chief Inspector Morris tilted his head ever so slightly, which apparently passed for sympathy amongst his kind.

"After Mother passed, I relied heavily on Alexander for advice and guidance. Father is a brilliant businessman, but he falls a bit short in the compassion category." Ollie sniffled.

"When did your mother pass away?" Mr. Blue asked in a voice implying he was stepping off the 'official' investigation and questioning as a friend.

"Just over a year ago," Ollie said, grief-stricken. "She was the balance, you know? We have no hope without her."

"You still have one another," Mr. Blue said. "All hope is not lost, Ollie. Hope is never lost if your motives remain true. Your brother and father will need you in the coming days. In the meantime, I would urge you to weep. Not all tears are bad."

Ollie Hampton looked at Mr. Blue, his eyes still running freely.

For a moment, Georgia thought he was going to say something rude or perhaps start screaming, but instead, he nodded in agreement.

Mrs. Duckworth looked like she was ready to jump out of her skin. "I knew it was poison the moment Alex fell," she said breathlessly. "That's how it works. You drink poison, and it kills you."

Yet Georgia had caught Mrs. Duckworth sipping her cocktail not five minutes after Sir Alexander dropped to the floor. She stifled the urge to point out the woman's obvious error.

"Yes, well, we are not sure what killed Sir Alexander," Mr. Blue said. "Mrs. Duckworth, did you see anything before he died? Perhaps some indication that he was in distress or anyone at the party who was behaving out of the ordinary?"

Mrs. Duckworth rubbed her temple in thought. "Distress? No, Emily is always a bit cold to me at these things, seeing as she is a fine and highborn lady. Alex got his title from her family. You know that, right? She comes from baronial stock, but she married down. Married for love, they say. I always liked that about Emily. She's still a bit stuck with her nose in the air. But that part about her I always liked."

"I was unaware," Mr. Blue said, pretending to write that down in his book.

"Emily and I have known each other for at least ten years, ever since she and Alex took up permanent residence here on the mountain," Mrs. Duckworth said. "I didn't know her before that. I knew the other Madisons, of course."

"Who are the other Madisons?"

"The parents. Alex and Emily moved into their place when his mum passed on. Just over a decade ago, I'm guessing," Mrs. Duckworth said. "We knew Alex before he got the title, though."

"I assume that is why you are refusing to address him properly?" Georgia asked.

"You seem to know them quite well," Mr. Blue said. "Mrs. Duckworth, since you do know them, perhaps you can help? Do the Madisons have any enemies?"

"Enemies?"

"Is there someone who would wish Sir Alexander harm?"

Mrs. Duckworth shook her head. "I can't think of anyone who would want to harm Alex."

"Are you quite sure?" Georgia asked. "You seem to be chewing on something, Mrs. Duckworth."

"Please call me Daisy, Duchess," she answered. Georgia had no intention of doing that. "I suppose it's nothing, but I seem to recall my husband once saying that Alex had some disagreement or unpleasantness with Mr. Hampton last year. It was something about the Madison's will. I don't think he ever said what it was precisely, but Donald seemed to think it was important."

When Mrs. Duckworth returned to the other room, Georgia faced Mr. Blue. "The Madison will?"

"Whenever a will becomes involved, one should tread carefully," the wizard said. "Wills tend to make people do extraordinary things."

"Daisy should have led with that bit of information," Morris said, his eyes twinkling. "I saw the look on your face, my lady when she suggested you call her by her first name."

Mr. Blue and Chief Inspector Morris both laughed as Georgia rolled her eyes.

Mr. Duckworth was barely conscious by the time he stumbled in. His wife's absence for questioning was the perfect opportunity for him to raid the Hampton liquor cabinet.

"Why don't we cut right to the chase," Morris said, as the witness would only be awake a bit longer.

Mr. Duckworth's eyes were bloodshot. "Ask away," he slurred faintly.

"Mrs. Duckworth told us you knew something about the Madison will," Morris said. "She implied you knew something about the nature of it."

"Daisy is a good wife, but a terrible gossip," Mr. Duckworth said.

"So, there was nothing important about the will?" Mr.

Blue asked.

Duckworth shrugged. "I know Sir Alexander had it changed last year. He mentioned it once or twice. You know our yards connect? The wives see each other over the fence. I see him pretty frequently out on the walking path." He winced. "I mean, I *saw* him. I suppose that won't be happening now. He was a good neighbor. The Duckworths and Madisons have always lived on the mountain, you know?"

"I did know that," Mr. Blue said. "I'm very sorry for your loss, Mr. Duckworth."

Mrs. Smythe sat primly under her giant flower-festooned hat.

Georgia had to admire the size of the hat and the way it swallowed all of her hair. Up close, the cap was tight. Mrs. Smythe must have exceptionally short hair to keep it sealed that way.

"It's getting late, so we will be brief," the Chief Inspector said. "Let's start with anything you might have seen. Did you notice Sir Alexander before he fell?"

"Of course," Mrs. Smythe said. "He's a great man of business who built a small empire out of nothing."

"He was, yes," Morris said.

"I mean he was, yes. What a terrible night this has been."

"So you took notice of him," Mr. Blue said.

"I had my eye on him for nearly an hour as that other young man... er..." Mrs. Smythe stammered.

"Mr. Turner?" Georgia said.

"Right. Fine chap. Anyway, yes, I was very near Sir Alexander and his beautiful wife for much of the evening," Mrs. Smythe said.

"How did he behave before he fell?" Mr. Blue asked. "Did he appear to be in distress?"

"Due to the arsenic poisoning, you mean?" Mrs. Smythe asked. "I remember you talking to Duchess

Goldenheart about it right after he collapsed."

"You have sharp ears," Mr. Blue said.

Mrs. Smythe shrugged. "It never hurts to listen to what people say around you, Mr. Blue. To answer your question, no, I saw no symptoms of poisoning before he collapsed. He was in fine spirits, laughing with his wife and young Manx Hampton. He was happy and did not appear to be in any pain. When he collapsed, I was completely shocked. If one were to predict who would fall tonight, I would never have guessed him."

"What an odd turn of phrase," Georgia said. "Why would you predict anyone falling?"

Mrs. Smythe tilted her head, causing her enormous hat to rustle. "Have you seen Mr. Hampton? He looks like death warmed-over, Duchess. Of course, it was more of a figure of speech, prompted solely by the events of the evening. Forgive me. Tonight was my first time seeing a person die. My late husband forbade my presence until right after he went to the great beyond. He spared me from seeing the act itself."

The act itself? Another odd turn of phrase. Georgia wanted to follow up on that but wasn't sure how. Instead, she decided to talk to Mrs. Smythe again, in private. Perhaps she would also the learn mystery of why the woman wore her hair so short.

Mr. Hampton was exhausted. Up this late and having his house held hostage while the constabulary investigated the death of Sir Alexander was taking a toll on him.

As he entered the study, Mr. Hampton spotted Georgia. "I am surprised to find you here, Duchess Goldenheart. I would not expect a lady to be part of these proceedings after ..." He gestured with his hand to where Sir Alexander's body was cordoned off from view.

"Ah, yes, Lady Georgia has agreed to sit with us to

offer comfort to those who were most closely affected by the events of tonight," Mr. Blue lied.

Inspector Morris seemed like he was about to object, but rethought his words and remained silent. Mr. Blue shrugged as if say 'it will be easier this way.'

Georgia let it go.

"I see," Mr. Hampton said. "Well, I am sorry for the trouble this causes you, Duchess."

"Thank you, Mr. Hampton. But I am here for you."

"I just have a few questions," Mr. Blue said.

"I would prefer it if the Inspector asked the questions," Mr. Hampton said. "No offense, but I don't believe in magic or wizards. Although your people were helpful back in the war, I still find it odd. I half expect you to freeze up and start talking to me with the voices of the dead."

"That's not really how it works."

"That's what Ollie was hoping for earlier," Mr. Hampton said. "You do realize that is why he invited you to join us when we encountered you on the path this morning? If the evening hadn't gone south, he would have cornered you and gotten you to commune with his mother from beyond the grave. The boy is obsessed."

"I think I would have preferred that to how the evening did go," Mr. Blue said.

Mr. Hampton nodded. "Now that you mention it, I would have preferred it too."

Mr. Blue looked to the Inspector. Morris shrugged. "I'll ask the same questions the wizard would, Mr. Hampton. Did you happen to notice if Sir Alexander was acting strangely before he collapsed?"

"I did not notice anything of the sort," Mr. Hampton said. "Alex behaved precisely the way he always does. He smiled and told my sons they were going to be great businessmen. He told his wife she is the most beautiful woman in the world, and he told me for the millionth time how glad he was we became friends."

Mr. Hampton, for a moment, reminded Georgia of his son, Ollie.

His eyes misted a bit, but he continued, "Alex was the best friend a man could have. He taught me how the business works, and he trusted me." He was answering the Inspector but looked between Georgia and Mr. Blue as he explained his relationship with the deceased.

Mr. Blue passed a note to the Inspector. "Mr. Hampton, what can you tell us about Sir Aubrey Algernon and his daughter?"

Mr. Hampton pulled himself together and breathed sharply through his teeth. "Ah, Manx or Ollie let you in on that one, I'm guessing. Sir Aubrey was a fine fellow. He was a good businessman, and we worked with him several times before making our move to consolidate. It was unfortunate he decided to be stubborn about things."

"We understand you put him into an untenable situation," Inspector Morris said.

"Indeed, we did," Mr. Hampton said. "It was probably the nastiest thing I have ever done. When I suggested we try it, I still remember the look on Alex's face. He was stunned, and then he just laughed. I think Sir Aubrey considered building a dock to bypass our trick but finally gave up. We bought it all from him at a reasonable price, of course. Sir Aubrey did not suffer financially, even though the whole affair bordered on nefarious. That's business for you. I suppose he stewed on it later. Why else come back with the lawsuit."

"He perished, though," Inspector Morris said.

"Perhaps you should investigate that death too, Chief Inspector." Morris was about to protest, but Mr. Hampton raised a hand. "Sir Aubrey was old. He died from some organ failure as any old man would. Honestly, if I could go back and find another way, I would. He was good at business, and we could have made money together. But I was foolish and impatient with his one remaining warehouse surrounded by the empire I was building on the docks."

"What about Sir Aubrey's daughter?" Inspector Morris asked.

"What about her?" Mr. Hampton countered. "She wanted to continue with the lawsuit. The silly girl loved her father and believed we wronged him, which may or may not be slightly true. But what can she do? Her husband put a stop to it, and I can't blame him. He has his hands full running those bakeries he inherited. Do you have any idea how hard running a bakery is?"

"Er… no," Inspector Morris said.

"It is a business where all of your stock goes stale within a day or two," Mr. Hampton said. "You have to sell it fast, keep your return on investment, and always be making more. Perishables require a constant turnover in stock, pre-stock, and you can never trust your distribution system. You are always on the search for fresh ingredients while marketing the hell out of everything. Nothing can go to waste, or you lose a fortune overnight. If anything, we should all be in awe of Price Bakeries. They managed to add two new bakeries in the last year alone, thanks to that whole bread pudding innovation."

"Bread pudding?" Georgia asked.

Mr. Hampton looked at her, and for the first time since they met, she saw a spark of life in his eyes. "Sir John Price realized his stock was going stale within two days," he said, almost as if they were the oldest friends, "so he brought in some old lady who knows puddings and gave her all the old bread and pastries. She went right in there and figured out a way to mass-produce the over-limit into puddings to last another two weeks. That is a phenomenal preservation of business assets. He rewarded her with a small mansion and stock in the company, as long as she keeps coming up with new recipes. She's living in splendor. The investment was far less than the resulting profit."

"What does this have to do with the lawsuit?" the Inspector asked.

Mr. Hampton laughed. "It has everything to do with everything. Sir John Price doesn't have the time or will to continue a failed lawsuit over a dusty old warehouse in the dry docks. He's too busy."

"That leaves his daughter, though," Inspector Morris said.

"What about her?" Mr. Hampton asked. "Her husband said no to the lawsuit. She has no recourse." He looked at each of them before the implication set in.

With the interviews over, and Mr. Blue about to leave, all Georgia could do was sit back and stare into the distance as she mulled the information over. Lady Emily was given a sedative and sent home before anyone could question her. They would have asked her the same questions they had asked everyone else.

No one had seen anything.

Georgia wondered how real detectives learned anything at all.

They relaxed with a cup of tea while the Chief Inspector organized the shipment of the glasses to the Order of the Blue guild house.

"Is it possible he wasn't poisoned?" she asked.

"It's possible," Mr. Blue said, "but right now, poison seems like the most logical choice. He had no other wounds on his body."

"You don't think it was a brain hemorrhage or some kind of heart attack?"

"He's going to the coroner, where they will do tests. These days, we know enough to figure out if one of those were the cause. If they find something, they will alert us," Mr. Blue said. "I could be wrong, but the damage to his fingernails and neck implies a lethal dose of poison. The fact that he showed no symptoms before he died is odd. Still, it might be possible he was poisoned and never realized it."

"I don't know much about poison," Georgia admitted. "But the idea he would have realized something was amiss seems the most plausible."

"I agree."

Georgia sipped her tea and shifted the topic. "Some of those witnesses weren't being entirely truthful," she said, finally. "I feel it in my bones."

"Nearly every one of them skirted something," Mr. Blue said. "It was in their eyes."

"Mr. Turner and Mrs. Smythe were already acquainted, did you notice?"

The wizard nodded. "Oh, yes," he said. "That was apparent."

"Perhaps when we get back from our walk tomorrow," she said, "I will call upon Mrs. Smythe and question her further."

"I think that is a good idea," Mr. Blue said. "I will go with you if you like."

Georgia nodded. "We also need to talk to Lady Johanna Price. What if she took matters into her own hands?"

"Agreed. We should track Lady Johanna down as soon as possible."

CHAPTER 4: WALK.

Mist clung to the morning air as Georgia made her way to the gate path. She was well-prepared in a sensible wool jacket, excellent walking boots, her hair pinned into a good leather hat, and the Sword of Goldenheart strapped to her back like a modern barbarian.

Mr. Blue waited at the gate, once again clad in his azure wizarding uniform and elegant walking cane. "You look ready for the day," he said, smiling brightly.

"I couldn't decide if I should strap the sword to my hip or make my ladies maid carry it behind me." Georgia laughed.

"You found the perfect solution. Shall we get started?"

She took a deep breath. "Okay. Yes. What would that first step be?"

"Walking and talking," the wizard said. He grinned. "We stroll up the Mountain of the Tree, and I will answer your questions? Perhaps tell a tale or two?" He held up a picnic basket. "The hike will take up much of the day, so I brought lunch."

"It all sounds perfectly civilized."

They set off. Without Mr. Hampton in tow, they arrived at the picnic spot from the day before within minutes.

"My uncle told me that it was my duty to take this office," Georgia said, "because I am the last of my family and because of the Articles of Unification, without which there would be no Three Realms."

"That is correct," Mr. Blue said. "Your ancestor, Godric Goldenheart, was the tie that bound the three ancient kings. Their regard for him and your family was so great they were willing to sit as equals over one realm made of three."

"This is not in any history book I ever read," Georgia said, arching an eyebrow.

"The Three Realms is over four thousand years old. It's easy to lose track of things like proper history," the wizard said. "Days become weeks, years become centuries, and everything eventually passes into legend."

"Where did the magic sword come from?" Georgia asked.

"It came from the Far West, more than five thousand years ago," Mr. Blue said. "The blade has a name. It is called *Anamagal*—the Sun Blade of the East—and was forged by the ancient Fay in the city of the Hidden Rock. It was carried across the world to our lands by the brothers Alaric and Redwald. They were the wizards who founded my order."

"Alaric and Redwald? *The Legend of the Midnight King*," Georgia said. "I read it in school."

"'Much that was once known by the children of men is now unknown,'" Mr. Blue murmured, quoting from the book. "'History lost will be the peril of the future.'"

"My magic sword is from an old fairy tale?"

Mr. Blue shrugged. "I wouldn't refer to it as a mere tale, but that is somewhat accurate. Everything about your family derives from the story—your title, the regard of the Three Realms, and the extraordinary physical prowess all Goldenhearts share."

"Physical prowess?" she echoed. "What do you mean?"

"I know you are physically stronger than I am," he said. "You know it too. You, Lady Georgia, are stronger, faster, and capable of feats greater than anyone you've ever met—with the possible exception of your late uncle and cousin. Am I not correct?"

Georgia nodded slowly. "I suppose. I always assumed it was just good stock and breeding."

"It is the best stock," he answered. "Your family goes back to the ancient days of the Aduna, the blessed ones who traveled over sea and land to settle this country. Your ancestors walked in the pale sun when the world was young, and the Fay lived among us. The first of your house was named Emeil Onaura, and he was a great hero who slew a terrible monster. His name roughly translates in the old language to Heart of Flame. From him, your family took the common tongue name of Goldenheart."

"Why am I only hearing this story now?" she asked. "It sounds like something Uncle Raymond should've told me at bedtime when I was a child."

"Some stories are lost to time, or known only to a few. As the tale goes, Emeil Onaura gathered his riders of the great plain. A terrible shadow lay across the world. From beyond the Western Mountains, news of the Midnight King came to his ear. Everything he heard filled him with dread, for the Midnight King was a lord of monsters, ancient spirits, and evil. Emeil Onaura thought to lead his people to safety in the Far East. Alas, to the east of the plains, lay the Mountains of Fire, where the Goblins of Dura Pluel held sway. Emeil Onaura opted to go north," Mr. Blue said. "He hoped to cross the great shelf where the sea was frozen, thinking to find the way south again to warmer lands far from the danger. The north, however, was the home of the Giants of the Heleg Vallu, who hated the children of men."

"Oh dear," Georgia said. The magic blade hummed. As the wizard spoke, the magic blade hummed in cadence with his words.

"The riders of the plains rode north, but the Giants ambushed them on the barren slopes of White Sky Mountain. You see, while the Giants hated all smaller creatures, they also hungered for their flesh. Many of the riders fell, only to be carried off. Emeil Onaura quickly realized if he were to save his people, he would need to find another way."

"I should think so."

"And so he took them into the south. Back across the plains, they rode, and down to the edge of the Great Wild Wood," Mr. Blue said. "But there was a danger waiting in the south. In those days, the Wood was the home of the Yarith, another tribe of the children of men. The riders of the plains traded with them and hoped to move safely through their lands. Emeil Onaura originally would have gone south before heading east, but the way would have been much longer. When he and his folk were forced to go that way, they found that the Yarith were gone. Their villages and places of worship were abandoned, and all signs pointed to a great evil taking hold. The Wood was dark and grim, and terrible creatures roamed everywhere. Once again, many riders fell, and Emeil Onaura was forced back. Finally, he returned to his home and wife."

"I was wondering about that," Georgia said.

"Wondering about what?" Mr. Blue asked.

"Sorry, you know how these old stories go. Poor Emeil and his riders are traipsing all over, while the wives stay at home with the children."

"Yes," Mr. Blue said, laughing. "There is an awful lot of gallivanting and leaving the wife at home."

"What if he comes home to find out Giants ate the

whole family," Georgia said. "I know, that sounds silly."

"No, it's not silly at all," Mr. Blue said. "Honestly, fear of having one's wife eaten by a Giant probably led to the gallivanting in the first place."

Georgia laughed. "Okay, what happened after that?" she asked. She had read *The Legend of the Midnight King* in school, but this whole chapter about Emeil Onaura—her ultimate ancestor—wasn't in the book. The published book was about the founding of the Three Realms and brave heroes. Georgia wondered how Emeil and the riders of the plains fit into the story of the Three Realms, along with her other ancestor Godric Goldenheart—who must have come along later. For that matter, the magic sword was still not mentioned.

"A great winter came to the plains. Next to the hearth, Emeil Onaura took counsel with the other chieftains. They did not know what to do, for everyday rumors came from the West—the danger grew. The Midnight King was building a mighty empire. He enslaved many people with the help of terrible monsters and dark magic. Tales circulated of other realms in the far west that resisted his unholy power. Hope flourished, and many of the riders began to talk about going to aid the west," Mr. Blue said. "They talked about helping, but they did not go."

"So, they waited," Georgia murmured. What else could they do? It all sounded like the ancients were listening to gossip. Where were the rumors of darkness coming from in the first place?

"One day, a great snow blanketed the plains, and all went quiet. The riders waited, but Emeil Onaura was restless. His mind returned to the question of the darkness. Would it come for his people now that they were unable to flee? Distracted, he rode out to survey the plains and gaze upon the Western Mountains. He rode far, making his way to the slopes where the plains ended. It was there where he spotted two ancient men on foot. Dressed in blue, they strolled through the ice and snow like it was a summer day.

Laughing and singing together, they approached him and bowed."

"Redwald and Alaric?" Georgia asked. "You mean the wizards who founded your order were there?"

"Yes, and they were, in fact, Redwald and Alaric," Mr. Blue said. "They greeted Emeil Onaura by name. He had never seen or met either of them before. Redwald said, 'We are returning from the West after a mission of great importance, lord of the plains.' Naturally, Emeil wanted to know everything of what they'd see. Was the Midnight King coming? Were the realms of the West winning their war against him? Right away, he sensed they were good folk."

"Of course," Georgia said.

"Alaric said to him, 'The danger is growing. The Midnight King conquers all who resist, and none in the West have the strength to continue their fight. Even now, the Midnight King sends his dark servants to your lands. He sends vampires, werewolves, ancient spirits, and even *bruja*.' Emeil Onaura was confused by the word. 'What is a bruja?' he asked. 'Dark professors,' the blue wizards told him. 'They offer corruption masked as a gift of power, and those who are weak in their minds and souls will be tempted by it. It is not the truth. No one needs to sell their soul for power or happiness. He hopes to sway your folk to his side to fight the lords of the West. You must find a way to get your people to safety. Your people are innocent. They have no history with this kind of evil'," Mr. Blue said.

Georgia gaped. "Good heavens," she said. "What happened next?"

"Emeil Onaura was dismayed, but the wizards gave him hope," Mr. Blue answered. "First, they presented him with the blade you wear." On her back, the sword sang merrily. Mr. Blue continued, "They also gave him a map. 'Go to the Mountains of Fire, to the east of the great plain. Take all of your people with you, not just the riders. Take everyone. Leave your home behind. We will meet you at the location marked on the map, for there is a passage beneath the caves of the Goblins. We will lead you to lands of the East, where the plains are greener and where you will find other free peoples. You will flourish in safety'."

"He took the sword and packed everyone up to go," Georgia said.

"He did," the wizard said. "It took a whole year, but Emeil Onaura eventually convinced the folk of the plains to migrate to safety. They traveled to the point on the map where the blue wizards indicated. Of course, there were other adventures along the way, and he found other heroes to stand beside him. There was also a whole side-story where Emeil Onaura and his friends had to leave the migration and perform acts of great heroism. They fought a dragon named Ayndarth, who was made of shadow and hunted stragglers in the darkness. Later, Emeil Onaura was taken captive by an evil spirit called Doria Nanette. Fortunately, he drove her away with the light of Anamagal, the Sun Blade of the East. Doria Nanette would go on to appear in many other folk tales throughout the centuries, and to this day remains a legend in some of the more remote parts of the Three Realms. So many tales, but I'll stick to the main one for now if you don't mind."

"We can revisit the other stories, I'm sure," Georgia agreed. "I take it, they made it to the mountains and got to safety? I mean, otherwise, we wouldn't be standing here talking about it."

"They did. The Goblins mistook the migrants for an invasion and tried to kill everyone. Emeil Onaura's people had to flee for the tunnel, and the blue wizards brought it down behind the refugees. For weeks, the folk followed the cavern in total darkness. All the while, the folk fended off the dangers of the underworld. Finally, they found the way through and back into the light. On the other side, they met the people of the Three Realms and were hailed as heroes. King Tobias, the first lord of the Three Realms, made Emeil Onaura a duke and Knight-Protector."

"That's wonderful," Georgia said. "This story is just as exciting as the one about the forming of the Three Realms. Why isn't it in the book, too?"

"Much that was known is lost," the wizard answered. "There was a time when all of the grand houses were like the Goldenhearts. They all have their tales of brilliant heroes and good people willing to do what was necessary. Those days are gone. The great families, even the princes of the Three Realms, diluted themselves."

"Oh, dear," Georgia said. "This won't turn into a warning about marrying into swarthy-skinned foreign families and ruining bloodlines, I hope."

Mr. Blue laughed. "Far from it. There is no such thing as ruining a bloodline by marrying the 'wrong type' of person. That is the whole point. We are all children of the same maker. The dilution comes from a lack of regard for the past. It happens when people are rash and imagine themselves better or more deserving than others. People don't like the old wisdom; it makes them think about dark nights and goblins. Magic doesn't sit well with people in these modern times. I assure you, the old days were real. They are still real. There are all sorts of beings and things around which we do not understand. We don't see the mysterious things now."

"Try telling that Mr. Hampton. He doesn't believe in wizards or magic. I know this because he told you so many times," Georgia smirked.

"Indeed. He will make a very unpleasant father-in-law for Lady Beatrice."

"Trust me, she's more than a match for him. Just give her time."

They followed the trail further up the lane for a mile, passing several houses. Finally, they arrived at a turn where the path headed up the mountain. Off to one side was another gate leading to the back lot of a sprawling home.

"Ah, a split in our path," Mr. Blue said, pointing at the

sign on the gate. Madison House.

Just across the fence, Georgia spotted Lady Emily Madison trimming a large Crown Princess rose bush. "Hello, Lady Emily."

Lady Emily looked up from her work, her eyes red and puffy. She gazed at Georgia without answering, then looked back down. Georgia thought the lady might simply ignore her, but she stood. "Hello, Duchess," Lady Emily finally mumbled, pressing the back of a gloved hand to her moist cheek. "I do not look presentable for fit company."

"You look precisely as you should. We happen upon you by surprise, after all." Georgia answered. "Please accept my condolences for your loss."

"Thank you. I'm afraid I don't quite know what to do with myself this morning. Despite the sedative I took, I didn't sleep a wink last night and couldn't stop crying. Well, I suppose that's natural. Anyway, I thought I would escape to the garden, but it is rather quiet, and now I am left only to my thoughts and memories. Normally, I can count on Mrs. Duckworth to show up and spoil the quiet. Alas, even she appears content to leave me alone. Would you like to come in for a cup of tea?"

"We would be honored to join you."

Lady Emily led them to a side veranda. She sent two maids to set up tea. Mr. Blue followed the ladies quietly, letting Georgia take the lead. A moment later and they settled in with biscuits and steaming cups.

"I knew you lived in the area," Georgia said, "but had no idea it was so close to Hampton House."

"We helped the Hamptons find their house." Lady Emily said. She turned to Mr. Blue "You are one of those blue wizards, aren't you? I didn't catch your name before."

"I am Mr. Blue," he said. "All of the blue wizards are either Mister or Miss Blue."

"I suppose that's convenient for you."

"Out in public, it is. At the guild house, it gets a bit confusing." He smiled.

"And you have a Miss Blue too? How extraordinary," Lady Emily said.

"We do," Mr. Blue said. "Miss Blue has an amazing mind and an uncanny memory. Her eye for detail is humbling, as she misses nothing."

"How extraordinary."

Lady Emily was being polite, but she might start weeping at any moment.

"May I ask you a few questions?" Mr. Blue asked.

Lady Emily sighed. "Of course. I will do my best to help in any way possible."

Mr. Blue tilted his head. "Lady Emily, did your husband complain of any stomach problems before the party? Was he ill?"

She shook her head. "No."

Mr. Blue nodded. "Was he afraid of anything? Did he express regret, perhaps for the way he treated anyone?"

"My husband was a shrewd businessman. He made hard choices, I think. There were old business rivalries back in the day. And yes, he might have had some regret, but not in the last few days. He was happy. He was relieved."

"Relieved?"

"Running a large dockside business can be taxing to a man," she said. "Alexander was happy to let go and enjoy his retirement. It was bliss."

"Did Sir Alexander have any enemies?"

She pondered the question before saying, "I should think so, considering someone poisoned him. If I were to guess, I would have to say Mr. Hampton did it."

"I say," Georgia gasped. "Are you certain this is an accusation you want to make? It's serious."

"My husband relinquished the business at some personal loss, yet I cannot think who else would have a motive." A lone, elegant tear rolled down her cheek.

Motive. That was a Cymbre word. "Forgive me. If this becomes too unpleasant, we will be happy to change the subject or leave you in peace," Georgia said quickly.

"I will never be at peace," Lady Emily answered, "unless you learn the reason why this happened." She dabbed at her cheek, stoically.

"May I pry a little more?" Mr. Blue asked.

Lady Emily nodded.

"When you say you cannot think who else would have a motive, does that mean you know of one for Mr. Hampton? The way you phrased the statement was precise."

"No. I cannot think why he would do this thing. Alexander treated him very well, and they shared a genuine affection. Alexander thought the world of him, even when Hampton was acting like a bore. It doesn't make sense, and I have to admit I wonder at the location."

"The location?"

"I hate thinking about this, but I must." She looked pointedly at Georgia. "I was trained to think." She was definitely from a Cymbre school.

"I understand what you mean, my lady," Georgia said, remembering something the sisters used to say. "Let your mind follow a logical course. The conclusion often happens before we see it."

Lady Emily dabbed her eyes again. She took a breath and laid out her case. "I do wonder why he would choose his own house for it. He is the first suspect, having a long history and potential financial complications with Alexander. Last year, there was a small matter of Alexander's will. He had Mr. Hampton listed as one of several beneficiaries but removed him." Ah-ha. The will.

Mr. Blue leaned in. "Why did he do that?"

"My husband did not see fit to tell me. That was not unusual, however, as I rarely questioned him on such matters. I only recall it happened because our solicitor had papers delivered for Alexander to sign, and he mentioned it in passing," Lady Emily said.

"Do you have a copy of the old will?" Mr. Blue asked.

"Perhaps along with a copy of the new one?"

"Mr. Clanahan, our solicitor, collected everything after the new document was signed. He took it all away."

"That's too bad," Georgia said.

"Mr. Clanahan will be here tomorrow," Lady Emily said. "Perhaps, Lady Georgia, you would like to join us again for tea? I'll send one of the footmen over to his office with a note asking if he has a copy of the old will."

Georgia took the new widow's hand and gently squeezed it. "I would be honored to join you for tea tomorrow, Lady Emily."

Mr. Blue closed the gate behind Georgia as they returned to the path up the mountain.

"A Cymbre girl just like me," Georgia said. "What a lovely coincidence. I suspect I would make a good detective. It doesn't seem too difficult. Follow the clues and eventually find the answer."

"I have never been a fan of coincidence," Mr. Blue said. "I have never met a wizard who was. First, by complete luck, we run into the last gate on the trail leading us directly to an interview with the grieving widow. She has tea and rather delicious biscuits waiting on the veranda, and it turns out she has the precise, and rather obscure, type of finishing as you. It is bothersome."

"In this case, it may work in our favor. If we can rule out the will, we can rule out Mr. Hampton as a suspect— or confirm him. Wait. You don't like coincidences?"

"Absolutely not."

"But, the world is full of coincidence."

"Agreed. The world is very cumbersome that way," Mr. Blue said. "However, it is not full of mysterious poisonings at dinner parties. Poisonings, I might add, that happen entirely too quickly for a natural toxin to take effect, and without the victim feeling even an inkling of discomfort beforehand."

Right. "Even with what we just learned, we may be no closer to the truth. Drat. I was hoping this detective thing would be easier."

"You, Lady Georgia Goldenheart, have a way of putting things I find refreshingly direct. I hope you don't mind me saying so."

"If it is a compliment," Georgia said, "how can I mind, Mr. Blue?" They smiled at one another, and the walk continued. She mulled over what they had learned so far. Why would Mr. Hampton do it? What does he have to gain? The Hamptons are thriving. Better yet, why murder the man right in one's own home? For that matter, why do it in front of witnesses?

"Mr. Hampton doesn't strike me as someone who would be rash. He's a bit rude, but that doesn't imply the capability for murder." Mr. Blue said.

"I concur," Georgia said.

The trail wound upward, past more cypress and cedars, and the air grew crisp with hidden pine.

Mr. Blue's breathing grew labored.

Georgia slowed her pace to accommodate the wizard. The terrain grew rocky while the wind picked up and stirred her hair. The trail turned again, and they arrived at a series of enormous roughhewn stone steps.

"This is the walk of kings," Mr. Blue said quietly. "In times gone by, the lords of the Three Realms followed this path upward. They were accompanied by the last of the Fay who would one day follow the sun and vanish."

"And now we follow the trail," she said. "What will we discover?"

"History. Legend."

The ancient steps were weathered and crumbling. Georgia gazed up to see how far they went and was startled to find they stretched all the way to the cloud-line. She turned and looked down. Oradale was quite far away now. To the east, she saw the Autumn Wood, cut through by the great River Pala, which formed the border of the Realm of Palas. Georgia walked across the first step to see the west. The River Findalon wound its way north, forming the border of the Realm of Findor. On the northern side of the mountain was the start of the Realm of Volusia. People always said Oradale was the meeting point of the Three Realms, but it wasn't. The Mountain of the Tree was the actual point where they came together. She breathed the crisp air. It was harder to take in, this high up, but still invigorating. Mr. Blue guided her to the next stone step, and they began the climb again.

Finally, Georgia arrived at a door on the side of the mountain.

CHAPTER 5: THE CORRIDOR.

The door was stone, slightly ajar, and inscribed with ancient writing.

"Do you know what the writing means?" Georgia asked.

"It is written in the tongue of the Fay, and says, 'Here begins the road under the mountain of the great tree of the east. All who walk this path follow destiny and face the test.'"

"What kind of test?" Georgia asked.

"It's always different," Mr. Blue said. "Your uncle walked this path with my mentor. He met the Grey Lady in the tunnels, and she gave him wisdom and counsel."

"Who is the Grey Lady?" Georgia asked.

"She is a Fay of legend. Her people have almost all abandoned our world, called back to their ancient homeland. A few, like the Grey Lady, still linger amongst us. Most of those who remain are like shadows and memory. They stay for their own reasons; some out of regret, others live in darkness without hope, but the Grey Lady stays to offer wisdom when she can."

"Did my cousin, William, also walk the path?"

"He did," Mr. Blue said, nodding. "I went with him. We saw only the darkness of the tunnels. There was nothing else."

There was just enough room for each of them to step through.

Mr. Blue went in first. "Join me?" he asked. "There is a path here. We will need to follow it upward to the top of the mountain."

"Goodness," Georgia said, pushing past the door into almost total darkness. "We are underground, Mr. Blue. Please tell me I am not about to be covered in cobwebs and spiders."

"Give me one moment." Mr. Blue fished a candle out of his jacket, and it lit on its own. Faintly, she could see the lines of a long stone corridor stretching out ahead, with only a few cobwebs. There were drawings and some writing.

"Is that graffiti?" she asked.

"These are the markings left by travelers for five thousand years," Mr. Blue said. He pointed to the drawings. "Here we have a warning about goblins, bogies, sprites, and other dangers. Here is a declaration of love by one whose name has eroded with time." They moved down the corridor with care, as the candle provided only so much light. The corridor turned, and the candle was the only light she could see.

She followed Mr. Blue and his little candle, expecting at any moment a stray breeze would blow it out. Luckily, that did not happen. They arrived at a narrow stairway, which led upward. The walls of the passage brushed each of Georgia's shoulders and the top of her hat. On her back, the magic sword hummed. They continued to climb.

"Bea would hate this," Georgia whispered.

"Any sensible person would," Mr. Blue whispered back.

Georgia felt fine.

The stairs ended. Georgia squeezed out of the passage to stand next to Mr. Blue. His candle glowed steadily but failed to pierce the blackness all around.

"Let's risk a little more light," Mr. Blue said, and the candle brightened.

To one side was a huge stone table with ancient writing, which—at first—looked like gibberish. Georgia walked closer and with some difficulty read the inscription, "'In the darkness, we sit.'"

"It's from an old proverb," Mr. Blue said quietly. "In the darkness, we sit quietly and wait until the end, when the world will be as brilliant as heaven."

"Evil will never hold sway when the world is as brilliant as heaven," Georgia said. Uncle Raymond used to say it occasionally.

"This way," the wizard pointed. "Watch your step. The floor is uneven. We are in the waiting room." They found a doorway and followed another corridor.

"When was this built?" Georgia asked.

"Just after the reign of the Three Princes, at least five thousand years ago," Mr. Blue said. "Prince Glendon Oakes of Findor, Prince Dalton Rose of Palas, and Prince Damon Mather of Volusia. They jointly ruled the Three Realms until the hidden folk came and waged war. All three princes died in the Battle of Belton. The hidden folk were defeated, but victory came at a terrible price. The great House of Oakes was utterly lost, while House of Rose had only one survivor, Lady Antonia Rose. The House of Mather fared better, as Prince Damon's youngest son, Tobias, survived. In a meeting of the greatest nobles from across the Three Realms, he was made king. He married Lady Antonia to seal the loyalty of the people and unite everyone. As a way to further that goal, Prince Tobias and Lady Antonia changed the name of their mutual house to Hart and took the buck, horse, and eagle as their symbol."

"Interesting," Georgia said. She had read about the royal house of Hart in history class at school, but she didn't know the part about the prince and lady both changing their names.

"King Tobias and Queen Antonia had this place carved out of the mountain. Originally, they hoped to make it a palace."

"But it was too dark," she whispered. "Nothing could live here."

"Indeed, it became the path for later generations to follow. On the mountain top, we will find where the ancients gathered to anoint kings, queens, and their children under the light of the stars."

"And the world moved on."

"And the children of men forgot what they should have remembered."

"Mr. Blue, today is going in all sorts of unexpected directions."

There was a faint light ahead. They entered another room with a smooth floor and a huge opening in the wall. Sunlight streamed in to reveal an empty banquet hall. The back wall was a vast mural depicting three warriors on horseback facing a large dragon of shadow. Off to one side, two old men in blue leaned on walking sticks.

"This would have been a lavish room, had they not abandoned their plan to build a palace," Mr. Blue said. "Originally, there were tables and chairs here. Time eroded them to nothing."

"Yet the mural remains," Georgia said.

"Legend says the mural was painted by the Grey Lady, and it will remain for as long she walks the world."

Georgia stepped over to the opening in the wall and looked out. Far below, the great city of Oradale spread to the horizon. "All those people below and no one knows this looks out over them," she whispered.

"You might be happy to know there are still many people who are aware of this place," Mr. Blue said. "It's never been a secret and is only lost to legend."

They left the banquet hall behind, heading back through another dark corridor. Mr. Blue's candle illuminated the way they walked. The next chamber was even more prominent with massive columns. At the same time, shadows grew all around. For a moment, Georgia missed the bright room with the mural.

Something moved beyond her sight. It scratched at the ground. "Do you hear that?" she whispered.

"Some sort of animal," Mr. Blue said. "Perhaps it is a rat or some other burrowing thing?"

Glittering yellow eyes peered out of the darkness, reflecting the candlelight. Still, they were not the eyes of a tiny burrowing creature. Whatever it was, the thing stood at near-human height. It followed them at the edge of the shadow.

"Do you see that?" she asked.

The reflection of eyes withdrew. The creature moved away from the light. Mr. Blue took a step toward it, and for a split second, Georgia thought it was a person.

"Is someone there?" Mr. Blue asked the darkness.

Only the silence answered.

Another noise drew their attention.

Georgia turned to find another pair of glittering eyes peering at them through the darkness—again, standing at human height. Cold fear pressed her chest.

"Mr. Blue, we should leave," she whispered. "I think we may be interrupting the residents."

Behind her, something hissed. Georgia and Mr. Blue spun around, causing his candle to flicker wildly. Someone stood very still in the shadow nearby.

"If you are a person, answer us. If you are not a person, you must go away," Mr. Blue said, his voice even and firm. "We mean no harm to anyone who dwells here. If you live here, we will happily move on and bother you no more."

Something, or someone, made a guttural, inhuman noise.

Georgia stepped closer to Mr. Blue. "This is not right," she whispered. Her skin crawled. "Lady Georgia, draw your weapon," Mr. Blue whispered.

"We should leave this place," she whispered back.

"Draw the blade, my lady. Do it now."

Someone grabbed Georgia's jacket and yanked her back hard. She whipped around. "Who's there?" A dark, hunched-over figure scurried away.

Georgia reached over her shoulder and drew the magic sword from its sheath. The blade began to glow and lit more of the room. She spotted several other shadowy figures ducking behind the pillars. A voice whispered from the darkness in a foreign language. The others whispered in response.

"They are calling for something. What are these creatures?" Georgia asked.

"Shadows from another time," Mr. Blue said ominously. "These caverns are sacred. These things are a warning. We should be on our way." He tugged at her arm, guiding her across the great room to the next door.

Georgia held the sword ready as they walked. The shadows continued gathering and hissing. They went up a set of stairs, turned another corridor, and saw faint light ahead. She followed closely behind Mr. Blue as he quickened his pace. Then, they emerged to warm sunlight. As they stepped away from the corridor, Georgia could make out the figures of the shadows, which had stopped at the edge of the day.

"For the record, I would prefer to find another way out of here," she announced, sheathing her sword. "Is there a way off the mountain?"

"We would have taken the other route here if not for two reasons. The first is the ritual: Every Knight-Protector must walk through the abandoned palace," Mr. Blue said. He blew his candle out and tucked it in a pocket.

"What is the second reason?" Georgia asked.

"This way was faster. The exit is not much further. Shall we?" They followed another trail through a thicket of beautiful old cedars to an open area at the top of the mountain.

Georgia caught her breath. Ancient stones stood in a

vast circle, and at the center grew a mighty golden cypress. The trunk was at least ten feet thick, and the branches rose a hundred more, reaching in all directions.

"Spectacular," she whispered.

"Behold the great Tree of the Mountain," Mr. Blue whispered. "The Tree was bought to this land as a seed-cone. The Men of Findor planted it in this sacred space. Its name is *Nimloden*."

"*Nimloden*," Georgia said. Dense sprays of rounded shoots produced gold, amber, and orange leaves, and hundreds of tiny oblong cones hung from the branches. None of the cones had fallen around the base, though. A gentle, whispering breeze rustled the high branches. The breeze continued, and the whispering was like a song.

Mr. Blue picked up the tune and sang:

> *Golden sky, this we see,*
> *Clouds are fleet, this we know,*
> *All the days, the world goes by,*
> *Nimloden stands, all alone...*

Mr. Blue's voice echoed off the mountainside, returning a moment later like a chorus as he sang.

"You could be a professional singer," she said. "I mean, if you hadn't chosen wizardry as your profession."

"Thank you, my lady," he said. Above them, the branches rustled, like the tree was laughing. "It's just about lunchtime. Shall we find a spot to eat before we begin the long walk down?"

"That's it?" Georgia asked. "I guess I thought there would be more to the ceremony. Don't get me wrong: I'm quite happy to be out of the shadow cavern."

"That's it for now. The ritual is specific. You come through the palace and see the tree," Mr. Blue said. "Let's find a spot to sit and dine. I don't know about you, but I find crawling through caves and running from shadowy figures tiring work. I'm hungry."

They found a spot at the edge of the great circle and sat with their feet in a patch of glorious sunshine. Beyond and to the south, Georgia saw the ocean. Below, the city spread everywhere.

"No one down there can see the tree," she whispered. "That's a shame."

Georgia and Mr. Blue dined on Caprese sandwiches with the freshest tomatoes, mozzarella, and basil. Also, there was a bowl of lovely tri-color potato salad with delicate onions, parsley, arugula, a touch of light vinegar, and just a hint of mustard. Mr. Blue drew out two bottles of fresh lemonade to go along.

"You have a wonderful cook," Georgia said around bites.

"Thank you, I made it myself," he said, smiling.

"So, the tree is thousands of years old, and it was brought here by ancient kings. You are a wizard, and I am a knight of the realms by inheritance," she said, sipping her lemonade.

"Correct. You are the realm's defense against evil. Dragons are specifically mentioned, of course. Belief, my lady, is the point. We walked up the mountain so you could see magic. You may never need to worry about fighting evil, but you are here to protect the free peoples from darkness," Mr. Blue said. "It is an awesome responsibility, but one I believe you can handle with time and experience."

"Especially since dragons are so rare," Georgia said.

"That is fortunate, yes. Again, as long as you believe and are ready, then we begin."

"How does this all work?" she asked. "I mean, practically-speaking. I assume, being a duchess, I will start to get invitations to parties, and people will likely want things. I don't have much experience with the world, but I know once a person gets a title, there are always people who start coming around."

"Quite likely, yes. And you should feel free to enjoy

that part of being Knight-Protector," the wizard said. "The more people you know, the more reason you will have to protect them from evil. I know it all sounds like something from a fairy tale. You have a magic sword, though, so I wouldn't be too skeptical. You have felt the blade in your hand, and you know in your heart what it is."

Georgia nodded. She could feel the magic humming from the sword.

"Okay," she said. "I choose to believe. I choose it."

Behind them, the great tree rustled its approval.

CHAPTER 6: LADY EMILY.

The next morning, Georgia was up bright and early. The walk down the other side of the mountain took the better part of the day, but the Hamptons barely noticed her absence. They spent their day talking to constables. Their home was a crime scene, and it might harm their reputation.

After escorting her to the back gate the night before, Mr. Blue set off to the city to check in with his guild and learn more about poisons.

Millie was set with the task of packing while Georgia went down for breakfast. After her errand with Lady Emily Madison, she planned to return to her home instead of sponging off the goodwill of the Hamptons.

Hampton House was very traditional, with breakfast laid on the sideboard and guests free to forage it.

Bea was already in the dining room, reading a copy of the *Youthful Ladies Journal* at one end of the table as she pretended to eat. Aside from a lone footman down the other end of the room, no one else was in the vicinity.

"Good morning," Georgia said, loading up her plate with mostly rashers of bacon. She also poured herself a generous cup of coffee.

"Good morning, Georgia," Bea said, folding up her

reading. "How was your madcap day with the wizard?"

"Weird. Wonderful. We crawled through a cave, and goblins chased us," Georgia said, tucking in without ceremony.

"That sounds ghastly. Are you serious, or are we playing our game again?"

"I am most serious. Mr. Blue took me through a cave, and there were mysterious creatures. I have no idea what they were, but they walked upright and were utterly terrifying," Georgia said. "We also had the most wonderful Caprese sandwiches. I got the recipe from Mr. Blue, who made them himself."

"Oh, Georgia, Caprese is simply tomato, mozzarella, and basil," Bea said. "What other parts of the recipe would one need?"

"Good point. Fortunately, Mr. Blue didn't see fit to mock me when I asked him to write it down," Georgia said.

"That's because you are a duchess and it would have been rude." Bea laughed.

"You make another good point. How was your day while I was away hiking?"

"I thought you'd never ask," Bea said, leaning in and lowering her voice to a whisper. "Ollie and I went for a stroll in the garden just after breakfast, and he said I was charming."

"You're halfway to the altar."

Bea laughed loud enough that the footman was startled. "It doesn't end there. Just before lunch—we didn't have Caprese, by the way—the Hamptons are more of a sour mayonnaise with cucumber bunch—what was I talking about?"

"You were wandering around the yard with Ollie after breakfast, followed by something before lunch."

"Right, it was Manx before lunch. I was in the side study, not the murder room, but the one where the women go, and he comes wandering in all sweaty. Apparently he does some sort of exercise thing to stay fit. Anyway, he was all out of sorts because he wanted to go into the men's study to find a book, but the coppers were there. Then he proceeds to tell me all about the great rivalry between the houses of Hampton and Madison," Bea said.

"Really?" Georgia asked. "That's interesting, because he told the constable the Hamptons and Madisons loved one another."

"He might have said that too," Bea admitted, "but not until after he told me his father was kicked out of Lord Madison's will because Lady Madison hates him. There was bad blood, and Manx implied the lady is not to be trusted."

"How shocking."

"Right? Do you see how useful I am when you are off trekking through marshes?"

"I certainly do, Bea," Georgia said. "But it was a mountain, not a marsh."

"Whatever. It still sounds terrible. Anyway, all of this puts me in a quandary," Bea said, rubbing her temple dramatically.

"How so?"

"Well, of course, Ollie is my first choice, but now Manx has become a bit more... well..."

"Sweaty and gossipy?"

"Precisely. I saw part of a muscle on his arm, Georgia."

"And he was chatty."

"I already said that."

Georgia shook her head. "Don't give up on Ollie. They are twins, after all. He might have a muscle too. Although I doubt he's gossipy. You know what they say about twins."

"No," said Bea, her eyes wide.

"I was about to make something up," Georgia admitted. Bea laughed, startling the footman a second time.

Georgia arrived at Madison House half an hour early and was admitted by the butler. Lady Emily was at the center of a storm of servants.

"Mr. Clanahan sent all of his notes ahead," she announced as Georgia walked in to find a sea of boxes and crates. One of the footmen was laying out folders on the side table like they were hors d'oeuvres at a party. "I had no idea my Alexander needed so much paper for his life."

"When my Uncle Raymond passed, his solicitor also had a room full of pulp to show me," Georgia said. "Do you need help sorting things?"

"The servants can manage it. Mr. Clanahan has his own system. They are setting it out per his instructions. Would you like a cup of tea?"

"That sounds delightful," Georgia said. "So, I take it you are a Cymbre girl, like me?"

"I thought you might be," Lady Emily said. She smiled, but then seemed to remember why Georgia was there. "I keep running over it in my mind," she said. "None of it makes sense. Alexander didn't have enemies. I looked through all of the correspondence in his desk and the safe, too. There was nothing odd in any of it. He kept excellent records. I found a summary of all the outstanding bills paid before his retirement, followed by a complete set of the current expenses. He had a way of keeping track of things that was very organized. That was one of the things I loved about him."

One of the maids walked in with a tray of biscuits. Seeing her mistress crying, the maid also started to weep. She set the tray down, tears freely rolling down her face, and hurried away. The maid was followed by a footman with a fresh pot for tea. The fellow's eyes were also red with emotion. Sir Alexander was clearly liked, even by his servants.

Mr. Clanahan arrived an hour later. Like all men in his profession, he had intimate knowledge of his clients' business affairs, while also being condescending to their wives.

"You will want to protect all assets with new legal issuances and safeguards," he announced in a tone that brooked no opposition. "If only to keep yourself from doing anything foolish, I recommend you name me your executor in all matters."

"I'm sure I can find my way without a legal guardian," Lady Emily said. "I have lived a while, Mr. Clanahan, and seen some of the world."

"You have a sizable fortune, my lady. Forgive my bluntness, but I wouldn't want you to squander or lose it. The papers are full of wild cat-fishing and kidnapping stories these days."

"Thank you, Mr. Clanahan. Your concern touches me," she said in monotone, the edges of her words laced with sarcasm. "That said, it's my decision whether I will squander my husband's fortune or not."

Georgia lost patience. "Mr. Clanahan, do you have the will? Do you have both of the wills?"

"Allow me to introduce Duchess Georgia Goldenheart. She's Knight-Protector of the Three Realms from Dragons, and keeper of the Sacred Blade," Lady Emily said before the solicitor could object. "Georgia is a very close friend from court."

"Oh, I see. It is a pleasure to meet you, Duchess," Mr. Clanahan bowed without blinking. "Well, this is highly irregular. Let us go through the assets first and discuss."

"Mr. Clanahan, you know the assets, correct?" Lady Emily asked. "I suspect you know where every penny is and where it came from."

"Oh, of course," he said quickly.

"Then I trust you will know what to do. I assume I should sell a few things off to simplify the estate?"

"Well, I wasn't going to put it—"

"It's fine. I am too distraught to think about any of it. Sell whatever you think you need to. Not the house, of course. Sell the other house, though. I never liked it, and

I'd rather live on the mountain where Alexander grew up and was so happy. Sell any remaining shares in whatever business you think I'm not fit to manage. Just make sure you get top offer so I can spend my remaining days in comfort. If it isn't worth selling, keep it, and we will hire a manager. Either way, get it done, Mr. Clanahan. Now, may I see both versions of the will?"

Mr. Callahan looked deflated at not being able to boss her around. He produced the two documents and handed them over.

Georgia and Lady Emily pored over wills, searching for Mr. Hampton's name. He was in the first will, as expected, but not in the second.

Lady Emily looked up at the solicitor, "Mr. Clanahan, in the first document, Mr. Hampton is awarded ownership of only one thing... er, Gladys?"

Mr. Clanahan shook his head slowly. "That was something I was going to mention, my lady. I have no idea what that means. Sir Alexander had me write it into the will a decade ago, and said he would explain later, but he never did."

"Do I own Gladys then?" Lady Emily pondered. "What or who is Gladys?"

"Perhaps it was a pet of some kind?" Mr. Clanahan suggested. "Maybe it was a dog or a cat?"

"Twenty years ago, we had a few dogs: Pointer, Scout... and that other one, what was it? Dodger? I don't remember," Lady Emily said. "They all died eventually. None of this makes sense."

"I think we need to find out who or what Gladys is," Georgia said.

"Perhaps you can ask Mr. Hampton about Gladys? Maybe the man will clear his good name," Lady Emily said.

Georgia shrugged. "Anything is possible."

❖

Georgia returned to Hampton House to find Millie waiting with everything packed in the carriage. The magic sword was strapped to the top like a weird bow.

Manx stood in the dark side of the foyer and Georgia almost missed him, but the opal on his ring finger caught a twinkle of light. For an instant, he looked like one of the shadows in the mountain. Then he smiled and stepped into the light.

"I hope you had fun," he said. "I mean, except for the tragic death, of course."

"Thank you for hosting me in your lovely home," Georgia said. "I take it Bea is already gone?"

"She went an hour ago," he said. "I didn't even get to say goodbye. She only has eyes for Ollie. Not surprising. He's always been the bright light in this house."

"One day, they will appreciate your darkness, Manx," Georgia said, smiling.

"I certainly hope so, Duchess," he said. "Thank you for being kind. I hope we meet again."

"I would like that very much."

CHAPTER 7: ANOTHER PARTY.

After what felt like an eternity, the carriage rolled into the driveway at Wending Way. Georgia loved the old place where as a child she lived when she wasn't at boarding school, and every room reminded her of her beloved Uncle Raymond. Wending Way was a solid stone manor, fronting almost on the street with a short gravel driveway. The structure was deceptively large, though. The first floor was built on an axis of right angles from the grand lobby. Unlike other great houses, Wending Way had one main staircase to the next floor. To the left of the lobby was the library and to the right sat the great dining hall. Behind it was a long wide corridor that went to the back of the house and connected directly to exceptionally large glass doors. They opened on a wide garden overlooking the spectacular Oradale Canal. In the summer, one could pull the glass doors open and enjoy the most delicious breeze throughout the whole floor.

Long ago, Uncle Raymond used to throw great parties on that back garden. Georgia looked forward to reviving the tradition.

The second floor was mostly bedroom suites and dressing rooms. There was another small study for the women, but Georgia never bothered with it. She preferred the library. The third floor was the attic, and also the servants' quarters. It was fine. As she pulled up, Georgia gazed up to see there was still a rather startling hole in the roof. She hoped to have that problem resolved soon.

The staff was waiting out front.

"Welcome home, my lady," said Mr. Derry, the elderly butler. He had served her uncle faithfully for as long as Georgia could remember.

"Mr. Derry," she said. "Hello, everyone." Next to Mr. Derry was Francis, the pristine footman. Francis was followed by Mrs. Cotton, the slightly harried cook. Mr. Ellsworth, the vaguely disinterested gardener, was next, and finally, the other girl whose name she couldn't remember. That was all the staff she really needed. She breezed past them with Millie in tow as Francis collected the luggage. "Millie, refresh my memory. Who is the girl at the end?"

"That's Eunice, my lady."

"Eunice. Right. And she does what again?"

"Eunice tidies up the fireplaces and all the rooms I don't clean, my lady. Generally, that means the ground floor, first floor, basement, and most of the second floor."

Georgia stopped. "Oh, dear, she cleans two-thirds of the house on her own?"

"I think she can manage, my lady."

"I'll think about hiring an additional maid. You have your hands full with me, after all."

They arrived at the library. On the table was a stack of correspondence—more letters of condolence addressed to: 'To Whom It May Concern.' She had to write back to those people, even though she had never met any of them.

"I shall tackle this tomorrow."

"My lady," Mr. Derry said, coming in. "This letter is from Lord Christopher Hart, the Earl of Cadwin." The Earl was a cousin of the king and one of the most influential people in the Three Realms. His estate was one-third of the Realm of Palas, and he was rich beyond measure.

"Right. That sounds important," she said, breaking the seal. It was not a letter of condolence but rather an invitation to a party, addressed directly to her—Duchess Lady Georgia Goldenheart of the House of Goldenheart, Royal Knight-Protector of the Three Realms from Dragons and keeper of the Sacred Blade and All That Implies.

What exactly did that mean? Were they expecting her to show up to the party with the sword in hand? The party was to be held in two days!

"Too late to decline, and maybe I shouldn't back out anyway with the added 'All That Implies.' Hm?"

"My lady?" Mr. Derry asked.

"I'll need to find a suitable gown and escort," she said. "The frock I can manage, but a fine gentleman is another matter. It can't be just anyone." She was pretty sure her butler wouldn't have any useful advice on the topic. "Mr. Derry, send Francis over to call on Miss Beatrice. I believe I will need her urgent assistance. Also, give Francis two bills, just in case he has to wait and wants lunch. Send him around to the main house with a note for Lord Wickham. I'll write that note in a moment, but we'll need to make sure he knows she's helping me as a friend, and not in any way that could be construed as service. Millie, we'll need a dressmaker—a proper one. I know you are talented, but this is a peril bigger than any of us."

"Yes, my lady."

She turned back to Mr. Derry. "On another note, how is our upstairs project going?"

"It is coming along quite well, my lady. The workers

have completed the removal of the rotting areas and replaced it all with fresh pine."

"Excellent, let's have a look," Georgia said. Mr. Derry followed her to the side stairs, and up to the attic where the servants were located. She arrived at the landing and smelled fresh-cut wood and heard the faint sound of tarps rustling in the breeze. Last time she was there, the attic landing was a dark area with a funky smell. Now the air moved and light streamed through the hole in the wall.

"Once the window is in," Mr. Derry said, "we will have the workmen put another layer of plaster, and then paint it all, as per your instructions."

"Excellent. No one took me up on the offer to have their room painted their favorite color?" Georgia asked.

Mr. Derry winced. He didn't approve of that sort of thing. "Miss Millie and Miss Eunice have opted for the pale Findor blue on their walls," the butler said. "Mrs. Cotton has requested a transfer back to her old room in the basement as soon as possible."

Initially, the attic was built with quarters to fit up to 40 staff members. Georgia never liked the setup, as it was cramped. She also had no plans to hire that many people to run a place with only one permanent resident. It was an absurd waste. Upon inheriting, Georgia hired workers to rearrange the entire floor to fit ten staff members. While the workmen were fixing the space, they discovered a rotting area on the south wall, so she had them take that part of the wall out, which left a massive opening. She promptly ordered a vast, bespoke stained glass window from an artist across town.

"Think of how pleasant it will be up there to walk with pale golden and lilac light in the hallway separating the men's quarters and the women's," she had said at the time.

"Oh my lady, that does sound wonderful. But we almost always get up before dawn and retire after dark," Mr. Derry had replied. "Who would see it?"

"Fine," Georgia said. "Imagine how pleasant I will find

the idea of it."

Now, months later, she looked around. The walls were fixed and stable with the tarps nailed down tight to cover the gigantic hole in the wall. All they had to do was wait for the stained glass window artist to complete his work.

"We should be receiving the new window in two weeks," Mr. Derry said.

"Will everyone be warm enough in the meantime?" Georgia asked.

Mr. Derry shrugged. He was from the old days when staff-members were servants, and they didn't complain about the cold.

Beatrice arrived a harrowing seven hours later, seeing as she was out with Ollie Hampton at some boating event. The Hamptons were all about boats. They owned half the docks in the city, after all. After that, Bea had to wait while her chaperone, a rather sullen woman named Mrs. Thornton, reported to Wickham. Fast-tracking Bea's dalliance with Ollie Hampton had to be handled properly. The Irvingdales could not afford even a whiff of scandal there.

"Sorry, let's get to work," she said, plopping down in the library. "I'm famished. Once we finish this, I'll tell you all about the wonderful day I had."

"Perfect. I assume you can stay over?"

"I think I should stay until your return from the party."

"Wonderful," Georgia said.

Bea had to write a note to her brother-in-law for permission. Georgia sent Francis back to deliver it to Irvingdale House. While they waited, they had tea and looked at the *Youthful Ladies Journal*. Fortunately, the turnaround was quick, given the situation, and the footman returned with Wickham's response within the hour.

Bea sighed, opening the note. "Okay," she said, "let's see if Wickham agrees to let me stay until after the party." Her eyes darted over the note. For a moment, she blinked with irritation but kept reading.

"May I ask what he said?" Georgia asked. "I can send him a note myself if it helps."

That offer made Bea cringe a bit. "No, it is fine," she said. "He says the following: 'Dear Beatrice, I received your request and was glad to know you are not wasting time on a trivial task, but rather helping your dear friend, Lady Georgia, prepare for a most important social occasion. I was also relieved to learn you will not be working in service, but rather as a special and highly-regarded friend would. Be certain you are not taken for granted and know we all await your return to the house with haste after the affair. For all of that, I give you consent to stay with Duchess Goldenheart until the day after the ball. —Lord John Wickham, Baronet of Irvingdale.'"

"Well, that doesn't sound so bad," Georgia said.

"I wish I had your agency, Georgia. This constant game of getting permission to leave the house is becoming tiresome."

"I'm sure Wickham is looking out for your best interests."

"He is afraid I will make a fool of myself in public," Bea said flatly.

They stayed inside that night. Georgia felt terrible, making the staff work late while she dined at the big table with her friend, but Mr. Derry appeared to approve of the formal arrangement.

Over dinner, they discussed suitable escorts. "You could ask Michael Talbot," Bea said. "He's still unattached, right?"

"Which one is he again?"

"He's the tall fellow from the Exchange with the weird nose," Bea said.

"Oh, right. Maybe. Isn't Michael a bit common for this?" Georgia hated calling anyone common but figured she was sparing him from embarrassment. Also, Mr. Talbot had a weird face. His nose was on one side, and it always distracted her. Inevitably, she would come home worried she spent the whole evening staring at it.

"Sir Oliver Cleeves?"

"He's too old. Also, he can't walk."

"True. How about Lord John Barrow, the junior partner from my brother-in-law Willoughby's firm? He's certainly not common, and his legs work."

"Suitable, yes, but also married. We don't want a scandal. It needs to be someone of a notable position, but not someone married or too old. What we need is a man people can talk to, but who won't turn it into a salacious article for the *Youthful Ladies Journal.*"

"Honestly, Georgia, they're going to write something about this either way. You are the only ducal knight currently living in the Three Realms, you are a woman, and this is your first real public appearance."

"Good point. Drat."

"Drat." Bea poked at her plate in thought. She looked up. "Wait. I've got it."

"Tell me."

"The wizard," Bea said. "He's young enough and can hold a conversation. Mr. Blue defies anyone's expectations and thus becomes acceptable because who has a choice? He has a royal writ on his person, and his guild is ten thousand years old. Granted, he's a tad strange, and people never quite know what to do around someone like him, but …"

"But so am I," Georgia finished. "I'm going to an Earl's party with a sword on my back. Why not bring a wizard too? Bravo, Bea!"

The next morning, Georgia sent a note to the Order of the Blue guild house inviting Mr. Blue to the party, which he accepted immediately. She checked the escort off her to-do list and focused on her gown next.

Millie found someone better than a mere seamstress—the renowned royal designer, Sir Lionel Rance. He appeared at the house in time for lunch with a mountain of fabric and four assistants.

Georgia's experience with dressmakers was limited to older seamstresses, who chatted excessively. Sir Lionel, however, was a strikingly quiet fellow dressed like a funeral director, but all in silk. His assistants, she noted, were immaculate footmen.

"Duchess Goldenheart, keeper of the Sacred Blade," he said, bowing deeply. "It is an honor to work with you. I will do my best to create the perfect gown for your grand evening. First, of course, I have questions."

"Forgive me, I have a few of my own," Georgia said, eyeing the footmen.

"You are wondering why there are no women here to dress you?" he asked.

"That would be my first question, yes."

"If you are uncomfortable, we can accommodate, of course. But these men are the best in my employ. They are consummate professionals who will treat you with the utmost care and respect. Also, I thought we might enlist your ladies' maid in the process. Miss Millie likely understands you intimately, and I trust her judgment. I have seen her references, and I feel I can teach her to mold your style accordingly after we are finished."

"That doesn't sound so bad. You said you had questions?" she asked.

"I think we should do something special with the sword," Bea said, cutting in. "She will be wearing it at the party."

"I quite agree," Sir Lionel said. "I think we should integrate Anamagal the Sun Blade of the East into your overall theme for the evening, and think about how you use it in the future during public appearances."

"Wait, you know the name of the sword?" Georgia

asked.

"Yes, I do," Sir Lionel said. "I am the greatest dress designer in the Three Realms. I research my clients before I meet them. Your ancestors traditionally attended events with the blade on their person. It was considered appropriate. Also, the current Knightly Orders: Buck, Eagle, and Horse—of which every Sir and Dame in the land, myself included, all have the option to wear a weapon to high social engagements. You outrank us all and should be wearing the blade. It is your duty. So I ask you, Duchess, would you prefer to present an air of great noble aloofness, stern, quiet dignity, or something younger and more spontaneous?"

"She's more spontaneous," Bea said, helpfully. "The gown will need to be fitted for dancing, too."

"I... uh... okay, yes, spontaneous and with dancing, if necessary," Georgia said. "Please, Sir Lionel, while we are doing this, I would prefer if you called me Georgia instead of by my title."

"You honor me, Georgia," he said without hesitation. "Do you prefer dark or light colors?"

"Dark," Georgia said.

"Light," Bea said, interrupting again. "She needs something to offset the wizard. Mr. Blue will be in black and blue.

"Ah, yes, we will need to consider the wizard." Sir Lionel nodded to one of the assistants, who wrote it in a book. "I will send someone to help him, as well. Georgia, would you give me this room to go over ideas while you have lunch?"

"Be my guest. I'll have the staff bring you and your people food." She turned to Bea. "I guess we should go to eat while Sir Lionel does his work."

Two hours later, they returned to find Sir Lionel hard at work. He was sketching furiously, even as three of the assistants draped fabrics over half a dozen wooden dress forms. To one side, there was a vibrant blue swath of cashmere. One of the assistants was actively cutting sleeves for a great coat. Next to him, another assistant was fashioning a broad hat. Beside him, Millie was helping another create a dazzling white silk gown with all sorts of detailed gold satin edging.

"Is it white?" Georgia asked. "I would think we would go with something more current like lilac?"

"People would expect that, and so we should not go with lilac," Sir Lionel said. "For your first appearance, I thought we might make it something timeless, but also just a touch over the top. Naturally, if you prefer lilac, we can do that."

"No. We go with timeless and over the top," Bea said. She looked at Georgia with urgency. "Right, Georgia?"

"Steady on, Bea."

Sir Lionel laid a startlingly blue sash over the gown. "I thought we might dress you in the colors of the flag, actually—white, blue, and gold. Currently, you are the only Knight-Protector in the Three Realms. What if we invoked that as a theme?"

The gown also had tiny little dragons stitched into the edging. "Oh, this is amazing," Georgia breathed. She looked at him. "Are you sure we should go against the current fashion this way?"

Sir Lionel's eyes twinkled. "My Lady Georgia, people like you do not follow fashion. You *are* fashion."

She blinked, hoping he was kidding. He wasn't. "Okay. Yes. Sir Lionel, let's go with this then."

"The wizard has agreed to let us dress him too," Sir Lionel said immediately.

"Really?"

"Of course he did. Mr. Blue may be the head of a five-thousand-year-old order of wizards, sworn to protect and counsel, but I am the premier dress designer, yes?"

"Yes," Georgia said.

"Never doubt the power of fashion," Sir Lionel said, winking.

Mr. Blue arrived at the precise time allocated on the invitation Georgia sent him, in a rather extraordinary blue carriage.

Mr. Derry allowed him entry to the house.

Georgia watched it all from the window while Millie put the finishing touch on her tiara.

"How do I look?" she asked, turning to Bea.

"You look like a queen," Bea breathed. "That headgear is incredible."

Georgia viewed herself critically in the mirror. Her black hair was threaded with gold wiring and pins made to look like solid gold stars. On her forehead, she had a second tiara shaped like the sun with tiny planets in a spray. The collar was an extraordinary gold leaf pressed to look like stars dripping off her shoulders.

"This is entirely too ostentatious," she muttered.

"How dare you," Bea said. "It's just ostentatious enough."

"Fine. I just hope we don't get laughed out of the room."

Millie brought the magic sword in its new sheath, which was patterned to look like the flag of the Three Realms. Carefully, she fastened it to Georgia's back.

There was a polite knock at the door.

"Enter," Georgia said.

Francis stepped in. "My lady, the wizard is... oh my goodness." The footman gaped. "Ma'am, you look like a goddess."

Georgia turned around and tried not to blush. "Thank you, Francis. Did you put him in the library with Sir Lionel?"

"Yes, my lady. I'm sorry. I didn't mean to gawk."

"Gawking is precisely what the occasion calls for," Bea said, getting up. "I'll go down and meet the men." She slipped past Francis, who was still staring.

"It doesn't look too gaudy?" Georgia asked him.

"I do not have words, my lady."

"Thank you, Francis. You may go." After he shut the door, she turned to Millie. "I suppose we should head down."

"Yes, my lady."

Bea had ushered the men over to the foyer so they could watch her descend the stairs. Georgia felt like a fool, but the look on Mr. Blue's face was worth it.

"My word," he said quietly. "That is some frock."

Sir Lionel smiled proudly.

Mr. Blue's outfit was a reverse parallel to Georgia's. Where her coat was blue with silver trim, his coat was white with gold trim. She wore a white gown, so his jacket and tails were vibrant blue and he wore a white tie. He also had tiny stars woven into his hair.

"Aren't we a pair?" she said. She turned to Sir Lionel. "From now on, you, and only you, will be my dressmaker, Sir Lionel."

"You honor me greatly," he said.

"Please convey our heartfelt thanks to your staff as well," she said.

"I certainly will. Have a wonderful time tonight, Georgia."

"Oh, not so fast," Georgia said, winking at Bea. "Before we go, we're all having a lovely drink and toast the night together."

Millie hopped up in the front with the driver, as she would be on-call all night.

"People make no sense," she said as Mr. Blue climbed in.

"How do you mean?"

"My ladies maid is about to spend hours waiting in a side room on the off chance I have a wardrobe problem, but she looks like she's going to her own party."

Mr. Blue smiled. "She is in some way. When she walks into the basement of the Earl's city house and tells them she's your ladies maid, they are going to treat her like a queen. She will sit in splendor in the lower room while younger maids ask her about her fabulous life. Meanwhile, older servants will stare daggers at her for no reason until the First Maid of the House tells them to stop being so foolish. For tonight at least, she is Lady Millie of the Downstairs. I think you should call upon her once and make a bit of a fuss. They should all go running to find her at some point. How lovely for her. You look sensational, by the way."

Calling on Millie to fix a pretend problem was a bit un-Cymbre, on the other hand, making Millie the center of attention seemed like a nice thing to do.

"So do you," she said. "We have a good ten minutes before we get to Cadwin House. What shall we discuss?"

"Poison, perhaps? None of the glasses had any in them."

Georgia straightened up. "But we saw the lines on Sir Alexander's fingernails and the strange rash on his skin. Are you quite certain?"

"I am. Miss Blue double-checked my work in the lab, and she misses nothing. There was not a trace of poison in any glass we took from the party," Mr. Blue said.

"Do you think we missed one of the glasses?" Georgia didn't relish the idea of returning to Hampton's house in search of the missing glass. Also, by now, any missed glass would surely have been cleaned.

"Currently, I think the murderer retrieved it before we could find it. The alternative—there was no poison, and we are barking up the wrong tree."

"Perhaps he did die through some other method."

Mr. Blue shrugged. "There is always a chance, yes. I feel like I am missing a piece of a puzzle. Honestly, it seems like an unseen force at work."

"Detecting is terrible," she said. "That poor man could have died from anything, and we have no idea how or why. What if he just died? What if it was his time?"

"It wasn't his time," Mr. Blue said. "It was murder."

Georgia couldn't deny his gut-instincts on the matter.

They pulled in to a long train of other carriages and came to a stop. "Where are we now?" Georgia asked, trying to see out the window.

"It looks like a side street before we arrive at the driveway to the Earl's house," Mr. Blue said. "There are at least a dozen other carriages parked on the street, and I cannot see how many are stuck in the driveway. We might be waiting a bit. Have you been to many of these parties?"

"I have attended several of the Hampton House variety, but this is new. I am both excited and experiencing mild dread for how tonight will proceed. How are you feeling, Mr. Blue?"

Mr. Blue smiled. "Being an 'official' wizard of the court has its perks. I get invited to at least one of the big parties every year, but never anything important enough to deserve a new outfit."

The queue took a while, but finally, Mr. Blue gave a card to the footman. "Duchess Lady Georgia Goldenheart of the House of Goldenheart," the footman proclaimed. "Knight-Protector of the Three Realms against Dragons and keeper of the Sacred Blade with Mr. Weldon Blue, royally-decreed head of the Order of the Blue Wizards, defender of the Three Realms, and advisor to our beloved court and king with the solace of a generation, as her guest."

Cymbre girls don't make themselves the center of attention, so Georgia was somewhere between giddy and terrified. All around, fine ladies were adorned in lilac, with a few spots of pink, eggplant, and lavender. She gazed down at her spectacularly white gown with blue piping and stars dripping from her shoulders. No matter what Sir Lionel might think about her being fashion instead of following it, Georgia almost turned around and fled. On her back, the sword hummed encouragingly. "Pull yourself together," she whispered. "It's only a ball. You are a duchess."

"I beg your pardon?" Mr. Blue asked.

"Nothing," Georgia said, smiling. "I am simply working myself up into a state of panic for no reason."

Mr. Blue smiled. "You belong here, Duchess Goldenheart. You are no longer a schoolgirl, and no one gets to tell you what is proper now. If anything, you tell them."

Georgia looked over at the wizard, who smiled his encouragement. She grinned wryly. "Your first name is Weldon?"

"Yes, it is," Mr. Blue said.

"I like it," Georgia said. "You have a good name."

"Thank you, Duchess. I think you are stalling now."

Georgia laughed, and stood taller. "Okay, let's do this, Mr. Weldon Blue." Mr. Blue fell in just behind her, and Georgia took the long, slow walk into the main ballroom. She didn't look directly at anyone, but rather held her head straight and smiled gently. All around were noblewomen wearing frilly dresses with fruit and flowers in their hair, while she was like a statue with stars on her shoulders and a sword on her back. The men gazed at her with shock or unabashed admiration.

Mr. Blue guided her past them all until they stood before a young and unobtrusive man barely adolescent. Still, he was a royal. "My lord, Earl of Cadwin," Mr. Blue said to the young man, "May I present Lady Georgia Goldenheart, Duchess of the House of Goldenheart, Knight-Protector of the Three Realms from Dragons, and bearer of the Sacred Blade."

The young earl took both of her hands into his own. "Duchess Goldenheart, your family is legendary. I cannot express my delight and humble admiration to have your presence here tonight. Thank you. I hope you enjoy our little party."

"I am deeply honored, Your Grace," Georgia said curtsying. He let her hands go.

The earl turned to Mr. Blue. "You also honor us, Mr. Blue. Finding you here tonight with the Duchess, I am hopeful for the future."

Mr. Blue bowed low. "Your Grace is too kind."

The earl turned and pointed to the room. "Please, enjoy the evening." Released, they entered the ballroom. Georgia looked around the room. The crowd parted where they went, and a few people gaped openly. She smiled at everyone. No one appeared to disapprove of her style choice after the initial shock of her entrance. In fact, several people raised a glass in greeting.

"We are officially here," she said to Mr. Blue. "Hopefully, we are a welcome oddity."

"We will always be an oddity," he agreed.

"Ah, but you are a necessary oddity," a woman's voice came from behind them.

Georgia turned to find a striking, red-haired woman in a black gown with intricate lace points. Atop her head was a wreath of fragrant roses, and her collar weave looked like a garden fence. "Lady Clara Gaye," she introduced herself with a curtsey. "Forgive me. I chose to speak before you did by pretending you were talking to me." Her eyes twinkled with amusement.

"Hello, Lady Clara, so nice to meet you," Georgia said. When she took Clara's hand, she noticed the woman's palms tattooed with eyes. "Oh, my goodness."

"They are my eyes to see the inner world," Lady Clara said.

"I think a clarification is in order," Mr. Blue said. "Duchess Goldenheart, meet the Witch of Volusia."

Georgia had heard of the Witch of Volusia in stories growing up. Each of the Three Realms had a Witch who spoke for the land itself and advised kings and princes alike. In the stories, the Witches all lived for hundreds of years while they waited for someone to be their successor to the role. The Witches are strange women of power who could be omens of good or evil, depending on the tale.

"Clara is a member of the Lunar Circle," Mr. Blue said. "They are a highly-regarded witch coven in the Three Realms, and if I am not mistaken... personal advisors to the Duke of Volusia?"

"That is correct," Lady Clara said. "We serve the duke just as you serve the king."

"Although, for the record, I have never actually met the king," Mr. Blue said. "He's not a great fan of wizards or the old ways."

Lady Clara frowned. "Really? Forgive me, I am hesitant to criticize royalty, but that seems short-sighted." She turned to Georgia. "Your Grace, I assume you have met the king?"

"I have not had the pleasure," Georgia said. "He might not be a fan of knight-protectors against Dragons."

Lady Clara shook her. "This is all very disappointing. We must get you into court."

Georgia answered, "Perhaps word of our attendance at the earl's party will get back to court, and things will change for the better."

"I suppose we shall see. How are you enjoying the party?"

Mr. Blue smiled. "I have a new outfit and people are staring at both of you in wonder. It's a lovely time." Lady Clara laughed.

Georgia peeked at the crowd, who were, in fact, now mostly staring. It isn't every day you see a wizard, a witch, and a female knight, after all.

"Say, Clara, I have a question, and you might have an answer," Mr. Blue said.

"Happy to help, old friend," she said, turning back. "Ask away."

"Have you ever heard of a poison like arsenic that kills the victim almost instantly, but without symptom or warning?"

Lady Clara tilted her head in thought. "Poison is not my specialty. We should perhaps talk to my witch sister,

Emelda, the Witch of Palas, but I do know arsenic takes time. To build up quickly, as I recall, it would require volume, and the victim would likely know something was wrong. There are other poisons like Polonium, which is colorless, tasteless, and almost undetectable. It breaks down the body's vital organs, and death comes within days. It is considered a better agent than arsenic in that way, but I'm not sure how painless or instant it is. The victim might still have some inkling. That said, polonium would be the quickest way to end someone's life. I assume you're not asking this out of mere curiosity. You've seen something?"

"A few nights ago, Lady Georgia and I attended a party where one of the guests abruptly perished. When we looked at the body, we saw signs of what appeared to be arsenic poisoning. Before he died, there was no evidence of discomfort. He was laughing and talking with several people," Mr. Blue said. "We also spoke with his widow, and she said he was in good health before the party."

"There you have the suspect part," Lady Clara said. "The widow may have been lying or mistaken. The simplest explanation is usually the truth."

"Perhaps," Mr. Blue countered, "but we took the cocktail glasses from the party to our chemist and found no trace of poison. If the victim was poisoned elsewhere, that would make sense."

Lady Clara pondered a moment. "It doesn't sound like it happened at the party. Perhaps it was before? Maybe at home?"

"I don't know," Georgia said. "Lady Emily was quite shocked, and she wasn't acting. I have been to her home and seen the effect his death had on her and the family servants. Does it make sense to say no one in his home—family or staff—was happy about him dying so suddenly?"

"Yes, it does make sense. That could still suggest the idea that the wife was mistaken about her husband's health." Lady Clara said. "Wait. Lady Emily? I read her name in the paper this morning. Wasn't her husband a wealthy merchant and Knight of the Order of the Horse— Sir Alexander Madison?"

"Oh yes, that is her," Georgia said.

Lady Clara looked at Mr. Blue. "If you would like, I can have my witch sister Emelda examine the glasses too. Another set of eyes? She's terrific and hates poison. If anyone can find it, she would."

"I'll have them sent over in the morning, and thank you."

"It is an honor to assist," she said. "You are quite certain it wasn't a heart attack or apoplexy, something that could be natural?"

Mr. Blue shook his head. "We are certain of nothing."

In the next room, violins arose in unison. The tune was at first upbeat but then drifted to the anthem of the Three Realms. A woman's voice echoed throughout the chamber, singing:

> *High in the halls of the kings, who are dead,*
> *We celebrate for the shadow was dread,*
> *All shall await the coming of the dawn,*
> *And let all be bathed in the light of the Sun,*
> *The Three Shall Become One,*
> *And let all be bathed in the light of the Sun.*

On Georgia's back, the magic sword hummed along. A moment later, the tune shifted again to something lively and fun. People began to push into the next chamber.

"It looks like the dancing has begun. Shall we migrate in that direction? I know Lady Clara is a fan of dancing, but how about you, Lady Georgia?" Mr. Blue said.

Before Georgia could answer, Lady Clara said, "Old friends have arrived. Please, wait a moment, so I may introduce you." Georgia and Mr. Blue turned to see a group of very fashionable people approaching them. Leading the group was a striking fellow with a pronounced jawline, reddish hair, and wearing a perfectly tailored tie, and black tails.

Lady Clara said, "May I introduce Lord William Reade, Viscount and primary aide to the Ear of Simsley in the realm of Volusia."

"Good evening," the Viscount said, bowing. "I must say it's lovely to see you here, my lady. You have the most interesting friends."

Lady Clara curtseyed. "Lord William, please meet Lady Georgia Goldenheart, Duchess of the House of Goldenheart, Knight-Protector of the Three Realms from Dragons and keeper of the Sacred Blade."

Lord William bowed low. Behind him, his entourage all lowered in unison. "Forgive me, Duchess, I did not recognize you and meant no offense speaking out of turn."

"Pleased to meet you, Viscount," Georgia said.

Lord William stood up, his eyes twinkling. "I assure you, my lady, all of the pleasure belongs to me." He turned to indicate his entourage. "Please meet Lady Lucinda Kilgore."

Lady Lucinda was a reddish-haired woman in a pink gown with a gigantic bow on her shoulder. The whole group was Volusian. Lady Lucinda looked a bit shy and kept her eyes to the floor as she curtseyed.

Georgia nodded in her direction.

"Meet Lady Carlotta Landsmere," Lord William said, indicating another redhead in a lilac dress. She seemed less shy, with better taste in clothes. Georgia did a head tilt to mix it up a bit.

Lady Carlotta smiled charmingly. "Duchess Goldenheart," she said. "I knew your cousin in passing. He was exceptional. Please accept my condolences for your recent losses."

"Thank you kindly, my lady," Georgia said.

"And finally we have Sir Richard Bourne, a knight at large. I believe he's from one of the knightly orders," Lord William said, indicating the last member of the group. He was also reddish in hair and face, but his tie and tails were impeccable.

Like Georgia, he wore a sword to the ball.

"Order of the Buck," Mr. Blue offered softly to Georgia.

Sir Richard looked at her almost too directly. He was more than a mere knight at large, and he waited for her to speak first.

"Sir Richard, I am still in the early days of protocol training," she said. "I would prefer if you address me freely and not look away. So it is said aloud, I pronounce this both as a duchess and as Knight-Protector."

Lord William and the ladies were taken aback.

"Duchess Goldenheart," Sir Richard said, "I would never presume to speak to the Knight-Protector without express leave and full consent. You honor me beyond my skill to express."

"Let's be as friends then," she said. "I would hate to disturb the party with too much formality."

"Wizards and witches," Lady Lucinda said. "What fun this is."

"We are headed for the dancing room," Lord William said, offering Georgia his arm. "Would you care to join us?"

Georgia looked at Mr. Blue and Lady Clara, who both smiled. She looped her arm with the Viscount and said, "Let's take the floor then."

They glided into the line of dancers.

Mr. Blue took Lady Clara as his partner, while Lord William asked Georgia to dance.

Georgia wondered if Sir Richard wouldn't be a good fit for Bea. If the Hampton family gambit didn't work out, her old friend could do much worse than a handsome young Volusian knight. Even Bea's horrid brother-in-law, Wickham, would find the match appealing.

Lord William was very charming, a good dancer, handsome, and a bit of a flirt. They spun around the floor and laughed. Several ladies fanned themselves provocatively when he passed.

Georgia laughed.

"What's so funny?" he asked.

"Everyone is funny," she answered as they spun around. Lord William smelled good. Not just covered in perfumes and oils but genuinely clean.

"Everyone cannot be funny," Lord William answered. "If they were, the comedians would be out of work." He took Georgia into a little twirl. As she went, she heard the magic sword singing happily, as if it were enjoying the moment.

The song ended. "Would you like another glass of wine?" Lord William asked. "I note your glass was white, and if I am not mistaken—a select vintage?"

"That would be lovely," she said. Lord William nodded and moved off to find a waiter.

Lady Carlotta idled at the side of the ballroom without her dance partner. Why wait? She hurried over and said, "Hello, my lady. I am on a mission, and I have questions," Georgia said. "We must speak like women. Alas, I am also pressed for time."

Lady Carlotta nodded. "I understand, my lady. Lord William is a Baron. He owns the estate of Cathrite, and as Viscount, he serves at the right hand of the Earl of Simsley. His family is quite well-regarded." She gathered her breath. "He's not precisely looking for a wife, I'm afraid."

"Forgive me; I'm not after the Viscount, my lady."

"You're not?"

"My question regards Sir Richard," Georgia said. She kept an eye out, just in case Lord William came stumbling back to overhear.

"Isn't Sir Richard a bit beneath your station?"

"Good heavens! If I were looking for a husband for myself, I wouldn't be hiding on the side of a pillar at a ball, Lady Carlotta."

Lady Carlotta looked like she wanted to die.

"Allow me to start over. I have a wonderful friend, Lady Beatrice Irvingdale, who is the fifth daughter of the Baronet of Irvingdale. She is looking for a suitable husband but is limited in what she can offer. Is Sir Richard suitable?"

"Yes," she said matter-of-factly. "He would be a sound match for Lady Beatrice. He is currently unattached, his family is near her level, and he will inherit a small estate upon marrying."

"I wasn't sure if either you or Lady Lucinda had a stake in this," Georgia said.

"Sir Richard is sweet, but completely beneath either of us," Lady Carlotta said. "He's a dear fellow, though. He has holdings, but they are too modest for either of us. He is a bit too earnest for my taste, for that matter, but really is a dear."

Georgia was reasonably sure that it would not be a problem. "Lady Beatrice has a quick wit. I suspect she could loosen him up."

Lady Carlotta smiled. "I like her already," she said. "How may I assist?"

"That's very kind of you, but I'm not sure what the answer is just yet. I've only just met Sir Richard, and Lady Beatrice certainly hasn't."

"I have the perfect solution," Lady Carlotta said. "I would love to invite you both to my aunt's party. We might arrange a moment for her to meet Sir Richard."

"May I ask, who is your aunt?"

"Lady Hermione Nisbett, the Dowager Countess of the House of Nisbett," Lady Carlotta said. Being the Countess of a House was a very different beast from being the Countess of an Earldom. A House was just a fancy title with nothing to back it up. On the other hand, Georgia was merely a Duchess of a House herself, so not much higher in station.

"I accept your invitation with great enthusiasm and

gratitude," Georgia said. "We all look forward to your aunt's party. The Dowager-Countess will, no doubt, delight all of us."

"I like Lady Clara, and Lady Carlotta has a sharp mind," Georgia said on the carriage ride home. "I'm not sure what to make of Lady Lucinda, though."

"I suspect we will be seeing a few articles about you in the coming days," Mr. Blue said, smiling. "Thank you so much for inviting me. It was great fun."

"It was, yes," she said. "A bit too crowded for my taste."

"Agreed."

They arrived at Wending Way, and Mr. Blue walked her to the door where Francis was waiting. "Thank you again," he said. "Once I have more information from Lady Clara and the witches, how about I pop around again?"

"Perfect. We will continue our investigation," Georgia said. She headed inside, only to find Bea waiting in the lobby.

"You must remember everything that happened tonight and spare no detail," Bea said.

They headed up to the second floor to her sitting room.

"You kept that sword on all night? How did that go over?"

"I think people honestly loved it... once they got over the shock. I will likely have to take it to other parties," Georgia said as Millie carefully pulled the scabbard over her shoulders. She was glad to be out from under the thing, even though the blade didn't weigh anything. "Thank you, Millie."

"Yes, my lady."

"Millie, don't wait up. I will change myself tonight."

Millie curtseyed and headed up to her room.

"At least she stopped arguing every time I want to change my clothes," Georgia said as Bea poured them nightcaps.

"You will ruin that ladies maid," Bea said, grinning. "I'll help you tonight, though."

"Aw, thanks, Bea. Now, sit a moment because I may have found a backup suitor-in-waiting, just in case those Hampton boys turn out to be a dead-end."

"What?" Bea sat down immediately. "Tell me this instant."

"There was a Knight of the Buck at the ball tonight. He is a Volusian, but quite a catch. His family is suitable, his manners are impeccable, and honestly, he's not hard on the eyes."

Bea laughed, delighted. "He sounds wonderful, actually, and the Volusian thing isn't a big deal. The Irvingdales are part Volusian too." Georgia raised her glass. They were just about toast when there was a crash on the next floor, followed by a blood-curdling scream.

Georgia dashed out of the sitting room. She cleared the first flight of stairs to find Millie with blood on her arm.

"My lady, run!" Millie gasped. "There's a— There's a thing up there."

"What kind of thing?" Georgia asked. Millie swayed. Georgia held her shoulders, steadying her, and peered into her wild eyes. There was another crash upstairs and a scream, but it was abruptly cut short. Who screamed?

"It came through the hole in the wall," Millie gasped.

"Like a bird?"

"It was more like a bat, my lady."

"Oh, Millie," Georgia said. "You've gone and gotten yourself hurt over a silly bat?"

"No, my lady, it wasn't just a bat," Millie looked up, trembling. "It was a creature—"

Georgia helped her down against the wall. "Millie, you're not making sense."

There was another thump, and Georgia distinctly heard

Francis say, "Oh my heavens."

"Georgia," Bea said behind her. She looked around to see her old friend standing there holding the magic sword, still in its sheath. The sword glowed and crackled as if it were electrified. "It just started jumping around. I thought I should bring it to you."

Darkness rolled like smoke down the stairs past Georgia's feet. From above, a terrible gurgling arose, followed by a charnel odor. She turned to see a dark human-like figure. The upstairs was in deep shadow, but the figure was darker. Faintly, she could make out wings.

"Millie, get behind me," Georgia said.

The creature scrambled down the steps on all fours, snarling with eyes that burned red, and roiling pitch for skin. The creature with roiling pitch for skin scrambled down the steps on all fours, hissing. It's eyes burned red as it stared at Millie. Georgia glared, not breaking eye-contact as the beast stood up in her face. It had great bat wings, awful talons, and a face better suited to one's nightmares. For a moment, it seemed like the thing might back away, such was the intensity of her gaze. She felt no fear, only odd indignation at its presence. Finally, it howled with breath reeking of death and blood. Georgia waited until Millie was clear, before she said to the thing, "You can leave my home or you can die in it." Instinctively, she leaned back as it swung a claw at her face. Then she moved against the creature. Georgia grabbed it by the arm and shoved the beast onto its back. She kicked it in the face so hard its neck made a sickening crack sound. Then she spun and grabbed the sword from Bea. She unsheathed the blade, which crackled with argent fire. "No? Not ready to leave yet?" she asked.

The shadow creature hissed and tried to tackle her, but Georgia swatted it away. She brought the sword down on its neck. Sparks exploded. The thing shrieked and crawled backward. Georgia pursued, slashing it across the face. She whipped the blade back hard. Sparks flew again, and the creature screamed.

Finally, it scrambled back up the stairs to the attic. Georgia turned to Bea and Millie. "Get Mr. Blue," she said.

"Georgia," Bea said.

"Find Mr. Ellsworth. If he still breathes, send him to the Order of the Blue at a full run. Do it now, Bea. I'm going up." Georgia didn't wait for an answer. Whatever that thing was, it was headed into the servants' quarters. She got to the top of the darkened landing. In the moment while her eyes adjusted, Georgia almost panicked from the blindness. Tarps were flapping over the hole in the wall. Darkness swallowed the attic.

Someone moaned. Georgia held up the glowing sword to see Francis laying in the corridor. He was barely breathing, and there was blood on the floor around his face.

"Francis," she said. "Tell me you live."

"My lady, run. There's a thing up here. I don't know what it is, but it isn't human," Francis said as blood flowed from a gash on his forehead.

"Thank goodness you live," she said. "Where are Mrs. Cotton and that other girl?"

"You mean Eunice, my lady?"

"Eunice. Right."

"I locked them in their rooms, my lady. It was out here in the hall."

"Unlock them and run for the other stairway. Get everyone out of the house."

"My lady, we can't leave you," he said.

"Nonsense," she said. "Do as I say and go."

Behind her, something stirred near the hole in the wall. Georgia heard a faint gurgling. She sprang to her feet as the creature came from above, slammed into her, and knocked the magic blade from her hand. She, and the creature, fell to the ground.

Francis shouted and tried to grab the thing, but it

slapped his hand away and hissed until he backed off.

"Francis, I told you to run," Georgia said through gritted teeth. "Do as I say." Reluctantly, Francis ran down the hall.

The monster looked down at Georgia, opening its mouth to reveal sharp, yellow teeth. She grabbed the thing by the throat and squeezed with one hand until the beast's neck popped and it began to writhe and choke. She punched the monster in the head with her other fist, knocking it across the landing. Howling, the creature instantly jumped to its feet and charged. Georgia kicked it in the face, rolled over, and snatched up the blade. In one movement, she rammed it into the creature's gut. With a gurgling whimper it slumped over and then blew apart in a spray of hot blood. All that remained was a sickening splatter as the magic blade glow faded.

The danger was gone.

"It was an Alpon—a kind of vampire bat," Mr. Blue said, standing in the library less than an hour later.

"A vampire bat," Georgia repeated. Usually, she would laugh at something so absurd but was still in shock.

"You were very brave, my lady," the wizard said. "A creature like that could have easily transformed you into a blood zombie—assuming it didn't kill you."

"What in the world are you talking about?" Bea nearly screamed. She was in the library too. Everyone in the house was there. Georgia had to make sure they were all alive. Fortunately, most of the staff was merely frightened and not seriously injured. Even Millie was okay, it turned out. Right after the creature exploded, the wounds on her arm mysteriously vanished.

"I know, this was frightening," the wizard addressed the household. "But the Knight-Protector was here. She defended you and will again if it comes to that. I assure you, you are quite safe now. This attack was a failed attempt by dark forces. I suspect it was a test of Duchess Goldenheart's mettle. She passed. Also, the Alpon was only able to come inside because there was a break in the wall. If the house were whole, no vampire bat or creature of darkness would be able to enter."

In response, Bea drank a whole martini in a single gulp.

"He's right," Georgia said, standing up and looking down at her once beautiful gown. She was a frightful mess covered in vampire bat blood, but she was also determined. "I will protect you."

Georgia looked at the faces of her staff, and her old friend Beatrice. She was glad they all lived and remained unharmed.

"If any of you want to go, I will not hold it against you. I promise. I will write any references you need. But if you stay, I will not allow another creature like what we saw tonight to hurt you."

"I am terrified," Bea said. "But I'm not leaving you here alone to fight vampire bats, Georgia. Also, you can't give me a reference. I don't work for you."

"I will not leave you," Millie said, her voice wavering a bit.

"My lady," Mr. Derry said. "We believe you will defend us. What kind of servants would we be if we abandoned you now?"

Georgia was pretty sure the gardener had already packed his bags. Nevertheless, she nodded. "Thank you, Mr. Derry, and all of you. First thing first, will you and Francis go up to the attic and hammer a few boards over the open spot? Just close it up for now."

"Yes, my lady."

"Thank you. We will clean up the mess on the south landing tomorrow. Mr. Blue, would you mind staying in a guest room tonight?"

"Of course," he said.

"Excellent. In the meantime, everyone is to sleep in the

resident quarters on the second floor tonight. Yes, even you, Mr. Derry. I know you have your quarters down in the basement, but I would feel better if we were all in the same place. Now, I'm exhausted, and my gown is ruined. Let's end this evening, shall we?"

CHAPTER 8: DRESSMAKERS.

Over the next week, the staff cleaned the attic, double-checked for vampire bats, and kept the hole in the wall firmly shut. Georgia almost canceled the order for the new stained glass window to put in a wall.

"Perhaps having a bit more light up there would be a good thing after all," Mr. Derry said.

"Perhaps it would," Georgia agreed. Light everywhere seemed like a good idea.

Georgia sent an inquiry to Mrs. Miranda Smythe, inviting her to tea, and another to Mr. Turner. She hoped to get a little more time to talk about the Hampton party. Perhaps see if the enigmatic Mrs. Smythe and Mr. Turner had further thoughts now that some time had passed. Mrs. Smythe responded the same day with an acceptance coupled with a counter-invitation to go shopping at the House of Felix dress shop the day after. It was a bold gesture but Georgia saw no reason not to attend.

"Ah, the dressmakers," Georgia said, looking over the invite. She had never been to an actual dressmaking shop before. She showed the counter-invitation to Bea.

"Amazing," her old friend said. "Imagine a room full of frocks already made but unworn."

"It must save time. Would you like to join us?"

"I thought you would never ask."

"Perfect," Georgia said. She sent for Millie and instructed her to come up with a suitable outfit for the outing. "Given the success of my all-white ensemble the other night, I'm curious to try it again. Sir Lionel said he hoped to instruct you on outfits going forward. Did he?"

"Yes, my lady," Millie said. "I have ideas if you need them."

"Every idea you have will be tried. Can you have something ready by tomorrow, Millie?"

Millie nodded, curtseyed, and then hurried off. She had a long night ahead.

Georgia turned back to Bea. "You need to get permission from your brother-in-law to go, correct? Is he expecting you home tonight?"

Bea threw her hands up and stomped her foot. "Yes," she said, "I have to spend more time with the family. Honestly, how will I ever find a husband? I am always stuck in the house."

"Lord Wickham must think you have one of the Hampton men locked down," Georgia mused.

"You are giving him too much credit," Bea said. "I honestly believe he enjoys the act of annoying me."

"I shall write to him a letter myself, begging for your company tomorrow," Georgia said. "Surely, he will not refuse me."

"Very well," Bea said.

Georgia sat at her desk and jotted a quick note and then sent Francis to deliver it. The note was quite simple: 'My Dear Lord Wickham—May I borrow Miss Beatrice tomorrow? Her company is such a great comfort, and I get lonely. Thank you. —Yours, Lady Georgia Goldenheart, Duchess of Goldenheart, Keeper of the Sacred Blade, and Defender of the Three Realms from Dragons.'

An hour later, Francis returned with a note from Bea's brother-in-law that said: "Dear Duchess Goldenheart— Yes, of course. I trust you will keep our Beatrice safe and reasonable. —Lord John Wickham, Baronet of Irvingdale."

Bea pouted when she saw the reply. "How tempting it is to say a bad word about him," she muttered.

"Now, we need to find out where the shop is, and we're all set," Georgia said, shaking her head. "Stop worrying about Wickham, Bea. We have other fish to fry."

Bea put her hands on her hips. "Georgia, you have no idea what it is like."

"I have some idea," Georgia said, smiling. "I have met Wickham, lest you forget."

"Well, yes, of course, you have—but that's not what I meant," Bea said darkly. "I mean, you have no idea what it is like to have limitations."

"I beg your pardon?"

"You know what I am saying," Bea said, uncharacteristically biting a nail. "I don't mean to sound small or petty, but sometimes it's a bit difficult to watch from the side as you run all over town without an escort at the drop of a hat."

Georgia understood. It was getting easier to forget what life had been like before she became a duchess. Bea wanted to be free—that's what marriage meant to her. Even if she wound up with someone who limited her movements all over again, at least she wouldn't be at the beck and call of her brothers-in-law, and chief among them being Wickham.

Georgia moved in and hugged Bea. "We'll get you there, dear friend. You'll see. You will find someone worthy of you, and it will all be better. Now, let's get ready to go shopping."

As it happened, House of Felix was on a side street off the Commerce Way, only two blocks from Georgia's solicitor's office.

Georgia and Bea took the carriage to a long row of brightly-painted lady's dress shops. The ones at the corner were all for common ladies, with mannequins on the walk displaying the fashion of the day. Pale lilac tea dresses stood in the sun, while women in sensible coats wandered past. As the street continued, the shops went upscale with fewer mannequins and practical jackets. Finally, they arrived at the end of the lane. There were no mannequins, only huge buildings, with one dominating them all. It was a striking five-story structure, painted charcoal grey, with full windows facing the street but nothing of the showroom from that angle was visible.

When the carriage pulled up, she shook her head in wonder. "How many times have I passed this very street without ever looking up? I had no idea this is where women went shopping for dresses. Certainly, I had no idea we would arrive at these odd temples."

"Let's not tell everyone that," Bea said as they hopped out. "People will think you are a snob."

"At this point, even I think I am a snob," Georgia said.

The doorman opened the front doors, which were a slightly darker shade of charcoal. The only indication it was a business was a modest letter 'F' on the pane. Inside, they found an enormous lobby of grey terrazzo. It was surprisingly minimal, with long black sofas along the south wall leading to a simple desk where a woman sat.

Well-to-do ladies and matrons mingled quietly amongst the sofas, enjoying a moment off their feet, while young waitresses brought tea carts. The women were all clad in pale lilac with a few yellow highlights. Every one of the women on the sofas gaped as Georgia glided past. Millie had done her work well, putting her mistress into a huge snow-white satin coat. The cuffs, collar, and nearly floor-length hem shot with a vibrant blue. That was a practical touch, as soot from the ground would be less noticeable. Georgia also wore her black hair pinned into an elegant wide-brimmed white hat.

Bea followed in a vibrant blue coat that set off her golden ringlets of hair with panache. She also had an adorable laced blue cap.

Georgia felt a bit silly, but the ladies who watched had a different opinion. Several curtseyed as she walked by, realizing she had a title of note, even though they likely had no idea who she was.

Mrs. Smythe was waiting near the end of the hall and curtseyed immediately. "How lovely to see you both again," she said, smiling. Her full-length coat was a vibrant yellow with white lace peeking out at the sleeves and collar. On her head was a form-fitting cap covered in fresh daisies that completely swallowed her hair. Not for the first time, Georgia had to admire the widow's boldness.

"Thank you for the invitation," Georgia said, smiling. She looked around the foyer. "I had no idea this place would be so minimal yet so impressive." Behind her, the ladies on sofas continued to watch intently.

"It is," Mrs. Smythe said. "House of Felix is the premier dress shop in the Three Realms." Mrs. Smythe turned to the woman at the desk, who had her gaze pinned to the floor. "Henrietta, will you take us to the room I reserved?" she asked.

Henrietta, the desk woman, curtseyed deeply. "Yes, of course, Ma'am. My ladies, will you follow me?" She led them to a side door inset in the wall. Behind her, another woman took her place at the desk. When they entered, Georgia hadn't noticed the doors lining the room. The doors were all set at an angle to make them appear almost invisible when standing at the front.

Henrietta led the party upstairs to a bright room with enormous windows, huge sofas, and a full tea set. The room faced an open space and a simple doorway.

Georgia had some idea what would happen, as she had questioned Millie extensively on what to expect. The free space was for the dress models, who would come in from the other room, parading around in the dresses for sale.

Several desk ladies appeared from another door and helped them with their coats. Once everyone settled, Mrs. Smythe pointed to the sofas. "They will begin when you are ready, Duchess."

Georgia sat down, and Henrietta, the desk woman, silently served the tea with her eyes averted. Neat trick, considering she didn't spill a drop. Once tea had been served, Georgia nodded, and activity ramped up around the model's door. Faintly, she heard someone playing the violin sweetly in the background. A moment later, a tall woman in a lovely lilac gown with an enormous train strolled out and took a turn around the room.

"Oh, that's beautiful," Bea said. The woman posed, facing different directions so that they could see the gown and its train from each angle, then turned and went back through the door. A moment later, she was followed by another woman in another lilac gown—this one slightly darker. After her came another.

"Fascinating," Georgia said. She grabbed a biscuit and looked at Mrs. Smythe. While the women moved around the room, she whispered, "I wanted to chat with you a bit, Mrs. Smythe. I wanted to pick your brain."

Mrs. Smythe's eyes twinkled. "You mean about the events of the Hampton party, my lady?"

"Yes. Is it appropriate to talk while the models are working? I'm afraid this is my first time in a dress shop."

"Perfectly appropriate, my lady," Mrs. Smythe said.

Georgia dove right in. "When Mr. Blue and the Constable questioned you, I thought I detected something not spoken."

Mrs. Smythe lifted an elegant eyebrow. "Oh?" she asked. "What did you detect?"

Georgia shrugged. "Perhaps I was mistaken, but when

they asked you about Mr. Turner, you said you didn't know him. It seemed, at the party, like you were old friends."

Mrs. Smythe looked down at her tea as if mulling. Finally, she shrugged. "I wonder if I might also ask you a few questions?"

"Is that not why we are here?" Georgia asked. "Bea and I are both hoping to find your friendship waiting at the end of all this."

Mrs. Smythe smiled broadly. "Oh, that is good news. I truly feel the same way about each of you for the record."

Another striking woman entered the floor, this time in a long pale yellow gown under a lilac short ermine-trimmed pelisse jacket. Her arms peeked out with marigold gloves to match the dress and an ostrich feather in her cap.

Bea rose from her seat as if she had seen the face of divinity. "How does one go about acquiring one of these pre-fabricated dresses?" she asked Henrietta, the desk girl. Her voice cracked slightly, making Georgia grin.

"I can arrange it for you, my lady," Henrietta said.

"Please do," Bea said. She turned to Georgia. "I love this place. I think I just bought a dress."

"It looks very much like you did," Mrs. Smythe said, laughing. "How do you feel about it?"

"I feel free? I feel wonderful? That was so easy," Bea said.

"Wait until you see the bill," Georgia said. She turned back to Mrs. Smythe. "Go ahead and ask your question."

If Mrs. Smythe was writing for the *Weekly Men's Journal*, she expected a whole discussion on the markets. Nothing of the sort happened.

"I understand you suffered a break-in at your house the night of the Earl of Cadwin's spring ball," Mrs. Smythe said. "Sources in the constabulary have hinted at something rather odd."

Georgia tilted her head. "Yes," she said. "There was a break-in that night. I'm not sure how to explain what happened. Honestly, I'm not sure anyone would believe me if I told them."

Bea shuddered.

"It was a creature," Georgia explained. "Mrs. Smythe, you do know about my unusual title and that I am frequently in the company of a wizard these days."

"Yes, of course."

"He believes the creature was a thing of the night—a vampire bat."

Mrs. Smythe sighed, looking vaguely annoyed. "Pardon me," she said. "Of course, I understand if you don't want to discuss it, but—"

"I saw the beast with my own eyes, as did most of my household. It had wings and came in through a hole in the roof on the third floor."

"My word, you're serious, aren't you?"

"She's as serious as the grave. I saw the vile thing, too," Bea said before taking a sip of tea.

Mrs. Smythe looked at Bea, then back at Georgia. "So the stories of you being a magical knight of the Three Realms is... true? When you sat in on the police interrogation after the party, I thought you were merely showing interest. Being a duchess, they could not deny you entry without it becoming a scene."

Georgia smiled and said, "Every word is true. The constable would have loved to turn me, a mere lady, away. But I had jurisdiction and he couldn't deny me entry even if he wanted."

Georgia hoped this wouldn't spoil their new friendship. Fortunately, she calculated correctly, as Mrs. Smythe regained her composure.

"Every rumor," Mrs. Smythe whispered, "is true about you." She set her tea down and said in a conspirator's whisper,

"I suspect you know, as there are regular rumors about me. I was hoping to write an article." Bea laughed. "I knew it. Mr. Adina is an anagram for Miranda."

Mrs. Smythe looked at Bea in surprise. "Oh, that. I'm sorry to disappoint, but I am not Mr. Adina, although I am writing under an assumed name, too."

"You don't write for the *Weekly Men's Journal?*" Georgia asked.

"Oh, good heavens. I could write for that paper, of course. My understanding of business is rather comprehensive," Mrs. Smythe said, not bothering with modesty. "No, I write for the *Youthful Ladies Journal* under the pen name of Mrs. Rowley."

"You're the one who pushed lilac in this season? Wait. That's not even an anagram," Bea said, disappointed.

Mrs. Smythe laughed. She looked at Bea sideways and said, "You have a delightful mind, Lady Beatrice."

"I keep telling her that, too," Georgia said. "So Mr. Adina is just that? He's just some fellow who no one can identify, but he is real?"

Mrs. Smythe grinned. "Oh, he's much more than that. Mr. Adina is Mr. Tom Turner."

"That is how you know him," Georgia breathed. "How has he been writing, though? Mr. Turner spent the last year in prison."

Mrs. Smythe shrugged. "How does anyone do anything these days? I suspect there is more to this prison alibi than we know."

Bea tilted her head. "Alibi? You mean you don't think he was in prison? Why would he tell people he was there if he wasn't? Something like that could ruin him."

"I agree, but I'm sure he wasn't there, at least not for a whole year." Mrs. Smythe leaned in as if anyone else were close enough to hear her whisper. "Two months after Mr. Turner was sent to prison, I was at the Majestrix Club on a completely unrelated errand, and I am quite certain I saw him in one of the gaming rooms."

"Isn't the Majestrix Club for gentlemen only?" Bea asked.

"Yes," Mrs. Smythe smirked. "But I was chasing down

a story, and one of the leads took me there."

"How did you get inside?" Bea asked. "They don't allow ladies in past the lobby."

Mrs. Smythe smiled gently. "I cut my hair and posed as a delivery boy."

Georgia burst into laughter. "Of course," she said. "I have been wondering how you keep those spectacular hats pinned so tight."

Mrs. Smythe grinned and rustled her hat side to side. "After it worked that time, I decided to keep it short, just in case I need to go unseen," she said.

"You mean you actually put on trousers and wander around? No one questions you?" Bea asked. She almost spilled her tea.

"As it happens, I'm quite slim," Mrs. Smythe said. "When I dress like a delivery boy, that is what I look like. No one gives me a second look."

"You are full of surprises, Miranda," Georgia said. "Okay, back to our investigation. Mr. Turner is Mr. Adina."

"Correct. We have a few mutual friends in the magazine world, and they told me about him," Mrs. Smythe said. "The Hampton party was the first time we were set in a room side by side. I was there to get a look at you, and hoping to get the scoop, as it were. At the *Youthful Ladies Journal*, we are always checking with the Office of Peerage for new faces. A brand new full-blown duchess appearing out of nowhere is like discovering a gold mine in your backyard. I was tracking you from a distance for months, but you didn't go to any parties or events. For a while, I wasn't even sure you were a real person."

"I was in mourning for my uncle," Georgia explained. "Anyway, you ran into Mr. Turner?"

"Tom was at the Hampton party to learn more about the big transition at Hampton Madison. He was following up on a rumor he heard," Mrs. Smythe said, stepping away from the topic of Uncle Raymond with polite speed.

"What rumor?" Georgia asked.

Mrs. Smythe shrugged. "He didn't tell me what it was. I do have a suspicion, however."

"Tell us," Bea said, setting down her tea.

"Sir Alexander Madison may have been thinking of coming out of retirement," Mrs. Smythe said. "One of my sources thinks he was about to tip the apple cart and force his way back into the company."

"Why would he do that? Lady Emily told me he was happily settled," Georgia said.

"It may be that the Hampton twins aren't nearly as good as their father at running the business," Mrs. Smythe said. "They have been losing shares on the market for the last few weeks."

"That might explain why Mr. Hampton wanted all of his old business contacts at their birthday party," Bea said. "Perhaps he hoped he could reassure them and show family unity. Instead, Sir Alexander died suddenly."

"And everyone was detained for the evening," Mrs. Smythe said. "Not the outcome he hoped for."

Georgia sat back. "So we do have a possible motive. Maybe someone wanted Sir Alexander out of the way?"

"That leads it back to the Hamptons, doesn't it?" Bea said, her marriage prospects dimming again.

"It certainly does," Georgia said. The last model had long since departed, leaving them alone. Even the violin had stopped playing. She stood up. "We should probably go. I would hate to hold this room all day."

Mrs. Smythe and Bea stood, and the desk girls returned immediately with their coats and a bill for Bea.

"Send this bill to Lord John Wickham, the Baronet of Irvingdale," Bea instructed the girl. She looked at Georgia. "If my horrid brother-in-law is serious about marrying me off, he'll appreciate the opportunity to assist with my dress budget."

"I'm sure he will," Georgia said. She looked at

Henrietta, the desk girl. "Send Lady Beatrice's gown to Wending Way, the House of Goldenheart. I'll have my ladies maid tailor it to her."

"Yes, my lady," Henrietta said, scurrying off.

CHAPTER 9: DETECTING.

Over the next few days, a plethora of party invitations arrived. Every party in town wanted Georgia in her white gown and magic sword. Five personalized notes arrived to invite her for tea with the matrons of other great houses.

"Mark my words; every one of those old ladies has the perfect nephew or cousin waiting to meet you, Georgia. Every one of them will be younger brothers of earls, dukes, and cousins to princes, with each weirder than the next and completely ready to give up his name in favor of yours."

"I'm not sure what the problem is," Georgia said. "Since no one can marry me without losing his name anyway, why not have it be someone happy to do so?"

Lady Clara and her witch friends finally reported back to the Order of the Blue.

Mr. Blue was prompt, arriving with a copy of the poison analysis in one hand and a copy of the *Youthful Ladies Journal* in the other.

"That was fast," Georgia said as he came into the library. "Francis, we'll take tea in here. See if Mrs. Cotton has any more of those ginger biscuits, will you? If not, we'll take anything."

"Yes, my lady."

"Which would you like to see first?" Mr. Blue asked, his eyes twinkling mischievously.

Georgia grinned. "Bea is still visiting, so let's wait on her before we read the *Journal?* She's at lunch with one of the Hampton's, but should be back within the hour."

"Poison report it is," Mr. Blue said. "You do realize Lady Clara was modest when she said her people would have less luck than my own at finding anything, right?"

"I didn't realize that, but it's good to know," Georgia said. "I liked her, by the way."

"She liked you too," he said. "When she delivered the papers today, Clara said she wanted to invite you to tea or some other social event. She won't, as it wouldn't be appropriate."

"Noted. I'll send a charming invitation to something, and we'll get this going. Bea's horrid brother-in-law, Wickham, is having a social next week. Would you care to join us? I'd love to see the look on his face when I show up with half the magical advisors of the Three Realms in tow."

Mr. Blue laughed. "I wouldn't miss it. Thank you." He pulled open the report from the witches, which was bound in a birch box with a lovely tree inscribed on the lid. Within were diagrams of glasses and several pages of poison descriptions. "She was kind enough to list out several dozen poisons, information on their effects, and how long they normally take to kill. Also, there are notes on potential discomfort. It seems unlikely Sir Alexander would have gone for an extended period without notice. He was too physically active. Most poisons would have limited his movements and drawn attention to his health. Lady Clara notes here that the glasses contained residue of borage with gin, wine, and juniper. One glass also had what appeared to be traces of perfume from a lady. Clara said it wasn't the most expensive perfume and was, in fact, rather cheap. Upon further review, her sisters realized it wasn't perfume at all but rather a mix of blood and butterscotch."

"Interesting," Georgia said. "Someone might have cut themselves, perhaps? Maybe when Sir Alexander fell, and everyone was running to and fro? Where would the butterscotch come from?"

"Perhaps that someone had candy in their mouth. Maybe this alleged person bit their tongue in the excitement, and some of it went back into the drink?"

"Ah, yes. The simplest answer again, of course."

"Further study of the blood revealed it to be from a bat," Mr. Blue said, looking up.

"Wait. Why didn't Lady Clara lead with that? We just spent time speculating about people running around eating candy."

"Butterscotch and the blood of a bat," Mr. Blue said quietly.

Georgia remembered the creature in the attic. Not for the last time, she missed Uncle Raymond and the simplicity of life before he was taken from this world.

"Have you ever heard the phrase *smelly kipper*?"

"You mean the proverbial red herring? Why, yes," Mr. Blue said. "Are you thinking the bat's blood was there to throw us off?"

"Maybe," Georgia said. "Let's go back and be analytical about this. We saw a man who appeared to be in good health fall over dead. The very same man seemed to be the victim of poison. Alas, we found none in his or any of the cocktail glasses at the party. Instead, we learn there was a bat's blood in one of the glasses, traces of it, that is—and we are no closer to finding the truth than before. We should review this from other angles, perhaps?" Her Cymbre training kicked in. "What do we know happened? Why, and then, I guess, how?"

Mr. Blue flipped a page in the report. "Right. We have only touched the surface of what happened and very nearly glossed over a reason why."

"I think we need to figure that part out," Georgia said.

Francis came in, pushing a cart full of tea and ginger biscuits.

"Also, I need something to write on. Maybe if we put it all together on paper, we can see the connections?"

Francis looked up from laying out the plates. "My lady, forgive me for interrupting, but would it help to have the old chalkboard?"

"The old chalkboard?"

"The master had it in here for years. When you went to school, we moved it to the basement for storage. It's still there."

"Yes, that might work, Francis. Can you bring it up now?"

"Yes, my lady." Francis hurried away.

Georgia turned back to Mr. Blue. "We've been so focused on how Sir Alexander died, we all but forgot to ask why."

"You are right," Mr. Blue said. "When you met with Lady Emily and the solicitor, there was a great deal of talk about money and property."

"The original will mentioned Gladys before it was changed," Georgia said. "We never found out who she is or how she could be owned by someone, as the document didn't have context. Mr. Clanahan, the solicitor, thought Gladys might have been a pet. Lady Emily thought the idea unlikely."

"Hm. Perhaps Gladys is a code?"

"You mean maybe Sir Alexander put it in as a joke or reference to something else?"

"People have been known to put absurd things in wills," Mr. Blue said in deep thought. "What if the only reason he removed Gladys was that, years later, he remembered the silly moment and acted?"

"Possibly, yes. There was also the rumor Mrs. Smythe mentioned. Apparently, Sir Alexander was planning to return to the business and unseat the Hampton twins," Georgia said.

Francis returned with Mr. Derry carrying the old chalkboard under a dropcloth. When they pulled the cloth away, there were still a few old maths formulae written at the corners.

"Fetch a bucket and cloth," Mr. Derry instructed Francis. He set down an old box of chalk sticks and turned to Georgia. "We'll have this clean and ready in no time, my lady."

Georgia watched, just a bit sadly, as they washed the old chalk marks away and made it ready for use again.

Once it was dry, she and Mr. Blue started writing.

"Sir Alexander," Mr. Blue wrote the name on the board with the word 'victim' in parenthesis. Below that, he wrote 'poison?'

To the side, Georgia wrote out 'party attendees,' with the names of Lady Emily, the Hamptons, Bea, herself, Mr. Blue, and the other guests she could remember in a column below.

Mr. Blue moved to the center, taking her cue and wrote 'motive.' Below that, he wrote 'money.' He drew lines from Mr. Hampton and Lady Emily over to 'money.'

"What are we forgetting?" he asked.

"Method and Opportunity," Bea said, wandering in with one of the Hampton twins by her side. Georgia wasn't sure which one he was, because he wasn't wearing a scarf to identify himself. "Motive is useless alone."

"I say, you have it all set up like one of those store novels," the Hampton boy said, looking at the board. He probably shouldn't be here to see this, but here he was.

"Ollie, would you say we are missing anything else?" Mr. Blue asked.

"Oh, it's Manx. I really wouldn't know," Manx said, delighted. "All right, method and opportunity—the latter being when a killer might strike?"

"Presumably," Georgia said.

"He must have struck at the party because we all saw Sir Alexander when he died."

"How do you know it is a he, Manx?" Bea asked. "They say poison is a woman's weapon, so a *she* could have done the nasty deed."

Manx nodded. "Quite right," he said, winking at Bea. Manx continued, "It did seem like a convenient time for poison, given everyone was drinking glasses of Ollie's disgusting punch. The killer must have been able to get at Sir Alexander's glass to deliver it. That could mean only one of two people."

"Who?" Georgia and Mr. Blue asked in unison.

"The first would be Mr. Bailey, our footman, who was serving. I saw him pass the tray by Sir Alexander and Lady Emily when they arrived. Sir Alexander accepted his glass, but his discerning wife declined in favor of a glass of champagne."

"And who is the second person?" Mr. Blue asked.

Manx hesitated. "That would be me," he said finally. "I poured the glass that went to Sir Alexander. That said, since I know I didn't poison him or anyone, I have to think Mr. Bailey wanted him dead."

Mr. Blue tilted his head, then took the chalk and wrote Mr. Bailey into the list, followed by 'suspect.' He followed that up by writing 'suspect' next to Manx's name. The young man nodded, looking more somber now.

"In all seriousness," he said. "Sir Alexander was like an uncle to Ollie and me, and Lady Emily like an aunt. Also, I cannot imagine Mr. Bailey doing this. He only started working for us recently and came with impeccable recommendations. Beyond that, one has only to speak to him to realize he doesn't have prerequisite evil in his demeanor."

"Could he have known Sir Alexander previously?" Bea wondered out loud. "Prerequisite evil isn't a legal term. I don't think."

Manx laughed. "Anything is possible. I suppose you will want to talk to him again?"

"Definitely," Georgia said. The footman seemed like an

unlikely murderer, but maybe he saw something.

"I should mention father will not like having the wizard back to question the staff," Manx said. "Sorry, old chap, but you were on thin ice with him before the party. Now that you're investigating the murder of his old business partner, he's had it with you."

"I suppose I could conduct the interview," Georgia said.

"That might complicate other things," Bea said, looking worried. She and Manx exchanged a glance, and he looked down. Of course, it would. Georgia introduced the Hamptons to Bea. If she went back there, causing trouble and being bossy, Mr. Hampton would almost certainly forbid his either of his sons from pursuing an engagement.

"What about our friend, the constable?" Georgia asked. "He's the law. Just send him to do the questioning."

"I think Father would let the constable talk to Mr. Bailey," Manx admitted, "and then he would fire the footman right after."

"We need to find a way to talk to Mr. Bailey again," Mr. Blue said. "Does he ever get a night off?"

"Of course he does," Manx said. "But it would still cause trouble. I'm sure he would go back and tell Father you spoke to him. Worse, that you sought him out to speak to him."

Bea snapped her finger, "I've got it. Manx. you can bring him to dress you for my horrid brother-in-law's social next week. Georgia will be there anyway."

"I'm bringing Mr. Blue and another friend as guests," Georgia said.

"You have a friend other than me?" Bea asked.

"Lady Clara Gaye, the witch of Volusia," Mr. Blue said. "She is dazzling, and I suspect you will love her, Lady Beatrice."

Bea grinned. "I already do. The look on Wickham's face will be priceless when he sees a witch at his party, and better yet, he can't do anything about it. Oh, and he said they would be playing bocce on the south green. Have you ever played it?" She turned to Manx.

"I'm sure I have," he said. "That's the one where you throw the little ball at the other ball, right?"

"You're practically an expert," Bea said. "There will be some sun, and it might involve a change of shirts before the evening cocktails?"

"That sounds reasonable," Manx said. "Father and Ollie are also going, so we will bring Mr. Bailey to manage our wardrobe. One of you can talk to him there. It would look like a coincidence."

Mr. Blue flinched at the word 'coincidence,' prompting Georgia to snicker. "Perfect," she said. "Now you see, Mr. Blue? The world is full of coincidences, and only you hate them. Everyone else finds them useful."

"On that note, I must dash. Good luck with the investigation," Manx said. He turned to Bea. "See you at the social. I cannot wait."

Bea curtseyed and said, "I look forward to our next adventure."

"Oh," Manx said. "You need one more thing on your chalkboard."

"What is that?" Mr. Blue asked.

"Alibis," the young man said. "None of us seem to have one." He left them with a wave.

"That was unexpected," Georgia said. "Why do I feel like we let a fox into the hen house?"

"How dramatic," Bea said. She spotted the *Youthful Ladies Journal* on the side table. "What have we here?" She snatched it up like lost treasure.

"There is a small article about Lady Georgia's adventure at the party," Mr. Blue said.

Bea scurried over to the sofa gleefully. "Come on," she said. "We'll solve the murder after we read this." She flipped it open and plopped down in front of the ginger biscuits.

"Our moment of truth arrives," Georgia said.

"Georgia, look at this. They have illustrations of your gown, and it looks beautiful. And this is more than a short article, Mr. Blue. Georgia, you will never guess who wrote this?"

"Mrs. Rowley?"

"Party-pooper."

Georgia settled in across from her friend.

Bea cleared her throat. "'The dashing young Earl of Cadwin has done it again. The party took place on the first day of spring, so there was still a nip in the air. The chill didn't stop the party-goers, as Cadwin House was full of lights, carriages, and the bold new fashion offerings of the season.' I love this," she said. "'We saw a veritable who-is-who in the carriage train, including old favorite Lady Rosamund Virtue in her signature lilting hat...' sorry, Lady Rosamund. Still, if I never read about your hat again, it will be too soon. Okay, let's get to the good part." Bea scanned down the page.

"Lilting hat?" Georgia asked.

"She has a bizarre growth on her forehead," Bea said, not looking up from the article. "All of her hats sort of droop over her face. Rumor has it; she tried to have it removed by a doctor, but they botched the surgery, and now she wears those hats constantly."

"Good heavens. That must be terrible."

"Honestly, my mother saw the mark once. She said it looked like a tiny dot. Rosamund is vain, though. Ah, here we are," Bea said, leaning forward. "'But the highlight of the evening was the arrival of Lady Georgia Goldenheart, Duchess of the House of Goldenheart, and Knight-Protector of the Realms from Dragons. You read that right, young one—a lady knight. Duchess Goldenheart stepped off her carriage and immediately broke with the current fashion, by opting for a long blue cashmere coat with exactingly detailed white and gold piping at the cuffs. The ensemble was designed by none other than Sir Lionel himself. Heads were turning.'" Bea threw her head back and laughed.

Mr. Blue settled in and poured them all cups of tea.

"'Even more surprising, the duchess wore a ceremonial blade across her back. It was decorated to resemble the Realms' flag, and stars on her head to invoke our regal future. Oh, she was a sight to behold, and it didn't stop there...' Wait, there's a sidebar here about the sword. Do you want to hear it too?"

"Yes," Georgia and Mr. Blue said in unison.

He smiled at her.

"I'll get back to the main story in a moment. 'Sidebar: The sacred blade of Goldenheart is an ancient symbol in the Three Realms. Duchess Goldenheart, being the last of her kind, may have committed a fashion faux pas by bringing it to such a lively party, but also upheld tradition, loyalty to the king, and that alone should be commended.' Aw, Georgia, you're a national treasure."

"A committee of faux pas, however," Georgia said wistfully.

"Committee or committer?"

"We may never know."

"Okay," Bea said. "Let's keep going. There's a bit more to the main article." She read on. "'The lady was accompanied by a striking fellow in a long white coat who turned out to be an obscure prestidigitator named Mr. Blue.' Oh, that's not good."

"It is fine," Mr. Blue said, smiling. "No one cares, as long as I'm not some cad swindling old ladies out of their retirement."

"Hm. I'm not sure I agree," Bea said dubiously. "'Fortunately, the conjurer was charming. When Lady Georgia transitioned in the hall from striking blue coat to even more stunning pure white gown, the wizard also changed to blue. We were amazed and realized just what a show was playing out at the court of the Earl. Lady Georgia appeared in a radiant evening gown of luminous white silk, custom-tailored by Sir Lionel. The evening was a tour de force of his work and made an impression across the party. The clever lady somehow switched out of her coat in the hall but kept the ceremonial blade attached to her back with ribbons and streamers so delicate the onlookers were amazed'."

"Well done," Mr. Blue said.

"Millie helped me out of my coat and back into the sword," Georgia said. "It's not magic. You saw it happen. It took all of one minute."

Mr. Blue laughed.

"Wait, there was more excitement," Bea said. "'Events took a new turn as an old face materialized in the crowd: Lady Clara Gaye, the Witch of Volusia. Who would have thought she would be at the same party? Lady Clara was also…' Oh my word, I so wish I had been there '…Lady Clara was stunningly garbed in funereal black with immaculate lace collar and lines. Her designer was none other than the House of Felix, known for their risky collections. Who would imagine black at a Spring party? Despite the shock, they chose the right model for their extraordinary gown. Lady Clara's famous red locks shone with white pearls and were a nod to the exalted company. She spent the entire evening shadowing the tolerant duchess. They spoke briefly before the wizard ushered the shining white lady away for more diverting conversation'."

"What? We talked to Lady Clara for nearly two hours," Georgia said. "And what is this tolerant duchess business?"

"Oh, that's what they always do in the *Journal*. It's a new lady rivalry," Bea said, looking up from the magazine.

"Excuse me?"

Bea folded the magazine across her lap carefully. "Every season at the parties, the *Journal* picks out a couple of court ladies, and they spend the next four months snubbing each other socially. It's good for the readers. Don't worry. There's a great détente in Autumn. The feuding ladies do social work or have a party together. The

Journal toasts them for being high-minded. It's all very dramatic, but it's not real. They just want to sell papers, Georgia."

"How extraordinary," Mr. Blue said. "Does this *Journal* do this with, er, gentlemen too? Or is it only the ladies?"

"Why would the *Youthful Ladies Journal* write about gentlemen?" Bea asked.

"Why would they choose to invent a rivalry at all?" Georgia asked. "Who else is in a rivalry?"

"They usually pick on gentry-level ladies," Bea said. "You know, my sister Bernadette spent a season in a bitter feud with Lady Cosumet. According to the papers, they nearly came to blows at the Harvey Vicars Ball two years ago. They had to stop, though. Bernadette was getting married."

"What?" Georgia gaped.

"I mean, that's what the *Journal* said." Bea laughed. "It's all in good fun. Bernadette loved it. When Cosumet realized they were selected, she even came over to the house to improvise scripts and figure out who their designers would be. Honestly, Georgia, why am I the first person to tell you about this? I've seen you reading the *Youthful Ladies Journal* many times."

"I guess I never read that much into it. Also, I'm usually more interested in the public warning articles—the cat-fishers and the kidnappers and whatnot," Georgia said. "What do you think this paper will make of me inviting Lady Clara to your social?"

"They might not cover it, or they may find a better set of rivals. It's unusual for them to target someone at your level. I suspect this was just a bit of friendly fun, given you know the writer."

"Lady Beatrice, you have dissected this most interestingly," Mr. Blue said. "I think you missed your calling."

"I refuse to teach school, Mr. Blue," Bea said. "I want a husband, and that is that."

"Fair enough," he said.

"Another odd thing," Georgia said. "They mentioned the designers by name."

"That's how they work the down-sell," Bea said as if everyone knew what that meant.

Georgia raised an eyebrow.

"Okay, there are these places called dress shops. They sell pre-made gowns, tea dresses, gloves, occasionally shoes, and hats to the ordinary public."

"I know what a dress shop is, Bea. Remember, we went to one just the other day, and it was fascinating." Granted, before the other day, she didn't know anything about dress shops.

"There are designers like Sir Lionel who makes glorious white silk frocks for duchesses at parties," Bea continued. "Sir Lionel, as it happens, is also one of the owning partners of the House of Felix."

"That's where Lady Clara got her dress," Mr. Blue said. "It was in the article."

"Correct. The rivalry is between the lofty white lady in the designer gown and the crass and feisty ginger-haired witch who gets her gown at the shops."

"The witch got her frock from the most expensive dress shop in the city," Georgia corrected. "That gown cost a small fortune."

"At first, everyone will be on the white lady's side because she's a patriot and not from Volusia," Bea said.

"What's wrong with Volusia?" Mr. Blue asked.

"It's full of Volusians," Bea answered.

Georgia laughed.

"Anyway, one complication was Lady Clara opting to wear black. That could have been something they didn't foresee because Clara decided on the color, or the nation is running out of the lilac dye. They decided to go black next winter when the next line comes out. I suppose it all depends on whether Lady Clara is her own agent or a pawn of House of Felix. We will know soon. If we see her at other parties in normal attire, it could mean nothing. If she gets a series of articles from it, the market is headed in another direction. Either way, the House of Felix will, logically, have an influx of business, and their investment in your gown, Georgia, will have paid for itself."

Georgia gaped. "That's right. Sir Lionel never sent an invoice for his services."

"And he won't send one," Bea said. "That beautiful gown you and the vampire bat destroyed was not only a gift to you, but you were a gift to Sir Lionel. No doubt, when Millie showed up at his door looking for a designer, he thanked the heavens."

"Okay, I know you said your horrid brother-in-law Wickham tells you about business things, Bea, but this is beyond the pale."

"Wickham didn't have to explain this to me, Georgia. I'm proud to admit I worked it out on my own."

"Honestly, Lady Beatrice, you should consider becoming a lady of business," Mr. Blue said. "Or become some sort of journalist."

"Bite your tongue, Mr. Blue," she said. "We have a social to go to in a few days, and there will be none of that modern lady talk there."

The next day, Georgia took Bea to see Lady Johanna Price. According to Bea's sister, Bernadette, Lady Johanna was known to take an early lunch every Tuesday at the Blue Epicure on Elton Street.

"Why are we accosting this lady, Georgia?" Bea asked. "And why aren't you taking Mr. Blue instead?"

"Lady Johanna didn't respond to my invitation to tea. I suspect she is far too busy to keep up her correspondence," Georgia explained. "We need to question her, though. I also liked how you handled yourself at the dress shop with Mrs. Smythe."

"Thank you, but I have no idea who this Lady Johanna is," Bea said. "I only asked Bernadette because you wanted to know."

As they boarded the carriage, Georgia answered, "Lady Johanna is the wife of Sir John Price, who owns the Price Bakeries."

"Are we getting apple fritters?"

"Not this time. More important to us, Lady Johanna is the daughter of a fellow named Sir Aubrey Algernon, who was a business rival of Hampton and Madison. They treated him rather shoddily, five years ago, and forced him to sell one of his warehouses. Two years ago, he tried to sue Mr. Hampton and Sir Alexander in court, but the case never made it to trial because Sir Aubrey died suddenly. Last year, his daughter allegedly wanted to continue the case, but her husband over-ruled it."

"Motive by proxy," Bea said thoughtfully.

"And we aren't taking Mr. Blue because I'm hoping not to draw attention and scare her off."

Bea turned to look at Georgia more closely. "You do realize you're dressed all in white again, right? I mean, everywhere you go, you draw attention."

Georgia shrugged. "I've decided to own my white silk, Bea. That said, I hope she will be properly stunned and tell us the truth."

Bea nodded. "You don't think she killed Sir Alexander, do you?"

"According to Mr. Stackhouse, my solicitor, there are some public records of what gets willed to whom. Lady Johanna received a sizable fortune from her late father, which implies Sir Aubrey wasn't destitute when he died."

"Motive behind the motive," Bea said. "When you first heard Lady Johanna was going to continue the lawsuit, you thought she was avenging her father for being ruined."

"Correct, but it appears he was suing because he was irked."

"Irk the wealthy at your peril," Bea said.

"Precisely. The loss of the warehouse had little to no effect on the overall fortune, and Sir Aubrey moved on to greener pastures—business-wise, I mean. I think the lawsuit was an attempt to save face, or possibly he just wanted to stick it to Hampton and Madison," Georgia mused.

"Listen to you talking all business," Bea said. "Kill one vampire bat and you *stick it to this and stick it to that.*"

They arrived. The Blue Epicure on Elton Street was an old establishment, having started more than fifty years prior as a coffee house. Over time, the menu expanded. Big pies and kettle dishes came in and went out. The fare shifted with the times. Two years ago, the place almost closed down, unable to compete anymore. The public lost its taste for coffee and large kettle pies. The grand old site almost died until a new investor came in and renovated. Last year, it reopened as a ladies' restaurant, where one might find all sorts of delicacies in a redesigned open-air dining room. The staff was all released from service. A story popped up in the *Weekly Men's Journal* that all of the old waiters were given pensions and were able to—shock—retire. The public began to watch the building with interest, even as it remained shuttered. One day, a fleet of workers came in and started the renovation. Articles began to appear in every paper of note, discussing the interest in the restoration of the Blue Epicure. Finally, it opened to great fanfare. The old waiters were replaced by a host of smiling young women. Tea was at the top of the menu. Every lady of note made time in her schedule to pop in at least once or twice a month. Amazingly, even businessmen were there for late lunches and taking meetings. It was like a fusion of all worlds.

Georgia's solicitor, Mr. Stackhouse, gave her the inside track—Lady Johanna was the investor and the mind behind it all. Georgia fully approved of that idea. He even told her where to find the lady.

"She's always at the Rose Booth," Georgia said as they

disembarked from the carriage.

They entered the café and looked around. The main room was a sea of little tables with social ladies enjoying their tea. The front of the building had massive windows that let the sunshine right in. Friendly waitresses ducked in and out of view to refresh the pots and biscuits. Further back, booths were named after a flower. The walls featured photographs of the city.

"How modern," Bea said as they approached the booths. "Have you ever seen so many photographs in one place?"

Georgia shook her head. Prints were framed and mounted on every wall where dozens of people stood admiring. "This makes me wish I had gotten William and Uncle Raymond to sit for one," she said.

Bea sighed. "We tried that once with the whole family, but it took forever, and Mother kept dozing off. They managed to get one print for us, but it looks like we are standing next to her dead body on the couch."

"Most of these are pictures of buildings, the mountain, the trees, and boats," Georgia said. They were all intentionally taken from unusual angles. It was as if the photographer were creating art with each image. They passed the booths, which each featured a bouquet placement featuring the name on the stall. There was a Daisy Booth, which had a lovely basket on the table, followed by gardenia, tulip, and so on. The back wall of each booth was covered in photographs. They arrived at the Rose Booth to find a well-dressed middle-aged woman enjoying a cup of tea. The woman was also watching the two of them approach with some excitement.

"Good day," Georgia said to the woman at the booth. "I am Lady Georgia Goldenheart, Duchess of the House of Goldenheart. Are you Lady Johanna Price?"

Lady Johanna nearly jumped out of her seat. "Why, yes, I am," she said. "My goodness, when I saw you wandering the aisle in that spectacular white coat, I knew you were someone important. A duchess, though? How extraordinary is that."

"This is Lady Beatrice Irvingdale," Georgia said, gesturing to Bea.

"It is a pleasure to meet you," Lady Johanna said.

"I wonder if we might join you for a moment, Lady Johanna?" Georgia asked. "We are here to see you."

"You are? Uh, yes, of course," Lady Johanna said, stammering.

Georgia didn't waste any time and slid right in. Bea followed suit. "Is it public knowledge you invested in the café?" Georgia asked quietly.

Lady Johanna blinked. "Not precisely, but it is not a secret," she said.

"Unfortunately, I have to ask you a few questions about a troubling matter. I hope you will not be offended by any bluntness."

"Now I am intrigued," Lady Johanna said. "Ask away, my lady."

"You are aware Sir Alexander Madison passed away last week, yes?"

Lady Johanna understood immediately, and her demeanor shifted accordingly. Fortunately, she wasn't unfriendly. "Yes, I read about it in a paper. I sent a note of condolence to Lady Emily right away."

"Naturally," Georgia said. "Now we come to the other troubling part... Your father was attempting to launch a lawsuit against Hampton and Madison."

"Ah, the lawsuit," Lady Johanna said, shaking her head slowly. "That was an unpleasant bit of business. I take it you have some personal stake in coming here today, my lady? I thought since you were blunt, I would be, too."

Bea grinned. "I like her," she said.

"I do, too," Georgia said. She looked at Lady Johanna. "I do have some investment in that I was in the room when Sir Alexander collapsed. I am also the Knight-Protector and have begun to assist the Order of the Blue in their investigation."

"Sir Alexander didn't die of natural causes then?" Lady Johanna said slowly.

"Indeed," Georgia said. "I'm so sorry we ambushed you, but I suspect you haven't read the letter I sent last week. At the same time, I had to come and ask questions. We thought if we did it this way, as civilized women, we could get you off our suspect list."

"Father's damnable lawsuit," Lady Johanna said. "What would you like to know?"

Georgia felt like her hunch was true: Lady Johanna was all business and innovation. She didn't have time for grudges or the past.

"Why did your father pursue the litigation after selling the warehouse?" she asked.

Lady Johanna shrugged. "I suspect he was holding a grudge. I'm sure you've met Mr. Hampton by now, so you know he can be an unsavory sort. Father trusted him at one time and was burned. The wound never quite healed, and he eventually decided to drag Hampton and Madison into court. Even if he couldn't win, he was determined to make them feel a bit of the sting."

"I understand you prepared to continue the suit when your father passed," Georgia said, keeping her voice gentle.

"I was, yes," she said. "My husband thought it was unnecessary, as Father made his point already. There wasn't much reason to continue when his health failed."

"Sir John overruled you then?"

Lady Johanna shook her head. "Oh no, he did not. John would have gone along with it if I insisted. What would the point be, though? The lawsuit would have meant drudging the past up again."

"You canceled the suit yourself?" Georgia said.

"Of course. I loved my father," Lady Johanna said, her eyes misting. "But in his later years, he was feeding on regret. It was unfortunate because he had a wonderfully successful life. He met my mother at a young age, and they shared a beautiful story even as he built an empire in business. The sale of one warehouse got ugly, but that happens sometimes. We were not adversely affected by it. If anything, the building was an expensive and difficult asset, as it was his only holding on that side of the docks. The dry docks also surrounded it, so even before they built their wall, getting carts in and out was a hassle. I would have thought him glad to be rid of it at the time."

"Why did he try to hold on to it then?" Bea asked.

Lady Johanna shrugged. "Why do men do anything? My father was a sensible fellow for most of his life, but we all have our moments."

Bea laughed.

One of the waitresses arrived with three bowls that smelled like heaven.

Lady Johanna perked up. "I hope you don't mind. I took the liberty of ordering us all a new dish we are trying out. It's a type of bread and butter pudding. I wouldn't want to presume, but you must know my husband's reputation with apple fritters is impressive."

"Oh, we are aware," Bea said, eyeing her bowl with enthusiasm.

Lady Johanna smiled. "Bakeries have a lot of leftover stock. My husband brought in a pudding lady to repurpose it. Here at the café, I have taken a portion of it and tried my spin."

Georgia looked down to find an apple fritter diced into delicate layers folded with hot butter, almonds, and creamy egg custard. "Good heavens," she said, pretending to be shocked. "I suppose now I must eat this."

Lady Johanna laughed, "Oh yes, my lady. You surely must."

Georgia and Bea tucked in, nodding their approval with each bite.

Lady Johanna was delighted but grew somber a moment later. "Oh, poor Lady Emily," she said. "I don't know her well. We have only met in passing, but she's always so dignified and respectful. I do remember seeing her with Sir Alexander at a couple of parties. They had genuine affection. She must be suffering."

"I agree," Georgia said quietly.

"And he was murdered," Lady Johanna said, shaking her head. "I find that especially surprising."

"Why?"

"Of the two partners in Hampton and Madison, one might almost imagine Mr. Hampton meeting a grim end. He's not exactly pleasant, even at the best of times. Not Sir Alexander, though. I really cannot imagine him being a victim of murder."

Georgia finished her bread and butter pudding and said, "Lady Johanna, thank you so much for talking to us. I must say, I love your café and look forward to returning."

"Thank you, Your Grace," Lady Johanna said. "This was the most pleasant murder interview one could imagine."

"We love the photographs," Bea said. "Never have I seen so many in one place."

Lady Johanna beamed with pride. "I hired a photographer to go all over the city and take them, especially for the café. His name is Carter Carterson, and he takes photographs as an artistic pursuit. Can you imagine having a name like that?" She snapped her finger. "He got a rather good shot of that old warehouse. Would you like to see it?"

"We would be delighted," Georgia said.

Lady Johanna led them over to another wall. They were treated to several photos of the dry docks with many ships, boats, and other structures all taken from delightful and dramatic angles. She pointed to one in particular of a huge building surrounded by walls. Georgia was about to look when something caught her eye. Another photo nearby featured a huge river yacht moored to an inlet. The name on the side of the boat was *Gladys*.

"Hello, Gladys," Georgia said to the photo. She pointed to it and looked at Lady Johanna. "Do you perhaps know anything about this boat, my lady?"

Johanna stepped over and inspected the photo. She shook her head. "No, I cannot say I do—although it appears to be moored to the other side of the warehouse." She pointed to the top of the photograph, where Georgia could see the shape of the building in shadow.

"Georgia," Bea said, leaning in very close to another photo. Her voice was grim—fearful even. "Georgia, come look at this." She leaned in close to the picture of the warehouse itself.

Georgia stepped over to get a better look. Bea pointed at a window in the warehouse. "Look closely," she whispered. Georgia leaned in to see a figure in the window. It looked like a silhouette, but she could distinctly make out wings on its shoulders—bat wings.

CHAPTER 10: WAREHOUSE.

Upon returning, Georgia sent Francis to the Order of the Blue with a note about the warehouse and the photo they'd discovered. While she waited, she changed into a sensible wool dress with long sleeves and solid walking boots. Millie found a stout grey coat in the attic, along with the old scabbard for the magic sword. It was tougher than the new ceremonial sheath. Georgia selected a modest black hat from her uncle's boxes, strapped the sword to her back, and was ready.

Mr. Blue arrived at two in the afternoon.

"It could have been a trick of the light in that photograph," Georgia admitted, "but it looked like that vampire bat was in the window."

He shook his head. "You found this and a photo of a boat named *Gladys* by chance?"

"I'm afraid so," Georgia said. "I know how much you hate coincidence, Mr. Blue."

"I am beginning to reassess my opinion on coincidences and am starting to wonder if they even exist. Perhaps it is because of fate you, the Knight-Protector, saw those photos."

"Whatever the reason, we should go over there and look for ourselves," Georgia said.

"I am concerned, my lady."

"You don't think I should go because I am a lady and could get hurt," she said.

"Well, I know you were built for this sort of thing, but as we face the idea of putting you in danger, knowingly, it worries me."

"It worries me, too," Bea said, walking in with some sort of leather band in hand. Behind her, Millie and Eunice followed. "Georgia, you had better not get hurt."

Georgia smiled. "I think it will be all right. We already handled the vampire bat. If anything, this might give a clue to its lair."

"If so, then that means its lair is on Hampton's property, which implies something dire," Mr. Blue said. "We are no longer looking at mundane poisoning, but rather something supernatural."

"Your labs couldn't find any poison," Georgia said, "but they did find bat's blood in a glass. You said yourself it sounded like a magic potion."

"You hear yourself talk, right?" Bea asked.

"We're already past the shallows, Bea. It's best to go with it."

"Indeed, I did say that about a potion," Mr. Blue agreed. "I have a bad feeling about this."

"At least you're going over there during the day," Bea said, holding up the leather contraption. "Georgia, I want you to wear this."

"What is it?" she asked.

"It's a leather wrap for your neck, my lady," Millie said. "Eunice and I stitched it together from one of the master's old leather braces. It's to keep the vampires from biting your neck."

Mr. Blue smiled. "Millie, that is ingenious."

"Thank you, sir," she said. "It was Eunice's idea. I just helped with it."

"Come now. It was just the one vampire bat. We're not up to vampires in the plural. Even I can't believe I just said that." Georgia took the neck wrap, and Millie secured it to her shoulders. "Thank you so much. That was sweet of you and, uh...."

"Eunice, my lady," Millie said.

Georgia once again made a mental note to write the girl's name down.

"Let's hope you don't need it," Mr. Blue said.

Francis brought the carriage around. "We'll be driving ourselves," Georgia told the footman. Mr. Blue climbed into the front, and Georgia joined him.

"Good heavens," Bea said. "Georgia, you look like you work here now."

"I will not put anyone else in danger," Georgia said. "Mr. Derry, we should be back by sunset."

"Yes, my lady," the butler said. "Please, be careful."

"Mr. Derry, if we do not return by midnight, you must send someone to the Order of the Blue. They are already aware of the situation, and will know what to do," Mr. Blue said.

"Yes, of course, sir."

Mr. Blue took the reins but didn't snap them. Instead, he spoke to the horse. "Take us to the docks on the west side as quickly as you can, please. Whatever route you think appropriate is fine." The horse snorted as if it understood every word, and they set off immediately.

"Okay, that was interesting," Georgia said as the carriage lurched forward. She had spoken to her mounts many times, but they never answered back.

"We should scout the area before going into the building. From what Mr. Hampton said in his interview after the party, it is abandoned," Mr. Blue said.

"Right. Let's see if the *Gladys* is still moored behind it, too," Georgia said. "I really wanted Gladys to be a cute little dog. That would have been so much better."

"I couldn't agree more."

It was an hour of cross-town traffic before they turned down Hampton Lane to the dry docks on the west side. The docks were bustling, and it took another half hour to get there.

"If we lose the light—"

"If we do, we should leave and come back in the morning." Mr. Blue finished the thought.

They made their way around the warehouse, walking past groups of dockworkers repairing boats in the dry dock. Georgia counted at least ten separate inlets, each with a project going. At the far side of the pier, a dozen small ships came for trade. The business was brisk. The warehouse was, as Mr. Hampton described, walled-off entirely from the landward side. The front face of the building had its little dock that was starting to fall apart from disuse.

"What a jerk," she muttered, thinking of Mr. Hampton. "How many people must have lost their jobs the day he decided to wall up this place?"

"Men of business are their own breed," Mr. Blue said. "Where do you suppose the *Gladys* is?"

Georgia looked around, trying to imagine where it would be, based on her memory of the photograph. "I think it would be this way," she said, leading them just to the east of the building along a side path.

They passed another ship set into a narrow basin on a dry platform. Next to that, they found the *Gladys* moored in a flooded basin. They walked around it entirely, getting a better look. Off to one side, a fellow who appeared to be a foreman approached. He was older with sun-dried skin. Still, he had the demeanor of one who gives the orders.

"Good day," he said. "May I help you?" He was polite enough, even if his tone said, 'what are you doing here?'

Mr. Blue held up a writ. "Good day," he said. "I am Mr. Blue. We are investigating with the full authority of the Crown. We need to look around and will be entering the craft. I assume you will not object?"

"You have a writ of the warrant?" the foreman asked.

"I have a Writ of Full Royal Authority to enter any domain or structure for any reason," Mr. Blue said, smiling.

The foreman took a step back. "Oh, I see. Well, uh, let me know if I can help?" He tipped his hat to Georgia and walked away quickly. Georgia watched as he rejoined a group of dockworkers, who all stared from a distance. What a sight she and Mr. Blue must be—a woman with a sword and a blue wizard.

Mr. Blue led her over the plank to the ship. The *Gladys* was a river barge, intended for rapid transport upstream. The vessel had a full deck with many hook-points for strapping down crates but rode high in the water.

"I wonder why this ship, in particular, was in Sir Alexander's will," Georgia said. She looked around, seeing at least two others marked with the Hampton Madison logo on the side.

"Interesting question," Mr. Blue said. "Maybe when the original will was written, this was the only vessel he owned? Sir Alexander may have acquired the others later but found no reason to list them after he sold his share of the business."

"That makes sense," Georgia said. They walked across the deck from port to stern, looking for anything interesting, before finding a galley door. With some effort, Mr. Blue pushed the portal open. Rust and the odor of rancid mold wafted into Georgia's nose as she stepped inside. "Charming."

The interior cabin was designed for bedding down or relaxation time with fold-down sleeping pallets mounted on the far wall and a table in the center. Everything was covered in thick dust. Along the opposite wall were a row of personal lockers. Mr. Blue poked through the lockers, but they were all empty. Along the rest of the wall, it appeared there were once hanging charts on hooks, but all of that was gone now. "When the ship went into dock, they must have taken the records away," Mr. Blue said.

"Accountants hate leaving charts lying around. You know, dust doesn't make an odor like this," Georgia said, looking around for a source. There were two other doors, leading further into the vessel. She opened the first to find a small kitchen. It was tidy, although the smell was stronger. "I guess boats just get smelly."

"They do when they sit in still water long enough," Mr. Blue said. "Judging by the buildup on the hull, I'd say the *Gladys* has been resting in this channel for at least two years."

"Hello?" a familiar voice came from the galley.

Georgia poked her head out to see one of the Hampton twins standing with the foreman and a few dockworkers.

"Ollie?" she asked.

"Lady Georgia, yes, it's me," he said, smiling suddenly. "You guessed correctly. When Gaffey came running to tell us a man from the Crown was here, he neglected to mention you."

"I'm sorry, Mr. Hampton," the foreman said. "I didn't mean to inconvenience you."

"Nonsense," Ollie said. "You did what you should, good man. Although, next time a lady with a sword strapped to her back pops in, you might want to lead with that." Ollie elbowed the foreman and laughed.

Mr. Blue followed Georgia out to the galley. "Hello," he said, grinning.

"Hello, Mr. Blue. Good to see you again. What brings you to the docks today?" Ollie asked.

"We're following up leads and checking on clues," Mr. Blue said.

"This old boat is a clue?" Ollie asked. "How

extraordinary."

"We think Sir Alexander originally listed it in his will but removed it later," Georgia said. "Do you know anything about the boat?" Intentionally, she left out the part about the will regarding Ollie's father and how the implication was trouble.

"Honestly, until you set foot aboard, I didn't even know it was here." He turned to the foreman. "Gaffey, run over to Irma and get the bill of lading. See if we have a manifest on file, will you?"

"Yes, Mr. Hampton," the foreman said, leaving immediately. Ollie dismissed the other workers. "We'll be fine, lads. The lady with the sword is quite friendly." The dockworkers all nodded, smiling, and shuffled out the door.

"It's sweet they are so protective," Georgia said.

Ollie and Mr. Blue laughed.

"We were just about to look in this second room," Mr. Blue said. "Would you care to join us, Ollie?"

"Okay," Ollie said, smiling. "I suppose it couldn't hurt to learn more about the old girl."

Mr. Blue opened the second door, which was a captain's office. A blast of cold air wreaking of mold and rust came out. As they stepped in, Georgia could see her breath.

"That's not natural," Mr. Blue said, looking around. He looked at the floor, poking around the desk with his walking stick. "Ollie, can you help me move this desk?" Ollie and Mr. Blue pulled the desk to the corner. Mr. Blue came back and knelt, holding the cane in the air. He closed his eyes and whispered something indecipherable.

"What do we have here?" Ollie whispered, a faint smile playing in the corners of his mouth.

Georgia shook her head. "Your guess is as good as mine."

Something changed. The air grew a little sharper and colder, and then the floor shimmered.

"My word," Ollie gasped as they stepped backward.

The floor glowed in places, and lines formed around Mr. Blue. It was a circle with tiny runes. The wizard stood and stepped over to them as the glowing area increased in threads across the floor. Numbers appeared in rings around the circle, shimmering across the floor. "It is for protection," Mr. Blue said. "Someone cast this here, years ago. The magic is still present."

"Wait. This is real magic? I mean, you're not having me on, are you?" He laughed nervously.

"I'm afraid it is genuine," Mr. Blue said. "Someone on this boat placed a magic circle here for a significant reason. I don't know what kind of circle it is, but I can feel its power. The fact we can even see it tells me it is potent."

The air grew so cold that Georgia's teeth began to rattle, so they stepped out to the galley.

Gaffey, the foreman, returned with a folder full of papers. "Thanks so much," Ollie said, accepting the ledger. "We're fine. You can go." He wasn't laughing anymore, and flipped open the folder.

Georgia sauntered over. "What do you see?" she asked.

"The *Gladys* went into dry dock two years ago," Ollie said, reading over the papers. Ollie tilted his head. "The crew reported two deaths and frightening noises in the rooms. Sir Alexander's name is on the bill of lading as the owner, so he ordered the ship to be set in and repaired."

Mr. Blue came over to listen. "Deaths," the wizard repeated. "Does it say how they died?"

"It does," Ollie said, shuddering. "One fellow was dragged into the river by an unknown creature. The second one witnessed the first's death and took his life right afterward."

"Chilling," Mr. Blue murmured.

Ollie flipped through the pages again. "Here we are," he said, reading. "The ship was a transport vehicle in Sir Alexander's name for about twelve years, until two years ago when it picked up a special cargo in Hendon. The captain reported the mysterious noises began immediately as the barge made its way to Oradale."

"Hendon," Georgia said. "That's a long trip."

"The ship manifest would have made it slower as they hit each port on the river route," Ollie said. "According to this, half the crew went missing in action by the time they arrived in the city. The captain was certain the boat was cursed, and the missing crew members were all dead, but Sir Alexander marked them as having quit without giving notice. Interesting, though…"

"What is interesting?" Georgia asked.

Ollie looked up. "Two things are interesting. First, when a crew member quits without notice, they are officially marked as 'not fit for further employment' at the company. Sir Alexander didn't do that, according to this. Instead, he gave everyone who served on the *Gladys* a job recommendation. There are little stars by each of their names. I should go back to Irma and ask her to look up the personnel files to see if this is in error or if it really went that way."

"That could be informative, yes," Mr. Blue said. He looked back into the captain's office, where the glowing circle was dimming. "What was the second interesting thing?"

"It might be nothing," Ollie said, squinting at the file.

"It's been my experience that everything is important at some point or another," Mr. Blue said.

Ollie showed the bill to Mr. Blue, pointing at the bottom. "That right there is the signature for Sir Alexander's final consent to dock the ship." Mr. Blue looked at it, then at Ollie as if in question. Ollie flipped the pages back to another spot. "That is Sir Alexander's signature to initially check the ship in after the voyage."

Mr. Blue squinted. "The two signatures are different. They are similar, but not identical." He looked at the second signature again. Georgia came over to look. The first signature was in a flowing, smooth hand. The second signature was like a shaky imitation. She also noticed something else—a faint correction in the name 'Madison' on the second signature.

"The 'd' was corrected," she said, "and the handwriting is overly-rigid."

"Someone signed for Sir Alexander, I suspect," Ollie said. "I've seen it before. The foremen occasionally sign my name to things when they know I don't want to be bothered. They're always getting it wrong, though."

"They misspell 'Hampton'?" Georgia asked.

"Oh no, I mean, they get my first name wrong. Everybody calls me Ollie, but it's actually Colin. Ollie was what Manx called me when we were little. He couldn't pronounce my real name," Ollie explained. "Anyway when that happens, we re-write over the original. You know, try to fit it, so the Port Authority doesn't get all worked up. They hate it when we cross something out. That 'o' is a write-over... although I can't imagine what it would have been otherwise."

Georgia took the sheet and held it to the light of the window. She peered closely and finally made it out. "It's a letter 't,'" she said. "It was changed to 'd.'"

"Whoever was signing wrote 'M-a-t' and then changed the 't' to a 'd','" Mr. Blue mumbled, squinting at the paper.

Ollie took the paper back and looked at it again.

Georgia noted his hand trembled. Was that from the unnatural cold, or something else?

"Well, that settles it. The person who signed was probably just one of the foremen doing so on Sir Alexander's behalf who misspelled his name. You must know half these fellows can't even read. Well, it might take us a while to go through the files," Ollie said. He looked at Mr. Blue, then at Georgia. "Perhaps we could meet tomorrow to go over what we find in the office?"

"That would be lovely," Georgia said.

Ollie cast another glance at the room with the magic circle before he exited the *Gladys*.

"There was something unnatural transported on this boat," Mr. Blue announced. "A circle like the one in the other room doesn't just happen. Someone had to put it there."

"I'm not sure I fully understand what any of it means," Georgia admitted. "Did something about that signature and Ollie's reaction strike you?"

"He was afraid of something, but not enough to tell us what—or he was cold. This room is freezing now."

"File it away for the future," Georgia said.

"Agreed. There are only scraps of information here, but it appears something came aboard the ship... something wrong and evil. Someone placed that circle as a way to protect himself if or when the evil got loose. I believe it did and may have killed several crewmembers."

Georgia gazed at the room, thinking. "When the ship arrived, Sir Alexander may have decided it was easier to put the boat into dry dock and leave it, correct?"

"I wouldn't be surprised if he assumed some sort of flu outbreak was the real culprit or didn't take any of it seriously. Rather than let the story get out, he quietly lets the crew go and set the boat here to wait until people forgot what happened. Eventually, he would put it back on the river, and that would be that."

"Except he never did put it back into work, and even removed it from his will," Georgia said. "I think you were likely correct about some of the will materials. He was probably cleaning house and realized there was no reason to list a singular boat after he sold his shares in the company."

"I wonder if Mr. Hampton knows anything about the *Gladys*," Mr. Blue said.

"Or, for that matter, if he even cares."

"We should probably keep moving. The light is going to fade in a couple of hours, and we still haven't looked at the warehouse," Mr. Blue said.

Georgia looked around. "So that's it for the *Gladys*?"

"For the moment, I suppose it is. We should take a trip up to Hendon, don't you think?" Mr. Blue asked.

"Isn't Hendon in Volusia?" she countered. Mr. Blue helped her across the plank and back to dry land. They strolled past the workmen, who were pretending not to be watching, and turned toward the warehouse.

"We should speak to Lady Clara before we go... If we go," Mr. Blue said, tipping his hat to the workers.

Barges rolled past, as they did at all hours, bringing grain and goods to the great city from inland up the river. Georgia glanced at the sky. The Sun was well past afternoon, but it was still fairly early. "We still have an hour or two of light," she said. "Shall we risk going into the warehouse?"

"If you feel confident about it, then I do," Mr. Blue said.

They headed back down the path and made their way to the building. The wall extended to the shoreline.

"What a silly thing to do, walling off a building like this."

"Yes," Mr. Blue agreed.

They went up to the front doors of the warehouse. The wind whistled through the broken windows, and nothing moved outside. Only the sound of her boots and Mr. Blue's cane tapping the ground as they walked intruded on the space. The walls were covered in graffiti messages and crude illustrations. Georgia tapped Mr. Blue's shoulder and pointed out one of the messages in particular. It said, 'Death Awaits Within.'

"That's not ominous at all," Mr. Blue said. He stepped up to one of the doors and pushed it open. "Not locked."

Georgia followed him into a large, grimy foyer full of great wooden desks and queue stands. The windows were boarded up, keeping the place dark. The walls had huge boards with notes for delivery and export. "The barge captains would have come here to register their manifests," Georgia said, looking around. The ground was strewn with old yellow ticket stubs, long since cut from their ribbons. Off to the side, she spotted faint human-sized footprints in the dust.

Mr. Blue moved over to an adjacent office. It was windowed and featured several old desks and filing cabinets. He poked through the cabinets. "It looks like they took all the receipts when they left."

"Footprints," Georgia said, following them to the door.

Mr. Blue fell in-step beside her. "You have a keen eye."

"Thanks. They're barefoot—someone with long toes."

"If you lived in a dusty warehouse, would you wander around without shoes?" Mr. Blue asked. Georgia drew the magic sword just in case. It flickered but didn't light up. What did that mean? It glowed in the presence of magic and evil; it didn't flicker. They continued down the corridor, listening for any sound. Next was a long series of locked office doors.

"You would think they might have more windows in a place like this," Georgia said.

"Who knows. Back in the day when it was open, there may have been more light coming." Mr. Blue fished out a candle, and it lit in his hand. He held it up to better see, and they continued.

Georgia held the magic blade low and steady. She wasn't entirely they would need it. For all they knew, the bare footprints were from legitimate people who simply had no shoes. They turned another corner to find a door marked 'storage level 1'.

Mr. Blue pulled the door open, and they peered at the gloom within.

"Still no windows," Georgia said.

"Or the windows have been boarded up. That is how it was in the front of the building," Mr. Blue countered. He held out his candle, but it barely dented the shadows. Carefully, they set foot in the room and followed the wall. The chamber was vast and appeared to be the main holding area for the warehouse. Perhaps only ten feet away were massive wooden shelving racks that reached to the ceiling.

"What was stored here?"

"Anything and everything, I suspect," Mr. Blue said. "Judging by those old racks, a lot of cloth was brought in from other parts. That one there used to hold cotton, for example."

Something skittered above, and Georgia stopped. "Do you think it's a rat?" she whispered.

"No," Mr. Blue said. He tilted his head to the right. A creature the size of a human crawled down one of the racks, its nails digging into the dry wood of the frame. The thing had red, glittering eyes.

In her hand, the magic sword flared with gold light, revealing more of the room. Georgia spotted other creatures crawling down the racks. They were quieter than the first one and moving fast.

"We should go back," she said, gritting her teeth.

Mr. Blue turned back to the door.

"Where you go, delicioussssss?" asked a terrible sibilant voice from the dark.

Georgia turned to see something like a man, but with skin that hung loosely on his face. His clothes were in tatters, and he seemed to have trouble breathing. His long fingernails clacked and scythed like scissors as his eyes burned with an unholy light. "You mussst sssstay," he hissed. "We eat."

"Blood zombies," Mr. Blue spat with disgust. "Stay back, foul creature. You have no power over us. All light is your enemy, and all fire is your bane." The blood zombie rushed forward, but Mr. Blue struck it with his cane, and a bolt of blue incandescence erupted. The creature screamed, falling backward in a haze of fire. The others hissed and gurgled.

"Seriously, we should leave," Georgia said as figures poured down from the racks. Another blood zombie leaped at her. She stepped to the side and brought her blade down, severing its head in one stroke. With a burst of orange and gold, her sword erupted in flame. While the sword was cool to her touch, the effect it had on the creatures was significant. They backed away in fear, recoiling from the glow.

"It hurts us," a voice cried from across the room. "Kill it." There were dozens of them now, gathering at the edge of her reach, blocking the door.

"We will have to fight our way out," Mr. Blue said.

Georgia strode forward and slashed at the nearest blood zombie. The sword tore through the creature like it was nothing. Screaming, it fell in a ball of flame. Two of them moved around her, trying to scratch at her heavy coat. She chopped the hands off the first one and kicked another in the face. Several more blood zombies lunged, dragging her to the ground. Snapping their teeth hungrily and tearing at her coat. One of them began chewing on her neck, but the leather guard Eunice and Millie created kept her from harm. Georgia brought the sword up and swung from a prone position, ripping through two of them at once. She kicked another off and got back to her feet.

She had no fear of these damned creatures.

Georgia swung around as the blood zombies gathered for another attack, quickly hacking the head off another. Shrieking, they pressed forward despite seeing many of their kind falling.

"They are not stopping," she said grimly.

"They cannot stop," Mr. Blue answered. "Their hunger is too great, and they are lost to the world."

Georgia spun and sliced through two more in a wild spray of blood and bone. Gore hit her face, but she kept going. Behind them, more were crawling down the racks. "There are too many, Mr. Blue."

"Georgia, get the door." Mr. Blue stepped past her and raised his elegant cane. "The darkness took you, but will not prevail," he said to the creatures. "I am a servant of the Sacred Tree. If you approach, I will burn you with the flame of Nimloden and send you to rest. Get back, shadows." A bright blue flame erupted around his walking stick, followed by a silent wave of force. The blood zombies were thrown back, with many spontaneously bursting into flame.

Georgia got to the door as the room caught fire. Mr. Blue followed. They turned to see dozens, maybe scores of blood zombies writhing in the racks above. White-hot flames ran up the dry wood, erupting in all directions. Georgia pushed through the door, slamming it shut, and ran back down the hall with Mr. Blue right behind. The blood zombies burst through, howling. Some were still on fire.

Georgia and Mr. Blue turned the corner, coming face to face with dozens more hissing blood zombies.

Georgia flung herself into the nearest door, breaking through to an office. There was a window looking out on another unlit room in the warehouse. She snatched up a chair and slammed it into the glass.

Blood zombies pushed into the room.

Mr. Blue spun about, and a burst of blue light flashed from his walking stick. "Be gone, spawn of darkness. You hold no power against the light."

Georgia jumped through the broken window, landing in the next room. For a moment, she reeled, having just decapitated at least five creatures and then thrown a chair through a window.

Mr. Blue hopped through the opening and tugged her arm. "Think about it later," he said as they ran again. Behind them, the creatures poured through the opening, snarling and clacking their talon fingernails.

Georgia turned another corner and came back to the lobby. She dashed to the door, hesitating long enough for Mr. Blue to catch up. The creatures stopped at the edge of the chamber, their feet going no further than the side of the light from the open door. Smoke from the burning warehouse began to pour in.

"Do not leave us," said one of the creatures sibilantly. "Stay forever."

"You are out of time," Mr. Blue said. "This building is burning, and you cannot leave it. By nightfall, it will be gone, and so will you. I'm sorry for the sad end you had. Now find peace."

"The master will not like what you have done here," the blood zombie said. "You will die, Wizard. You and your Knight-Protector are finished."

"Go to darkness and do not return," Mr. Blue commanded.

He turned and followed Georgia into the daylight as the warehouse went up in flames behind them.

Georgia reeked of smoke and death when she got home.

"What happened?" Bea asked as Georgia walked in. Behind Bea were Millie, Eunice, Mrs. Cotton, Mr. Derry, and Francis. Georgia was sure Mr. Ellsworth, the gardener, gave notice already, but then he came in, too, pushing a cart full of tea and biscuits.

"Oh, it was fine," Georgia said. "The warehouse almost took out the dry dock, but then the rain started, and it all ended rather suddenly. Mr. Blue really does have wizardly powers."

"My lady, forgive me, but we were worried," Mr. Derry said.

She looked at him. Derry had served her uncle for decades. He had to have seen something akin to what she looked like tonight—covered in soot and disheveled. Behind him, the rest of the staff looked both relieved and frightened.

She offered them a reassuring smile. "There's nothing to worry about. Both Mr. Blue and I are fine."

Francis poured tea while everyone waited. Bea sat

down and patted her hand. Someone said something. The air was still. Georgia felt fear, and then it was gone, and she felt nothing. Her eyes stung, and then they didn't.

Monsters.

A male spoke to her. She heard her name several times. Someone seemed upset. Another voice arose after that. She could hear a song—the magic sword, Anamagal, the Sun Blade of the East. Georgia listened, feeling comforted. The song picked up, but this time it was a woman singing the same tune. The sword joined in, and Georgia drifted off with it.

Eventually, Mr. Blue began to speak. He was talking to someone.

"Oh no, Lady Georgia isn't the first. There have been other Knight-Protectors who were ladies."

"How amazing," a female voice said—Bea, Georgia realized. "Why have we never heard of this?"

"Five thousand years is a very long time," Mr. Blue said. "Much of what we see in the world that seems new is actually quite old. There are tales of heroes and heroines throughout the ages, and we must never forget about hope."

"I'm not feeling so hopeful, Mr. Blue."

"I understand, Lady Beatrice, but it is in those moments when hope is most critical. It reminds me of the tale of Lady Gwendolyn Goldenheart, who was a great force for good."

"What a pretty name," Bea said. "What happened to Lady Gwendolyn Goldenheart?"

"Why, she saved the Three Realms from certain disaster. Who knows, perhaps even the world," Mr. Blue said. "Now, this was back in the year 3904 of the Current Era, more than a thousand years ago. At that time, some of the laws and customs were different. There was no prohibition on ladies from owning land or having titles. It was dependent only on the firstborn in any family. Lady Gwendolyn was the eldest in that generation of

Goldenhearts, so she became the Duchess of House Goldenheart, and Knight-Protector."

"Huh," Bea said. "Go figure."

"Word came of a growing evil in the hinterlands of Filhampton, deep in the realm of Findor. Lady Gwendolyn and her kin rode to the rescue with all haste. People spoke of the sky burning red with a great mist that clung to everything. It poisoned all it touched, and many lives were lost. When the Goldenhearts arrived, they saw the devastation and wept for the innocent. It was the work of Mehira, queen of the vampires, who returned after millennia. They thought she was gone for good, destroyed in the last Battle of Midnight, but there she was. Now, over the many centuries, Mehira regained her power. In fact, she was greater than ever and held the gift of life or death in her hands. The Goldenhearts rode to her dark fortress, the Tower of Angum, where they found an army of night creatures amassing. They knew they were too few to resist such a horde and planned to return to the Three Realms to raise the war cry. Alas, Mehira sensed their approach and wove a great spell. Her power lulled them all to sleep. When the Goldenhearts posed no threat, she set her night wolves upon them to feast."

"Horrible," Bea said. "Mr. Blue, is this really the story you should be telling when Georgia is stuck in this terrible coma?"

"This is a healing sleep," he answered. "If Georgia can hear us, perhaps she will appreciate the adventure. Shall I continue or leave it for another day?"

"Please continue," Bea said. "Sorry, Georgia, now I want to know what happened."

"Lady Gwendolyn awoke to the sound of her kin eaten by the night wolves. She leaped to her feet and took up Anamagal, the Sun Blade of the East, and slew the night wolves on her own. Sadly, many of her family were now dead. It filled her with a rage, and she strode to the very gates of Angum, shouting, 'Queen of Vampires show yourself! Face the wrath of the Goldenhearts'," Mr. Blue said.

"Good for her," Bea said.

"Mehira was filled with fear, as Lady Gwendolyn's rage was great. In her hand, the Sun Blade burned with a terrible power, and the Vampire Queen knew she would fall if she appeared. Instead, she fled into the depths of the tower to hide. When she didn't appear, Lady Gwendolyn raised the blade high and smote the ground where the base of the tower met the earth. It cracked, sending a fissure deep into the structure, and the tower fell. The Vampire Queen Mehira was sealed in and has remained so to this day. Never again did she bring evil to the children of men."

Georgia drifted after that.

She heard a woman's voice say, "Do not lose hope."

Fresh air and the scent of cinnamon wafted into her nose. Georgia opened her eyes and looked around. On a nightstand, beside the bed, sat a plate of cinnamon cookies and a fresh pot of tea, and sitting in a nearby chair was Lady Clara Gaye, the witch of Volusia. Lady Clara looked brilliant in a black linen morning dress with white ermine trim at the cuffs and collars. Her hair was sensibly tied, and she was reading a book with spectacles on, no less.

"Hello," Georgia said.

Lady Clara looked up, smiling brightly. She set her book down, along with the spectacles, and leaned in. "Welcome back to the living," she said, almost conspiratorially. "Everyone will be so relieved."

"What happened? I remember I was sitting in the library, and—"

"You had a bit of a blackout," Lady Clara said. "I think it may have been a form of shock, my lady."

"Shock? Nothing shocks me," Georgia said.

"Meeting the darkness and seeing what it can do to innocent folk will shock anyone, I suspect," Lady Clara said. "Mr. Blue told me about the warehouse. That sounds like the most horrific thing I could imagine, and I can imagine a lot." She helped Georgia sit up and poured a cup of tea.

"How long have I been asleep?" Georgia asked.

"I coaxed you to sleep two days ago," Lady Clara said.

"Coaxed me?" Georgia asked.

"I sang to you until you slept. Before that, you were in a state of catatonia," Lady Clara said quietly. "They got you up to the bed, but neither Bea nor Mr. Blue could shake you from staring at the wall. It is a wonder your eyes didn't dry out."

"Catatonia," Georgia repeated. Her eyes did sting a bit, now that she thought about it.

After getting her settled, Lady Clara stood. "You'll need to talk to a few people, I'm afraid. Are you up to it?" Lady Clara didn't wait for an answer as she opened the door and signaled to someone on the other side. "She's awake now. Tired, but awake."

Bea hurried in, beaming and tearful at the same time. "Oh, Georgia," she said, hugging her tightly.

Behind her, Mr. Blue poked his head in and smiled.

He let Millie in, followed by Eunice and Mrs. Cotton.

"I assure you, I'm fine. Lady Clara said it was just a bit of catatonia. I'm assuming that's something akin to a coma, correct?" Georgia asked.

"Georgia, you are not allowed to make jokes," Bea chided. "We were so worried."

"Bea and the staff have barely left your side since you collapsed," Lady Clara said. "I rather think they should all get some sleep, or they will be no good to anyone."

"My lady, I've got to get the soup ready for her ladyship," Mrs. Cotton said.

"Nonsense, you must get some rest," Mr. Blue said. "Mrs. Cotton, I will make supper for everyone and bring it up to your rooms."

"What? Why I've never heard anything so strange. Is this how wizards behave in their own homes?" Mrs.

Cotton asked.

Mr. Blue winked at Georgia and then pushed everyone but Bea and Lady Clara out into the hall. Faintly, Georgia heard Mrs. Cotton say, "Next that woman will be dusting our rooms and cleaning the windows."

Bea rested her head on Georgia's shoulder. "He's probably right. I should go, too. I'm so glad you are not dead."

"Now that you mention it, I'm also glad about that," Georgia said.

Bea stumbled out of the room, stopping for a moment at the door to smile reassuringly. Then she was gone.

Lady Clara turned back to Georgia. "You will want to get some rest. Eat these cookies first, though. Mr. Blue will be back with the soup, but anything you eat now will help."

"I have no appetite right now," Georgia said. "It's all coming back—those people, the blood zombies. We need to find their families and tell them what happened. They must be worried sick."

"It will be done, all in good time, Duchess. Ollie Hampton thinks most of them were dockworkers."

"Really?"

"He told us the business had been losing employees at a surprisingly high rate for several months. His father chalked it up to most of the workers being lazy or unreliable. Still, Ollie said something about it didn't sit right. He said he assumed it was some sort of mismanagement at the docks, or perhaps there were bullies on staff. He had even begun to think it might be a rival company terrorizing his workers," Lady Clara said. "He had quite a few ideas about it."

"Well, of course. Who would think the workers were turning into blood zombies and hiding out in the long-abandoned warehouse?" Georgia asked. Maybe a cookie was a good idea, after all. She took a bite, and her mouth began to tingle. The cookie was not sweet, nor was it the savory kind. She took another bite, trying to figure out what precisely the taste was. It was both crunchy and slightly chewy. Georgia had another. It was fresh ginger and something else. Was it cinnamon? She looked down to realize the cookies were gone. She had eaten them all.

"Well done," Lady Clara said, pouring another cup of tea. Mr. Blue appeared in the doorway with a cart and a tureen of potent chicken broth. The aroma was intoxicating. He also had a plate with steaming hot bread, butter, a carrot, and an apple. "Now tuck into a bit of this. You'll likely need another night of sleep before you start to feel human again."

Mr. Blue set a tray across her lap with a bowl and bread.

After she ate, Georgia slept for the rest of the day, but at least she wasn't in a coma.

Georgia was back on her feet and feeling much healthier when Ollie Hampton arrived two days later. He had several dockworkers in tow, all carrying boxes of files.

"Father was rather put-out about this," he said. "He didn't like the idea of you and the wizard poking through our personnel files. I asked if he would rather have the constables come and do it. He changed his tune after that."

They started laying out stacks of papers. "Where do we begin with this?" Georgia asked.

Ollie pointed. "These files go back two years. Before that, we found nothing odd. Every single one of these people vanished relatively recently, Duchess. Irma and I went through all of them, just trying to see if there was a reason that made sense, and none of them do."

"How many people are we talking about?" Georgia asked. The dockworkers laid out file after file.

"At least a hundred people are missing," Ollie said.

"They came to work at our docks one day and never returned to see their families."

There were dark circles under Ollie's eyes. For that matter, none of the dockworkers seemed in much better shape. Every man carrying boxes looked like he was on his last legs.

"Lady Georgia, there is an epidemic. The building you burned down—we talked to the families. I think all of those men were abducted, murdered, and transformed into the creatures you encountered."

Georgia watched them stack the files. Each one placed so she could read it easily. She looked at the workers and Ollie and knew they wanted her to figure out how this could happen.

"You believe they were the un-living? Creatures from beyond the grave?" she asked.

"I saw the magic circle on the ship. Mr. Blue stood over it and called for it. We both saw that. He didn't play some parlor trick. It was there already. Later, I read the report about the warehouse—scores of strange creatures who could have been human but were not—and all burned on the spot," Ollie said. He looked at the dockworkers and then turned back to her. "We came back after you and Mr. Blue left, and looked at the last glowing traces of the magic circle. I could feel it on my skin. I don't know how the magic works, but we could all see it. After that, we started looking through the personnel files and found so many people gone. Honestly, how could this happen right in front of us? I'm always up at the office. I suppose, I could see how I would miss it. My father is quite demanding, but I walk the docks several times a day," Ollie said. He punched himself in the leg. "How could I miss it?"

"We all missed it, sir," one of the dockworkers said to Ollie. "We missed the signs. You were not alone. I kept thinking it was just people being people, but it wasn't."

The dockworkers went outside to wait.

"Are you okay?" Georgia asked him.

"Every time I think about it, I kick myself," Ollie said. "I walk past the slip where the *Gladys* is tied every single day. I've been walking past that slip for five years. For the last two years, that ship has been sitting right there. The other day, when you and Mr. Blue arrived, was the first time I ever noticed it."

"You supervise a rather large dock," Georgia said.

"Duchess Goldenheart, the *Gladys* is capable of transporting more than half a ton of cargo," Ollie said. "I'm not trying to argue, but that is one big boat. How could I miss it sitting in our slip for two years?"

"I don't know what to tell you, Ollie," Georgia said.

"After you burned down the warehouse, we held a séance."

"Pardon me?" Georgia asked.

"I know, it's silly," Ollie said. "I tried to talk to my mother."

"What happened?" Georgia asked.

Ollie leaned forward. "We did it on the ship, not over where the warehouse was. I thought for a moment, after what Mr. Blue said about it being a magic circle, we could call out and maybe get an answer. I hired another wizard— a fellow from the Magestrix Club. I mean, they all seem so certain even as they spew nonsense. Mr. Blue barely speaks, but I didn't want to bother him."

"He would have advised you not to do it," Georgia said. "Ollie, you know that."

Ollie nodded. "I do, Georgia. I do. You don't mind if we use names?"

"I would prefer it," she said. "What happened?"

"The Magestrix wizard arrived and went on at some length about the magic circle. He was very impressed. He said some goddess created it. I told him it was there already, and then he tried to do the séance. We were all standing there holding hands in a circle and feeling foolish when he just stopped and gave the money back. I just sort of sat there, I suppose, but that wizard was out the door.

He told me I should let it go. He said several things."

"Like what? What did he say?" Georgia leaned forward.

"He told me the ship was cursed, and I shouldn't try to use the magic circle. He suggested we burn the vessel, actually," Ollie said, shaking his head. "I guess I just wanted to try it. I needed to talk to Mum. I needed to, you know?"

"Yes, I understand," Georgia said.

"We did not succeed," Ollie said. "It went nowhere, and I left feeling like an idiot."

"I'm sorry, Ollie," Georgia said.

Georgia strolled through the front foyer of the Edmunds Building and up to the receptionist. She was fully decked out in her great white coat with the magic sword strapped to her back and donned a spectacular wide-brimmed hat.

"I am Lady Georgia Goldenheart, Duchess of the House of Goldenheart, Knight-Protector of the Three Realms from Dragons and keeper of the Sacred Blade," Georgia said. "I have no appointment, but I would like you to summon Mr. Adina."

"Mr. Adina?" the receptionist asked, gulping.

"That is his pseudonym. You may know him better as Mr. Tom Turner," Georgia said. "He works here. If you do not summon him, I will go up and search for him myself."

"You can't go up there," the receptionist said. "This is the *Weekly Men's Journal*."

"I certainly can. I will simply return with a Royal Writ of Full Entry," Georgia said. "I'll give you five minutes to decide what to do." She stood by as the receptionist hurried upstairs.

Less than five minutes later, Mr. Tom Turner appeared.

"Duchess Goldenheart," he said, "To what do I owe the pleasure of your visit?"

"Mr. Turner, I am here to ask questions. You haven't

responded to any of my letters, so I thought I would take a chance and find you myself," she said. "Is there somewhere you would find more comfortable to talk, or shall I begin right here in the foyer?"

"My apologies. I fell a bit behind in my correspondence."

"That happens when you are leading a double life," she said pointedly.

"There's a lovely place we can sit, just around the corner. Perhaps we will be more comfortable there," Mr. Turner said, ushering her out the door.

Georgia glanced back to see the receptionist falling into her chair with relief.

Mr. Turner guided her around the corner and found a comfortable café. He walked in like he knew the place well, and selected a booth with no other tables nearby.

Georgia was barely in before they brought a steaming pot and a tray of sweet biscuits.

"This is better," she said. After everything that happened over the last two weeks, she found herself less inclined to the gentle approach. "I would apologize for not giving you prior notice, but I was afraid you were avoiding me."

"I might have been avoiding you without really intending to. That whole night at the Hampton House was a disaster on a personal level. I know I should be more sympathetic to the Madisons and help the constabulary. Still, I'm sure you know by now about my family tensions."

"I know only what Chief Inspector Morris deigned to tell me, Mr. Turner," Georgia said. "He told us you were his nephew, and there was family trouble."

"So you can see why I avoided it all."

"The explanation makes sense, but you are a trained observer. I need you to go back over your memories of the night of the party," Georgia said.

"So you are working with the police?" Mr. Turner

asked.

"I am, yes," she said. "Mr. Turner, I must confess my patience is at an end. For two weeks, we have been struggling with the mystery of how Sir Alexander died. Since then, I have encountered many strange, surreal, and frightening things. I would very much like to move forward now. What do you remember from that night?"

"I remember Mrs. Smythe, who was just as delightful and brilliant as rumored. You and your friends were also a cheerful lot, and if the evening had not gone the way it did, I hoped to strike up friendships with your group."

"We felt the same," Georgia said.

Mr. Turner smiled. "Sir Alexander seemed happy. I know you were thinking about poisons. I have since done some research, and I must say I cannot imagine him poisoned quite so suddenly. I know the symptoms matched arsenic. Mr. Blue said as much when we cleared the room. I'm just not sure I believe that theory."

"Do you have another idea?" Georgia asked. After dealing with vampire bats and blood zombies, she had plenty of wild and far-fetched theories. Still, it never hurt to ask.

Mr. Turner shook his head. "I'm not sure you would believe me if I told you. I've been digging."

Georgia leaned in. "Mr. Turner, at this point, I am prepared to believe almost anything. The absence of a reasonable explanation opens the door for the unreasonable."

"What an interesting way to put it." Mr. Turner looked around the room as if concerned someone was listening. Finally, he leaned closer. "I think a curse killed Sir Alexander. I know what that sounds like, but I promise you I am not insane."

"After the week I have had, I will take you at your word," Georgia said. "Tell me more about this curse?"

"Sir Alexander wasn't drinking when he fell. The man was chatting and amiable, but set his cup down untouched.

He was talking to Manx Hampton and just keeled over. The coroner found no trace of poison in his blood."

"You read the coroner's report? I haven't even read it yet."

"I bribed someone to slip me a copy," Mr. Turner said, smiling mischievously. "You haven't seen the report because someone is keeping it from being released."

"Who?"

"I don't know who," he admitted. "But the coroner told me it was someone with power and money."

"May I see your copy of the report?" Georgia asked.

"Funny, you should ask," Mr. Turner said. "Yesterday I came home to find my place ransacked. At first, I thought I had been burgled. At the paper, we see a rising rate of home invasions, but none of my valuables were missing. I have a pair of solid gold cufflinks that were on the dresser in my room. They went ignored. The only thing missing was the copy of the report."

Georgia sat back. "I need to see that report," she whispered.

Mr. Turner nodded. "I need to reference it again too. I was preparing my notes for a story on the incident, and my editor is breathing down my neck."

Georgia stood. "Only one thing to do," she said. "Go see the man you bribed and bribe him again."

"Really?" Mr. Turner stood up. "If I take you to him, and he's amenable, will you let me see it too?"

"Yes, that sounds fair," Georgia said. "First, we need to take a side trip. Would you care to join me?"

"Lead the way, Duchess," he said, grinning. "Where are we headed?"

"We need to swing by the Order of the Blue guild house," Georgia said. "I think Mr. Blue will be interested in this new development."

They headed out. The café was only a few blocks from the guild house, which was a small tower on the top of Oakes Street.

"You know," Georgia said as they walked, "Bea and I wondered if you knew Mrs. Smythe already."

"Only by reputation," Mr. Turner said. "She has scooped me more than once, though. When she walked up at the party, I must admit, I almost said something unkind. You've met her, though. How could anyone be unkind to that ridiculously adorable hat?"

"I like Mrs. Smythe very much, and yes, she has excellent taste in hats. May I ask you a personal question, Mr. Turner?"

"Sure," he said. "I have a feeling I already know what you will ask."

"You were rather publicly arrested, but you continued to write articles under your pseudonym during your time in prison. How did you do that?" Georgia asked.

Mr. Turner laughed. "As I said, my lady, I bribe people to do things.

"That's all good and well, but some of the information in your articles required firsthand knowledge."

"That's because I was there in person," he admitted. She stopped and gaped. Mr. Turner grinned. "Oh, my lady, I have shocked you. I bribed the guards to let me in and out of prison when it was useful to do so."

"You escaped and returned?"

"Quite simply, the answer is yes. I knew I had to serve out my sentence, or I would never be able to live in the Three Realms. Also, I was framed for a crime I did not commit. I had to find the real culprit and clear my name. In the end, when I did just that, the authorities had no choice but to let me live free again. They even forgave the escapes, as I was innocent from the beginning," he said.

"What was the crime?" Georgia asked.

"I was charged with bribery and fraud against a royal judge," Mr. Turner. "It is deliciously ironic, yes?"

Georgia laughed. "Wait. Did you learn to bribe people to clear your name of bribery then?"

"Oh yes," Mr. Turner said, laughing. "I became the

thing they accused me of, in the end. That said, I was indeed framed for the wrong crime. The real culprit was never caught, but I managed to extract a partial confession out of the judge. It was enough for my uncle to reopen the case and proclaim me innocent of all charges."

"If the Chief Constable knows you are innocent, may I ask why he was so hostile the other night?"

"My uncle hates being wrong more than he cares about doing what is right," Mr. Turner said, flatly. "He's very stubborn."

At the corner of Oakes Street, they took a left toward the Order of the Blue following a long green hedge. "Have you ever been to this tower?" Georgia asked.

"Me? Oh, no, never. I mean, I have ridden past in carriages," Mr. Turner said. "Now that I think about it, I've never actually seen it. I understand it is nothing like the Majestrix Club."

"I should think not," Georgia said. "The Majestrix is a gambling hall."

"Only the first three floors," Mr. Turner said. "The fourth floor is for the elite club-members, who are all taught the art of sorcery and conjuration. I know, because I was a candidate for the fourth floor when I was arrested."

They arrived at a huge, bright blue wooden gate in the hedge. "I suspect this is the door," Georgia said. She knocked politely. A moment later, the gate swung open to reveal a garden beyond. A tiny older man in a solid blue butler uniform said, "Hello, Duchess Goldenheart."

"Hello," Georgia said. "Forgive me, I do not know your name."

"Please call me Mr. Blue," the butler said.

Mr. Turner chuckled.

"Hello, Mr. Blue. Would you kindly fetch … err, Mr. Blue? I need to see him."

"I'm sorry, my lady," Mr. Blue, the butler said. "Mr. Blue is not here right now. Would you like to come inside and wait? We have some lovely tea cakes."

"How long will he be gone?" she asked.

"I do not know," the butler said. "He never returns when I want him to, only when he sees fit."

"Naturally," Georgia said. "A wizard arrives when he means to."

"Exactly, my lady."

She thought for a moment. "Very well, Mr. Blue, when the other Mr. Blue returns, will you inform him that Mr. Turner and I are en-route to bribe a coroner to give us a legal document? If he would like to join us, we would like to see him. Hopefully, it will only take us another hour or two before we complete the task. At that time, we will adjourn to my home to read the stolen materials."

"I will pass along your message, Duchess," the butler said with a bow.

Georgia turned to Mr. Turner. "Shall we catch a carriage to the coroner's office?"

"Right away, Duchess." Mr. Turner flagged down a cab, ushered her aboard, and gave the driver directions.

"You spoke of the Majestrix Club," Georgia said, settling into her seat. "I remember the night of the murder, you mentioned running into Ollie Hampton there."

"Yes, I saw him at the club, and he invited me to the birthday party," Mr. Turner said.

"So, you got your membership back after the prison fiasco," Georgia said.

"They had to give it back to me. My family has a lifetime renewing membership, and the whole incident revolved around the club. The alternative would be a public spectacle, and no one wants that," Mr. Turner said, shaking his head. "The judge was a member there. It was all part of some internal plot. That club is very political. Judges, notable peers, and noblemen are all members. You might be shocked at what happens behind those doors."

Georgia smiled. "Mr. Turner, very few things shock me anymore. I take it they aren't going to teach you the secrets of sorcery now, despite your return?"

"I suppose that remains to be seen. Ollie was just asking me the same thing, but I don't know how to help him."

"What does Ollie need from you?" Georgia asked. "Can you tell me more about that?"

Mr. Turner leaned in. "Duchess Goldenheart, I will tell you this about Ollie Hampton, but I must ask you not to repeat it."

Georgia sighed, "Very well. I will not repeat it."

"Ollie is desperate to talk to his dead mother. He is fixated on her. I do not know if it is merely the grief of a son or something else—but he will not let it go. Mrs. Hampton passed away just before I was entangled in the bribery scandal. Right away, Ollie was after me about the Majestrix Club's fourth floor. He knew I was a candidate, and he was desperate to have a séance. I chalked it up to sorrow and did my best to get someone at the club to hold the ceremony for him. I remembered the loss of my mother, and I wanted to be a good friend. Unfortunately, the bribery debacle happened, and I was sent to prison. While I was there, Ollie was a good friend and wrote constantly—but you know, he also kept asking about séances and sorcery. I finally had to tell him in a letter I would never be allowed on the fourth floor. He was very upset."

"I'm sorry, Mr. Turner," Georgia said.

Mr. Turner threw his hands up. "I felt bad that I couldn't help him, but also confused. Why didn't he just ask his brother?"

"Manx?"

"Sure," Mr. Turner said, "Manx has a fourth-floor membership. I'm sure he's not a conjurer or involved in anything ridiculous like that—he doesn't strike me as the type to go in for sorcery, if you get my meaning."

"I do get your meaning," Georgia said.

"One would think he might introduce his brother to

someone, though."

The carriage rolled up to the Office of the Royal Coroner on Blake Street. As they entered, Georgia said, "Shall I assume you will do the talking, and I will do the paying?" She pulled several folded bills from her purse.

"That sounds like a marvelous arrangement, my lady."

They turned a corner to find a door marked 'Mr. Blasey, Assistant to the Coroner'. Mr. Turner knocked politely.

After a moment, a young man with spectacles answered. "Hello, may I assist you? Oh, it's you," he said.

"I need another copy of that document," Mr. Turner said, keeping his voice low.

Mr. Blasey shook his head. "I can't do that. It's too risky."

"How much will your bribe cost?" Georgia asked.

"Excuse me?" Mr. Blasey said. "Who is this woman? Is that a sword on her back?"

"She's a friend," Mr. Turner said. "You might want to address the duchess formally."

Mr. Blasey blanched. "You're Lady Georgia Goldenheart. I knew your uncle."

"Lovely," Georgia said. "Did he bribe you too?"

Mr. Blasey took a step back, then darted covert glances up and down the hall. "Yes," he said finally. "How much are you offering?"

Georgia handed him a wad of bills. "How is that?" she asked.

Mr. Blasey nodded. "It is a proper bribe. Return tonight at midnight, and I will have the copy ready. I'll need to go get it from the locked file after everyone leaves."

"Excellent," Georgia said. "I look forward to bribing you again sometime."

"I look forward to it too, my lady."

An hour later, Georgia and Mr. Turner arrived at Wending Way to find Mr. Blue waiting. "How did the bribery go?" he asked.

"We have another appointment with the fellow," Georgia said. "He has to find the right moment to steal the report and copy the contents."

"Ah, yes, that would take some planning. So the coroner finished the report, but they never sent it to us?" Mr. Blue said. "Mr. Blue, the butler suggested it might be a government cover-up."

"Maybe, but I think someone very rich is involved who doesn't want us to see what was in the document. I already read it once, though. I remember most of it. The body had no evidence of poison, sickness, or even a logical reason for death. He stopped living. That is why I think it was a curse that killed Sir Alexander," Mr. Turner said.

"Fascinating," Mr. Blue said. He turned his attention to Georgia. "We have seen a vampire bat, a magic circle, a warehouse full of blood zombies, and now we learn Sir Alexander died by unnatural cause."

"Vampire bat?" Mr. Turner said. "What?"

"I did mention I've had something of a week, right?"

"You forgot to mention the extent of your week, though," Mr. Turner said. "No wonder you didn't blink when I said it was a curse."

"We still need to see that coroner's report. It is evidence. If this all boils down to standing in front of a judge, we will need to present a case. Also, it may provide a clue to the murderer," Mr. Blue said. "What time is it available?"

"The coroner's assistant said to come back at midnight," Georgia said. "Mr. Turner needs to see the document too. He's writing an article about the murder."

"A public declaration of what happened. Good. We have six hours then," Mr. Blue said. "Perhaps we should go to dinner and make an evening of it."

"I have another idea," Georgia said. "Gentlemen, dinner will be served in two hours, right here at Wending Way, and I will be wearing formal gloves. I will invite a few more people. What do you say?"

"I'll get my tie and tails," Mr. Turner said. "See you soon."

An hour later, Lady Clara Gaye walked into the library in a stunning floor-length satin black gown with gold leaf trim at the collar and cuff. Her hair was up and layered with pearls.

Georgia was all in white silk. She wore long blue satin gloves to accentuate the white but wore her hair down.

Bea was in a stunning lilac tea dress. Usually, the look would be too casual for dinner, but she accented with a white ermine half-coat. The effect was quite modern, but also very chic.

Mrs. Smythe arrived a moment later, clad in a marigold silk gown with green buttons instead of lace. It was, again, a very bold choice. Her cap was a bouquet of fresh-cut daisies.

"Hopefully, this will be the first of many lovely dinners we share as friends," Georgia said.

"I could not be more excited," Lady Clara said.

Mrs. Smythe turned to Lady Clara. "You are the Witch of Volusia, my lady."

"I am. You are not Mr. Adina, but rather Mrs. Rowley?"

"Correct."

"Mr. Blue and Mr. Turner have arrived," Mr. Derry announced from the doorway. He and the staff were in full regalia. Georgia realized she would need to throw these dinners more often if only to keep Mr. Derry from jumping off the roof. Suddenly, she remembered something Uncle Raymond said when she was home from school for the summer holiday and he threw a dinner party at the spur of the moment. When she asked why, he told her, "Sometimes a butler needs to buttle. We all do what we must, dear Georgie."

Mr. Blue entered, wearing a stunning black tail and tie. The only blue on his person was a silk ribbon on his lapel.

He looked quite dashing. Behind him, Mr. Turner entered in pristine black tail and tie.

"Good evening, ladies," Mr. Turner said. "Goodness, what a gathering." He nodded to Lady Clara but took Mrs. Smythe's hand and kissed it. She blinked, blushed, and then smiled.

Mr. Derry came over and said, "Dinner is ready whenever you are, my lady."

"Give us half an hour," she answered. Making the staff wait was almost entirely against Georgia's nature. Good Cymbre girls didn't inconvenience anyone, servant or not. Still, this was an excellent time to enjoy the moment. She looked at Mr. Derry, and he nodded happily.

Bea stepped over. "I think Mr. Turner and Mrs. Smythe may have something in common. You should sit them together." Georgia nodded and hurried over to Mr. Derry.

"Put Turner and Smythe together at the table," she whispered. "We are matchmaking, Mr. Derry. Whatever you give them from the menu, be sure it has no foul odor."

"Yes, my lady," the butler said, and went directly to the dining room to move the place cards.

Georgia turned back to find Mr. Blue grinning from across the room.

Half an hour later, the party moved into the dining room. Mrs. Cotton set out a menu of duck and sauce, greens in a savory tray, and a side of delicate macaroni pie. The wine flowed.

After the first course, which everyone seemed to enjoy, Georgia raised a glass and said, "Thank you all for coming. I know that we each met under different circumstances, but I must say I am delighted for tonight."

They raised their glasses.

She continued. "Each of you is an investigator in some way. Tonight, Mr. Turner, Mr. Blue, and I will be going to pick up the coroner's report. I bribed a man to deliver it illegally. But as my Uncle Raymond would say, we do what we must. We already know what it says, but our hope is when reading it, we see some clue to the identity of Sir Alexander's murderer."

"Oh, dear," Bea said. "Georgia, is this the right moment to talk about this?"

"Yes, it is," Mrs. Smythe said. "Does this mean you eliminated all of us as suspects?"

"No," Mr. Blue said. "The least likely suspect is Lady Clara Gaye, the Witch of Volusia because she was not at the party the night Sir Alexander died. The rest of us were there, so we are all technically suspects, along with the others not invited to tonight's dinner."

Lady Clara tilted her head. "Yet, because you said this, Mr. Blue, you admit you do not think anyone here is the murderer."

"Correct," Mr. Blue said. "I freely admit that. I may be proven wrong, of course."

Georgia nodded. "I don't think anyone here is the murderer, either. For that reason, I ask for your assistance. Each of you has the mind to see what we might miss. We know Sir Alexander died suddenly. We know it looked like poison, even though he had no symptoms before. At the same time, the autopsy showed no such weapon. We need other ideas. If it wasn't poison, and his body was whole, what was it? Why or how did he react that way? The autopsy also showed no heart attack and no apoplexy. Mr. Turner thinks Sir Alexander died as a direct effect of being cursed."

"Cursed?" Mrs. Smythe asked. She leaned her head in with Mr. Turner.

"There are curses that can kill," Lady Clara said, quietly. "But a mere mortal could not cast one. Creation of element to destroy, yes that is possible. A wizard could create fire. A witch could sing to bring the wind to destroy. Saying a word and simply killing another with it? No, a mere human could not do such a thing."

"Are we seriously talking about monsters again?" Mrs.

Smythe asked.

Bea looked at her. "I assure you, I saw the vampire bat here at Georgia's house. I heard the magic sword call out and tell me to take it to Georgia's hand. Mrs. Smythe, magic is real, so why not monsters too?"

Mrs. Smythe was about to object but seemed to think better of it.

Georgia stepped out the carriage in a sensible wool dress and black coat, with the magic sword strapped to her back. Behind her, Mr. Blue and Mr. Turner climbed out. The Royal Coroner's Office was closed. Down the lane, there was activity at the Jester's Pub. A man sang and danced with a bottle in his hand.

"Revelers work at all hours," Mr. Blue said.

"Perhaps after we get the report, we will join them," Mr. Turner said, grinning, "Although, I might prefer simply going home after this."

"I agree," Georgia said. "Let's get the report and talk in the morning. I will have a full breakfast waiting on the sideboard. My butler will be thrilled to learn about it."

Mr. Blue chuckled. "He is very old school, Lady Georgia."

"As I am learning. Tonight, I told Mr. Derry to set up a dinner party with forty-five minutes to spare. For a moment, I thought he might start dancing with joy," Georgia said. "For that matter, the whole staff seemed so happy."

"They want you to be happy," Mr. Blue said. "It's simple. Their ability to please you might also help ensure their continued employment. Perhaps I am cynical?"

"Seems like an astute deduction, Mr. Blue."

Mr. Turner led them to a side door. "This is where the bribes are distributed," he said with a wink.

Mr. Blue laughed.

Just inside, they found a small side office with electric lamps already lit. On the desk was a folder marked

'Madison.' Mr. Turner opened it, revealing a stack of papers.

"Good old Blasey. He knew we couldn't wait to read this and even left the lights on."

"Blasey?" Mr. Blue asked.

"That's the name of the fellow I bribed," Georgia said, smirking. "It's my first bribe, actually."

Mr. Blue grinned.

Mr. Turned leafed through the folder, pulling subfolders out. "This is another crime scene assessment." Mr. Blue took that folder and began leafing. "This is a toxicology report." He handed it to Georgia. "And this is a witness addendum." Mr. Turner took that and began reading.

Georgia scanned through the report. No trace of arsenic or polonium or any other toxin. The coroner was baffled and requested a second, third, and even a fourth test before concluding poison was not involved.

"No poison," she said.

"The witness addendum includes additional interviews with the servants," Mr. Turner said, reading. "Typical."

"Typical? How so?" Georgia asked.

Mr. Turner rolled his eyes. "My uncle has a bad habit of glossing over anyone who lives downstairs."

"He was less thorough interviewing the staff?" Mr. Blue asked.

Mr. Turner nodded. "It's as if they weren't in the room, too." He read aloud. ""All servants accounted. Footmen were working and saw very little. Maids were… uh, this part is a bit hard to read, but it looks like he wrote 'gone.'"

"I wonder if we should go back and re-question some of them," Georgia said.

"Interesting," Mr. Blue said, reading his folder intently. "Georgia, this document has a legal hold on it, signed by the widow, Lady Emily Madison. She invokes family privacy and requests all information to be left confidential and secret."

Georgia shook her head. "Why? She was very clear about wanting the truth to come out."

"She changed her mind. Wait," Mr. Blue said, peering closer at the page. He handed it to Georgia. "Look at the signature."

Georgia peered at it. It clearly said 'Lady Emily Madison', but then she realized the 'd' in the surname was a little off. "Oh, dear," she said, understanding. "The letter 'd' was originally written as a 't'."

"Where have we seen that before?" Mr. Blue asked.

"Uh... Where have you seen it before?" Mr. Turner asked.

Georgia looked up. "We saw it at the Hampton Madison dry docks. One of the sign-in reports for a ship had the same problem. Ollie Hampton speculated that a dockworker must have signed on Sir Alexander's behalf then. He said whoever did it probably misspelled the name, then realized and corrected the letter."

She handed the report to Mr. Turner, who also peered at the signature. "It's definitely a marked letter. Whoever signed this spelled 'Madison' as 'Matison'?"

"Maybe," Mr. Blue said. "We should not speculate on it yet. There may still be a rational reason for all of this."

"Mr. Blue, the last time we saw 'd' and 't' switched-out, we also saw a magic circle followed by a warehouse full of blood zombies," Georgia said. "I am beginning to appreciate your stance on coincidences—I don't think they exist."

Mr. Blue grinned at her. "I couldn't agree more, Lady Georgia."

"Where do we go from here?" Mr. Turner asked.

"Let's take all this back to my house," Georgia said. "I had Mr. Derry fix up a couple of guest rooms. You are both welcome to stay over tonight. In the morning, we can pick up the reading over fresh coffee and scones."

❖

Sometime around 5 am, Millie woke Georgia with a tray of tea, toast, jam, bacon, and a boiled egg. "The wizard is downstairs, my lady," Millie said. "He was out all night, and just returned."

"See to it that Mr. Blue has breakfast waiting in the library on the sideboard," Georgia said, between bites of bacon. "I know, we normally serve in the dining room, but today is an exception."

"Yes, my lady."

"What about Mr. Turner?"

"He's still asleep."

"Do not wake him," Georgia said. "It was a late night, and Mr. Turner doesn't have my endurance—or for that matter, the fortitude of a wizard. When he gets up, ask Francis to help Mr. Turner bathe and dress, if he needs assistance. I doubt he will need help, but make the arrangement just in case. After that, be sure he knows we are in the library."

"Yes, my lady," Millie said. Georgia got dressed, grabbed the coroner's report from her nightstand, and went downstairs to find Mr. Blue ensconced in the library with several folders.

"Ah, my lady," the wizard said. "I take it, Mr. Turner is still asleep?"

"It was a late night," she said.

Mr. Blue shrugged. "I took advantage of the extra time to do a little bit more detecting."

Georgia set the report down, saying, "What did you learn?"

Mr. Blue sat with another folder, and pulled out a sheaf of papers. "This is a legal document from the Housing and Land Commissioner—signed by Lady Emily Madison." He handed her the document and pulled another out. "This is a letter of reference for a parlor maid who left employment under good terms, also signed by Lady Emily. We might compare the signatures with the one from the coroner report."

"How did you find a letter of reference?" Georgia asked.

"I went to Madison House and asked for it," Mr. Blue said, smiling. "Lady Emily had a copy on file."

"Did you tell her why you wanted it?" Georgia asked.

"Yes, I did," Mr. Blue said. "She told me she never signed any document from the coroner and didn't hesitate to pull these papers upon request."

Georgia took both documents and compared the signatures to that on the death certificate. In the land bill and reference letter, Lady Emily's signature was clear and swoopy. In the coroner report, it had a certain kind of swoop but was also a bit jagged.

"The person who signed was hesitant."

Mr. Blue produced another document. "This is the Lading Bill from the dry docks."

He handed it to her. The signature was very similar.

"How did you get that in the middle of the night?"

"I snuck in and stole it."

"Okay." Georgia looked up. "You think the person who signed for the ship also signed the death certificate?"

"Yes," Mr. Blue said. "Both times, we see the mistake with the letter 'd,' but also note the same jagged hesitation in the script. I think it's a fake but done by someone not experienced in the art of forgery. I think it is someone nervous and acting after the fact."

"So many questions," Georgia said.

"When this all began, our first thought was a poisoner—someone with a likely grudge against Sir Alexander. Naturally, our prime suspect would be his old business partner. They have a long history, and we could find no one else with a bona fide vendetta. Later, we discovered the development with the warehouse previously owned by Sir Aubrey Algernon and his plans for a lawsuit. He died before he could launch the suit, but his daughter opted to abandon it. The daughter told us he died from natural causes, and so far, we have no indication otherwise."

"From the meeting with Algernon's daughter, we learned the connection with the *Gladys* and the warehouse full of blood zombies," Georgia said. "I do not think it is a coincidence. Then, there's the misspelling of 'Madison,' both times in direct connection to the victim. Merely misspelling a name isn't conclusive of anything, per se. We have the semblance of coincidence, yet I think none of it is."

"I agree," Mr. Blue said. "It is all intentional. Based on that and the fact the coroner found no trace of poison in the body, we must assume dark magic killed Sir Alexander."

"I'm not sure how to follow these leads," Georgia admitted. "Until the sword came to me, I had never even seen real magic. I didn't believe it even existed. Now we are to try and find a magical murderer?"

"We still have one outstanding clue," Mr. Blue said. "It's a bit of a trek, but we did learn the haunted ship came down the river from the village of Hendon in the far north. Perhaps we should take the journey there and see if it is the ultimate source of this evil?"

"It's worth the attempt, but we can't leave for a couple of days. Tonight is the Volusian party, and the day after tomorrow is the Irvingdale Social. I committed to both events, and it's too late to get out of either," Georgia said.

Mr. Blue smiled. "That's fine. We will need to arrange our transportation to Hendon. It's not like the old days when we would hop on a couple of horses and ride for five days across the country. These things require planning."

Georgia laughed. "Millie will need, at least, a day to select my wardrobe for the trip. Very well, how about we plan to go Hendon at the end of the week?"

"Perfect. I will arrange a large coach to take us upland. At this time of year, the thaws are only just starting, and

Hendon is quite far north. The river may be crowded," Mr. Blue said.

Mr. Turner appeared in the doorway.

CHAPTER 11: VOLUSIANS.

Right at dusk, Georgia and Bea rolled into the driveway at Nisbett Manor for the big Volusian party, situated only a block from the Hampton's house.

"Does everyone live on this mountain?" Georgia asked as the driver pulled the door open.

"They do," Bea said, stepping out. Georgia followed, and they made their way past piles of horse dung under a bright array of festive lanterns toward the great house. "Be careful," Bea said. "The horses have been here, and we are not the first arrive."

At the front door, Millie appeared at Georgia's side and carefully strapped the magic sword to her back. After that, she laid a white ermine stole over Georgia's shoulder. Bright white silk with startling gold trim dominated Georgia's new gown, off-set by deep blue buttons. Her collar was stitched with gold wire and rode up the back of her neck where it fanned out like a divine clamshell to frame her face. After seeing Mrs. Smythe's excellent use of buttons the night before, Georgia opted out of lace altogether. Without the frilly element, it felt like she could move without worry. Millie checked both of their feet for dung, finally nodding her approval like some sort of military general.

Bea was sharp in a floor-length satin gown of slightly-darker lilac hue with a high collar. She wore her hair up with a modest silver tiara from her mother's collection. Georgia approved. Bea might be a fifth daughter, but she was still an Irvingdale. Why not make the point?

Millie scampered around her and Bea, making sure everything was in order, even as they entered a vast marble foyer strung with multi-colored lanterns. Festive music drifted in from an adjoining room, where young people in formal wear lounged. Off to one side, two women shared a hardy laugh, and one of them spilled her drink, which made them laugh even louder.

"Less pomp, more flirting," Bea said. "I like it. It's very Volusian."

"A happy and unpretentious people," Georgia said. "It makes me wish my own family was a bit less Findorian. I'm so glad I brushed up on Volusian protocol before we left the house."

Bea laughed. "You mean when we had that pre-game cocktail? Georgia, you are both the most and the least pretentious person I have ever met."

"Thanks, Bea. I'll take that as a compliment." Georgia turned to Millie. "Do they have somewhere you can be until I need you, Millie?" she asked.

"Yes, my lady," Millie said. "I will be just behind those doors with the other maids."

"Off you go," Georgia said.

Millie curtseyed and went into the side room.

Georgia turned to Bea. "Shall we enter the party?"

Together they strolled through a set of double doors to

find a large ballroom bustling with people. Unlike the Earl of Cadwin's ball, this one had no footman to announce people. The custom up north was to walk in with a smile, so that is what Georgia did. Several fine ladies curtseyed as Georgia passed. They were all clad in black as if the night were a funeral. Georgia paused, taking the whole lot in, and then nodded once in passing. The curtseys continued as they made their way across the room. Bea stayed one step behind her.

When a waiter crossed their path, Bea stepped over and fetched two flutes of champagne, further illustrating their difference in rank without making a fuss about it.

"Every lady in the room is wearing black," Bea said, looking vaguely panicked yet excited. "I knew it. We are looking at a fashion revolution."

Every Volusian woman was wearing a witch-black gown. A few non-Volusian ladies stood nearby, reliably clad in lilac, and looked out of place.

"You're right. That said, I think we are doing quite well here," Georgia said, nodding to another woman who was still in a full curtsey. "Refresh my memory, Bea: without a footman, are we essentially introducing ourselves?"

"That is precisely what we are doing," Bea said, startled to find another woman curtseying to her too. She smiled and nodded, releasing the woman.

"The curtsey ends when I arrive," said another lady, who was smiling. She was older and dressed in a black gown with huge white feathers on her head. "Duchess Goldenheart, I am the Dowager-Countess Lady Hermione Nisbett. You honor me greatly with your attendance."

She and Georgia nodded, being near equals. Bea waited behind Georgia with her eyes down.

"You honor me with your superb invitation," Georgia said formally. "I must say, your home is amazing yet comfortable, Countess."

"Thank you, and spoken like a true Volusian," the Countess replied happily. Behind her, Georgia noticed

Lady Carlotta Landsmere smiling at the floor.

Lord William Reade, the Viscount of Simsley, strolled up in elegant black tie and tails. "My lady Countess and Duchess Goldenheart," he said happily. "What a pleasure to see you finally meet."

"Lady Hermione and Lord William allow me to introduce Lady Beatrice Irvingdale," Georgia said before the window for proper introductions closed. Bea curtseyed immediately to the Countess, then to the Viscount.

"Pleasure," Lady Hermione murmured.

"Well met, Lady Beatrice," Lord William said, grinning. "You're an Irvingdale, eh? I believe I know one of your kin in the form of Lord John Wickham."

"He is my brother-in-law, my lord," Bea said.

"He's a fine chap, too," Lord William said. "His investment turned my brother's estates right around after last year's big freeze." He looked at Lady Hermione. "Oops, I didn't mean to start talking business, my lady."

"Your brother is Sir Reginald Reade?" Bea asked. "I remember that. The entire summer peat crop would have gone if he hadn't devised his new grinder. You must know your brother was the real hero there. He may have discovered a whole new refining process that could revitalize the northlands. As a result, the autumn holdings in Findor will remain stable well into the winter months. That said Lord Wickham will be so happy to hear such kind praise. I hope you don't mind if I relay your compliments on the timing of his investment."

"My goodness, yes, by all means. I've never heard a lady speak so succinctly about business."

"Forgive me," Bea said. "I don't mean to presume."

"You do not presume. Far from it," Lord William said, looking at Bea as if she had just started doing acrobatics. Georgia knew Bea had a mind for business, but this was some in-depth and specific knowledge. Lord William's broad chin jutted at Bea, and for a moment, Georgia was afraid there would be words of disagreement. Instead, he blushed and looked away.

Bea smiled at the lord and began to blush, too.

"Perhaps, Lady Georgia, you and I could speak alone?" Lady Hermione said. She looked at Lord William. "My lord, would you mind leaving us a moment to speak in private? I must have the ear of the Duchess. Lady Beatrice, may I have a word with Duchess Goldenheart? Perhaps you and Lord William could go find a waiter and bear us with your patience? I promise it will not take long, and beg both of you to forgive the request?"

"Of course, my lady," Bea said, curtseying.

Lord William smiled and took her by the arm. They walked away together.

"Unexpected," Lady Hermione said. "Did I misread what just happened, or has Lord William found a Lady he might actually deign to speak to without sounding like a smug know-it-all? Better yet, an Irvingdale lady. What better way to see if they have anything in common than to put them to a mutual task and see where it goes."

"I was under the impression the plan was to introduce her to Sir Richard Bourne," Lady Carlotta said.

"Sometimes, we mere mortals cannot predict the path life will choose," Lady Hermione answered. "It appears to be an odd match, but perhaps not. I have a mind for this sort of thing, and I know something rather delicious."

"What do you know?" Georgia asked.

Lady Hermione leaned in close. "Lady Clara Gaye wrote me. You know she is the Witch of Volusia, yes?"

"I believe that is common knowledge," Georgia said.

"Clara told me Lord William's great aunt by marriage is the Dowager-Countess Lady Harriet Cunningham. She can pass, by proxy, the title of the Barony of Elton, west of Oradale, and she's over one hundred years old," Lady Hermione said. "Some people think she might live forever, but of course that is absurd."

"Good for her, though," Georgia said.

"I couldn't agree more, but Lady Harriet favors Lord

William as an heir to both her fortune and her husband's. Still, there are several other families with an equal or even better claim."

"I'm not sure where this is going," Lady Carlotta admitted.

"I have not gotten to the best part," Lady Hermione said. "You see, Harriet's maiden name is Dale."

"Lady Harriet comes from another branch of the original family that preceded Bea's family, the Irvingdales," Georgia said, blinking rapidly. "Surely, Bea is no direct relation to Lady Harriet. It would be known. I mean, there cannot be more than three Dales left in the world."

"I'm quite certain the families are too distant for it to be anything but half of a name in common," Lady Hermione said. "That said, if Lord William and Lady Beatrice did find a match, even though she is plainly beneath him—well, I wonder if Lady Harriet wouldn't find it a compelling reason to include her favorite great-nephew in her will?"

"That is a long road to follow," Georgia said.

"True," Lady Hermione admitted. "But wouldn't it be a charming tale for them to tell their children? Oh fine. Let's get Sir Richard in the room next and see what happens. I love this sort of thing."

Lady Carlotta smiled, shaking her head. "Imagine if, all along, Lord William simply needed the right Lady who could stimulate his mind, amongst other things?"

"Let's not get carried away, Carlotta," Lady Hermione said, winking.

Lady Lucinda Kilgore and Sir Richard Bourne wandered past. "Oh, hello," Lady Lucinda said.

"Duchess Goldenheart," Sir Richard said, bowing deeply.

"Sir Richard," Georgia said, "Please rise and be at ease." The week before, she had read up on the formal interaction with another knight and was ready this time.

"What fun," Lady Lucinda said. "I see you've brought

your sword again, Lady Georgia."

"I did," Georgia said. "It's more or less expected these days."

"Sadly, no wizard, though," Lady Lucinda said.

"Perhaps he will join us next time. I am going to see him tomorrow, so I will pass along your good wishes if you like," Georgia said. She turned back to Sir Richard. "I wonder if I might pick your brain a bit, Sir Richard."

"I am at your disposal," he said immediately.

"On Friday, I am going on a journey to the Volusian northlands: specifically, to the village of Hendon," Georgia said.

"Why would you go there, Lady Georgia?" Lady Hermione asked.

"Duchess Goldenheart is pursuing an investigation, I believe," Sir Richard explained.

"Correct, Sir," Georgia said, wondering how much he already knew. "We are headed to Hendon to follow a lead. I wonder if you know enough about the region to recommend lodging."

Sir Richard looked at Lady Hermione, who shrugged. "Hendon is the border village for the Earldom of Simsley. Lord William has a house on the other side of the county. We've all been up in the area several times. As for Hendon itself, there is only one place a traveler could stay."

"Do tell?"

"You will want to stay at Pere Castle," Lady Hermione said. "It was an ancient fort from the days before the unification of the Three Realms that lay abandoned for centuries. About a decade ago, investors went in and turned it into one of those lodges for skiing. Now it is quite the holiday spot."

"Be wary, though," Sir Richard said. "Pere Castle is said to be haunted."

"Haunted?" Georgia repeated. She had already run afoul of a vampire bat and a building full of blood zombies. Why not a haunted castle, too?

"According to all of the travel guides, that's one of the selling points of the hotel," Lady Hermione said. "Some people enjoy being scared as much as they love skiing."

"A haunted hotel in the Volusian northlands sounds perfect," Georgia said.

Bea returned with Lord William, followed by a waiter bearing a tray full of champagne.

Georgia grabbed a drink and toasted. "To the northlands."

"To the northlands!"

"That was so much fun," Bea said as they climbed into the carriage. "What a charmer Viscount Lord William was. I am almost embarrassed I took up so much of his time, but it was such a pleasure."

"I'm glad you enjoyed it," Georgia said, sliding in next to Bea. She nodded to the driver and the carriage pulled out. "Bea, I should tell you something."

"What is it, Georgia?"

Dark tree shapes rolled by the coach window. "There is a possibility of a match between you and Lord William," Georgia said, choosing her words carefully. There were so many ways this idea could go wrong. Perhaps she should hold her tongue.

"Georgia, that is almost laughable," Bea said, shaking her head.

"I'm serious," Georgia turned toward her friend. "Lady Hermione said Lord William has a dowager great-aunt from House Dale with no one to directly inherit. She might be favorable to a match and leave him her estates if he finds a bride from a suitable family from another branch of her line. You could be that bride."

"You are being serious," Bea said, biting a fingernail. "Georgia, I don't know about that. What if we pursued it, only to lose the few prospects I have? I mean, House

Dale? I cannot possibly be related to this dowager. My family would know."

"Think it over," Georgia said. "Talk to Lord Wickham and see what he says. If he overrules the idea, then you're still free to pursue the Hamptons."

"Right," Bea said. "This evening just got complicated."

CHAPTER 12: IRVINGDALES.

Georgia stepped out of her carriage and squinted at the gardens around Irvingdale House. Beyond was the bocce field, where it was already hot enough to make the air shimmer. She nodded her approval. The Hamptons would have their footman attending them. Mr. Blue and Lady Clara were in separate carriages, so it was just her and Millie. Speaking of Millie, she had taken some inspiration from Sir Lionel's designs and fashioned a lovely tea dress for the occasion. Georgia stepped out of her carriage in a dignified white saree cotton skirt attached to a blue lined straight bodice with gold stars running down the back.

A small crowd of onlookers gathered at the gate to Irvingdale House behind them.

"Duchess, we love you!" a woman's voice came from the gate.

"Oh my word," Georgia said, smiling and waving. "That's new."

"Yes, my lady," Millie said.

Another carriage pulled up, and Mr. Blue popped out,

looking dapper in a sharp white shirt, blue waistcoat and single-breasted tails. His gray breeches were narrow and conservative. The whole outfit was topped with a blue hat. The crowd at the gate approved clapping.

"Goodness," Mr. Blue said.

Another carriage rolled up. An older couple Georgia didn't know stepped out and hurried inside without looking back.

"We might not be a universal hit," Georgia said.

Mr. Blue smiled.

Lady Clara Gaye stepped out of the next carriage looking breezy in an all-white tea dress with delicate lilac lace at the cuffs and donned a broad white hat. "Hello, Duchess. Mr. Blue," she said as the coachman helped her.

"Welcome to the social," Georgia said. "No more 'Duchess,' though. We have graduated to 'Lady Georgia,' I think."

Lady Clara curtseyed, much to the delight of the crowd at the gate. "What is that all about?" she asked as they turned to head inside.

"Lady Georgia has a fan club," Mr. Blue said. "There was an article in a magazine, and now she is famous." They passed through the front of the great house and found their way to the bocce court.

"I read it, too," Lady Clara said.

"You saw the part where it said I was merely tolerating you?" Georgia asked mortified. "If they knew how you sang me to sleep after the blood zombies trauma, do you think they would write something so shallow?"

"Reporters always write those little articles," Lady Clara said. "Think nothing of it, my lady. Next week it will be someone else."

"Bea has a theory about that," Georgia said. "In fact, here she is now. Perhaps she will have additional thoughts on it."

"Georgia!" Bea called out, hurrying across the lawn. "Mr. Blue," she said.

"Lady Beatrice," the wizard said, nodding. "Thank you for the invitation."

"You are most welcome. Georgia, have you seen the size of the turnout this time? Wickham has outdone himself. I've already seen two countesses and an earl wander past. Last year, we were lucky to have the old retired knight down the lane. Now we are an event. There's so much to tell you. I talked to Lord Wickham about you-know-who."

"About Lord William Reade, the viscount?" Georgia asked in a whisper.

"Yes," Bea said, her eyes darting from side to side. "Let's try to avoid embarrassing anyone."

"Who are we not embarrassing?" Georgia asked. "Just so I know what we are talking about."

"I don't want to embarrass Ollie," Bea said, glancing around. Ollie Hampton was standing some twenty yards away at the edge of the bocce game.

"Okay, but I am fairly certain he can't hear us at this distance," Georgia said. "Please continue."

Bea leaned in. "I went to Lord Wickham and told him what the Dowager-Countess told you about Lord William's great aunt."

"Good. What did he say?" Georgia asked.

"He said it sounded too good to be true."

"Wickham thinks the Hamptons are the only option then?"

Bea smiled, but her voice betrayed regret. "He went further than that and negotiated directly with Mr. Hampton. It is done, Georgia. All of the levels you imagined: House of Peers of House of Commons and the blending of the two families. That is precisely what Lord Wickham proposed, and Mr. Hampton accepted. Ollie proposed this morning. I accepted his proposal, and I am not to think about Lord William Reade again."

"Oh, my goodness," Georgia said, sitting back. "You are engaged then."

"I am," Bea said, holding up her hand. On the ring finger was a diamond the size of her knuckle.

"I say," Mr. Blue said, "Lady Bea, congratulations."

"Thank you, Mr. Blue," Bea grinned, and looked very convincing.

"Oh. Oh, dear," Georgia said. "Bea, that's wonderful. Tell me you're happy."

"I'm happy. I'm delighted."

"What about Manx?"

"Manx? He didn't ask me," Bea said. "I'm sure they will sort it out. Honestly, they probably did already. I didn't even think about him."

"I'm so happy for you, Bea," Georgia said.

"You deserve it. You remember Lady Clara Gaye, the witch of Volusia," Mr. Blue said.

"Lady Beatrice, congratulations," Lady Clara said.

"How could I forget the one who sang Georgia to sleep after that horrid catatonia? Consider me closer than a sister, Lady Clara. Oh, what a nice dress," Bea said. "White, I see. Is it a total capitulation? That was quick."

"Lady Beatrice, you are wonderful, and thank you. I'm sorry, I don't understand the comment about my dress, though," Lady Clara said.

"Bea has a ghastly theory; we are all pawns of the press and dress design industry," Georgia said. "She was second-guessing your next public outfit after the ball at the Earl's house after the article came out in the *Youthful Ladies Journal*."

Lady Clara blinked rapidly. "You know, there might be something to your theory. This tea dress was a gift from Piedmont House. They sent a whole cartload over, just this week. I was quite taken aback, but this one stood out. I just loved it and couldn't resist. Since they insisted, I kept the whole lot—although I did give several of the sturdier items to the *Working Poor Woman Foundation*."

"You know, my sisters and I have an entire room full of coats we never wear. I believe I will send a note to that organization, too. In fact, we should do a drive to collect coats and scarves while it is still the summer season. People love to give away things they aren't using, even if they might wind up needing them later," Bea said.

The green was filling up as more guests arrived. Bea had to be attentive, so she wandered off with Ollie and Manx in tow. Her four sisters, Bernadette, Bridget, Barbara, and Bonnie, all gathered in a line to welcome guests. At the end of their line was Bea's mother, Lady Irvingdale, reclining in a chair.

Georgia went over and greeted each in turn and watched them awkwardly curtsey now that she was a duchess.

"You don't have to do that," she kept saying.

"Yes, Georgia, we do," Bonnie said finally. "Now go see Mother before we are all permanently exiled."

Georgia approached Dowager Lady Irvingdale. The matriarch of the family tried to get up but was struggling. "Don't you dare stand up," Georgia said sternly. "How are you, my lady?"

"Old and weary, Georgia, and you're ruining the fun. You should be enjoying your new title. Everyone should be fawning, and you should be checking suitors off a list. Why are you Goldenhearts all like this? Your Uncle Raymond wouldn't allow it either."

Georgia knelt beside her chair. "You are like a mother to me, Briana. I will not change that now. I'm sorry, but it is the way it must be."

"You're a good girl," Lady Irvingdale said, patting her shoulder. "Bea told me all about your rivalry with the witch of Volusia. I knew Lady Clara's mother. The Gayes are a lovely and old family. They have that same entail the Goldenhearts do. No matter who the heir is, anyone who marries them must take their name. Oh Georgia, I cannot tell you how many times in my youth, Lady Clara's mother dragged me to every soup kitchen in town. Now tell me, what about suitors for you, dearest?"

"No suitors, I'm afraid," Georgia said.

"That's too bad. A woman like you should have a fine gentleman to rely upon, even if you are in a position not to need it—I take that back—*especially* if you are not in a position to need it. When I was younger, I would have said you should have the security of a man no matter what. In your case, I must re-think things and say a man might merely be fun and comforting. What about the fellow in blue? He looks dapper, or is he one of those lifetime bachelors we see at court?"

Georgia looked at Mr. Blue, who grinned and waved. "Actually, he is a wizard."

"You're spending your time with a witch and a wizard. Now I've heard everything," Lady Irvingdale said, laughing until she coughed. "Oh, now I remember—Order of the Blue. Those wizards protected us in the war. That would explain the outlandish clothing. You are living in an exciting time, Georgia, and coming into your own just as your dear Uncle Raymond wanted. I'm happy for you, even if you must die a spinster."

Georgia was almost shocked but saw the mischief in Lady Irvingdale's eyes as she said that last sentence. Instead, Georgia laughed. "Your daughter, Bea, is a bad influence on you."

Lady Irvingdale laughed again without reservation. She smiled at Georgia with affection, as if she was one of her daughters.

"I have held up the queue too long," Georgia said, patting her shoulder.

"Go," said the lady. "Have fun, and laugh, Georgia. Not that you ever had a problem there, but laugh anyway."

"Thank you, my lady," Georgia said, getting up. She rejoined Mr. Blue and Lady Clara.

Mr. Blue handed her a glass of crisp raspberry tea over ice. No borage at this affair. "We should talk to Mr. Bailey," Mr. Blue said. "The bocce game is underway, and Mr. Hampton has gone to watch his sons play in it."

Mr. Bailey was laying out shirts for the Hampton twins in the basement when Georgia, Mr. Blue, and Lady Clara found him. He was a good-natured, quiet fellow, like most good servants.

"Mr. Manx hinted you might come to speak with me," he admitted. "I wish I could help. I only remember taking the tray and passing it about."

"Do you remember the moment Sir Alexander took the glass? Do you remember how you moved through the room before that?" Lady Clara asked.

Mr. Bailey thought for a moment. "I suppose so, my lady. We always go the same way. Mrs. Billingsley, may she rest in peace, had a way she preferred and was quite specific."

"Mrs. Billingsley?"

"She was the head of the house, the chief maid," he said. "Mr. Davenport was butler, so he was the boss, of course... But he was quite young, and she trained him. Mrs. Billingsley ran the house for years. When she passed away last year, Davenport told us to stick to the routine, you know? At the parties, we always move in pairs—one leans into the right of the room and moves through the outer area before we take a position on the edge. The other walks through the middle and then goes left. That way, no party guest gets missed, and there are no complaints."

"I see," Lady Clara said.

"It sounds elaborate," Mr. Blue said.

"Just a good way to keep everyone happy," Mr. Bailey said. "Fine folk like you come to these parties expecting service, but it gets confusing with everyone moving about."

"Suddenly, I feel better about being a wallflower," Georgia said.

"Folk like you are our favorite kind, my lady," said Mr. Bailey. Then he blushed. "I'm sorry, my lady. That was rude."

"Not at all," she said. "I now have a reason to stay put at every party, Mr. Bailey."

"Can you recount the evening when Sir Alexander died?" Mr. Blue asked. "I arrived at just about six that evening, and you met me at the door, as I recall. What happened before that and after?"

Mr. Bailey mused. "We returned from the picnic, where the master first met you, Mr. Blue. I remember that. After we came back down the trail, I helped Mr. Hampton get his clothes sorted for the evening, before putting him down for a nap. He slept for about forty-five minutes. I ran to the chemist to pick up pills for his foot. It always swells after these affairs."

"What happened after that?"

"I got back and helped Mrs. O'Leary with a few odds and ends. She was unpacking some old silverware, and a few of us jumped in with the polish. We got it done quickly and put everything away."

"Then what happened?"

Mr. Bailey shrugged. "Of course, we knew the party was coming for weeks, so most of the preparation was done. I went from room to room with Mr. Davenport, and he inspected everything one last time. All the dishes were accounted for, all the glasses, all the silverware. Everything was where it should be, with only the usual exceptions."

"What are the usual exceptions?" Georgia asked.

"My lady, in any large house, there are always a few items floating in rooms. Mr. Manx had a glass and a couple of forks in his room. Mr. Ollie had a saucer he forgot. Sometimes these items go missing for short stints. Mrs. Billingsley would have known about them from day one. Still, Mr. Davenport views it as unavoidable and not worth tracking every little thing. As long as the guests are happy and the master is pleased, he takes the little things in stride."

"Interesting," Mr. Blue said. "Did you notice anything unusual about the day of the party? Was anyone behaving strangely?"

"What qualifies as strange, Mr. Blue?" Mr. Bailey asked. "I would hate to speak ill of my employers."

"We see your position there," Lady Clara said, "and we promise to keep anything you say in the strictest confidence."

Georgia had no idea why the fellow would trust Lady Clara's word on anything. It's not like he had ever met her before.

"Mr. Manx was in a bit of a state, as I recall," he said. "Forgive me, but Mr. Manx was rankled by the encounter with Mr. Blue on the hillside at lunch."

"He did express a bit of skepticism about wizards," Mr. Blue said. "My very presence was a bother."

"He and his father share a healthy disregard for magicians," Mr. Bailey said. "Mr. Ollie is different. He loves the magical stuff and even has books on it in his rooms."

"What kind of books?" Georgia asked, amused.

"I think it is mostly about séances. Ever since Mr. Ollie's mother, Mrs. Hampton, passed away, he has had an interest. You know, the very moment she died, the clock in the back foyer stopped ticking. It never worked again."

"When did Mrs. Hampton die?" Lady Clara asked.

"She passed about a year ago. It was just a day or so before Mrs. Billingsley went. They were both in bad health at the same time. I remember thinking the house would never be the same," Mr. Bailey said.

"You mentioned the clock stopping," Lady Clara said. "What time was it left at?"

"It was six o'clock, my lady, right on the mark."

"The clock faced down," Lady Clara said, looking at Mr. Blue.

"Does that mean something you know that I do not, Lady Clara?" Mr. Blue asked.

"It is an ill sign," she said quietly. "Also, it is an odd coincidence the clock stopped on the very hour and not a minute or two to either side."

Mr. Blue nodded. "In other words, you don't think it was a coincidence at all."

"I don't believe in coincidence, as you know," Lady Clara said.

"I do know," Mr. Blue said. He looked at Mr. Bailey. "Well, this has all been very helpful, Mr. Bailey. Just a quick recap—you served the drinks on the right side of the room at the party. Who took the left side?"

Mr. Bailey shrugged. "Mr. Davenport took that side. We lost a footman earlier in the day, so he had to fill in."

"Lost a footman?"

"Clancy. He fell ill quite suddenly and went to see his family to recover. He hasn't returned yet. I suspect Mr. Hampton will have him replaced if he doesn't come back soon. The master has no patience for that sort of thing."

"Interesting. You also served the drink to Sir Alexander, correct?"

"No, that wasn't me," Mr. Bailey said. "Lady Emily wanted champagne, so I stepped off to fetch it. Mr. Hampton himself got Sir Alexander's drink."

Mr. Blue looked up. "He did?"

"He handed him his drink, in fact," Mr. Bailey said. As he said it, his expression changed, and his face grew pale.

"You have remembered something, Mr. Bailey," Georgia said.

"I guess so. Mr. Ollie gave his father the drink. I don't know if I remember anything at all, though," Mr. Bailey said quickly. "It's just a little odd thing."

"Tell me."

Mr. Bailey shrugged, "Mr. Ollie handed his father the drink and then sort of darted across the room. He was so quick about it, he knocked a glass off Mr. Davenport's tray as he went."

"Oh, dear," Mr. Blue said.

"That contradicts something we heard," Georgia said. "Mr. Manx told us he gave the drink to you—not his brother—and you gave it to Sir Alexander."

"Oh, no, my lady. Mr. Manx was clear across the room. He couldn't have given the master the drink," Mr. Bailey said. "And I never touched it. Mr. Ollie gave it to his father, and then he, in turn, handed it to Sir Alexander. Mr. Hampton would never drink if one of the guests were empty-handed. He's very traditional."

"Mr. Hampton poisoned Sir Alexander?" Hampton was Lady Emily's first suspect, Georgia remembered.

"It looks like Manx lied to us, too," Mr. Blue said. "He said he poured the drink. But if Mr. Bailey is telling the truth, it was his brother who did the deed."

Lady Clara shook her head. "What if Sir Alexander was not the intended victim?" They stopped walking.

"That is an interesting idea, Clara. If we are still going with the poison in a glass theory, and the glasses were floating around the room in all directions, it could be our glass went to the wrong person."

"Or maybe it was given to the right person, but he gave it away," Georgia said. "Maybe the glass was intended for Mr. Hampton all along. When Lady Emily sent the footman for champagne, he handed his glass to Sir Alexander to be polite, not realizing what he was doing."

"Why would Mr. Hampton's son hand him a glass of poison?" Lady Clara asked.

"Perhaps the son wanted to kill him." Mr. Blue raised an eyebrow.

"But to do it in front of so many witnesses?" Georgia asked. "Why not wait for a better time?"

"What if he wanted to muddy the water with other suspects and wasn't worried about witnesses?"

"It seems like a terrible risk," Georgia mused.

"Hm," Lady Clara said. "This is a good point, and we still have no clear motive for any of it."

"I would assume wealth is the motive," Mr. Blue said.

"I agree," Georgia said. "We haven't heard anything

about grudges or hidden lovers, so it must track back to money. At the same time, Ollie Hampton is wealthy himself. He lives in a great house, has servants, and appears to want for nothing. He also knows his father, when he dies, will leave him with a fortune and a company. So, why murder anyone?"

"Pardon me," a woman's voice said behind them. "Are you Lady Georgia Goldenheart?" Georgia turned to find a genteel older lady in a beautiful pale blue tea-gown and modest tiara. "I am Lady Osibeth Crighton," she said. "Countess of Vexbury. It is such a pleasure to meet you in person, Duchess Goldenheart."

Georgia and the countess curtseyed.

"The pleasure is mine, Your Grace," Georgia said.

"May I be bold and steal you away for a moment?" Lady Osibeth asked.

"Of course you may." Georgia nodded to Lady Clara and Mr. Blue as the older woman guided her off to one side.

"My lady, when I saw you on the green, I was completely taken by surprise and delight. I wanted to extend an invitation," the countess said. "In a month, we have a little boat race at our house on Crichton Dock, and it would be wonderful if you could attend."

"That is so kind of you," Georgia said.

A young man wandered over, dressed in bocce clothes. He was rather tall and bore a resemblance to the countess.

"Here's my nephew, Sir Alfred Crichton. We call him Alfie around the family, though. Alfie, let me introduce you to Lady Georgia Goldenheart, Duchess of the House of Goldenheart."

Alfie didn't look like an Alfie to Georgia. He looked quite a bit taller, more flaxen-haired, slightly over-muscled, and more handsome than she would have thought likely for an Alfie.

He bowed deeply. "Your Grace, it is a pleasure." He even had a lovely voice, deep but gentle.

"The pleasure is mine, Sir Alfie," she said, not quite sure what to call him.

"Alfie is my sister's youngest," Lady Osibeth said. "I'm surprised you two have never met. I believe you are about the same age."

"I attended a Cymbre school growing up," Georgia said. "It was a bit cloistered there, and I'm only just making my way into proper society."

Lady Osibeth must have known all of that already. Alfie was quite likely unmarried with no inheritance of his own and ready to give up his name. The countess smiled. "Well, I do hope you can make it to our boat race. We would love to see you again. Isn't that right, Alfie?"

"Yes," he said, bowing to Georgia again, this time even lower. "I hope I see you again, Your Grace."

Minutes later, Georgia was back with Lady Clara and Mr. Blue. "I see you met the nephew," Lady Clara said. "I'm pretty sure they created him in a laboratory."

Georgia laughed, whereas Mr. Blue didn't find the statement humorous.

"Pardon me," another voice said behind them. Georgia spun around to find yet another lady of note, complete in pale blue and tiara. "I am Lady Constance Greenheart, Countess of Grandhall. Are you by chance Lady Georgia Goldenheart?"

Georgia glanced at Lady Clara, who raised an eyebrow. She turned back to Lady Constance. "I am she, Your Grace. It is a pleasure to meet you."

"Not half the pleasure it is for me," Lady Constance said, almost breathless. "My lady, may I perhaps take a moment of your time?"

"Of course," Georgia said, guided away again. She looked back to see Lady Clara grinning. Mr. Blue started smiling too. The absurdity of it all was catching up with him.

"You know, I was quite shocked to find you here today," Lady Constance said.

"I have been a close friend of the Irvingdales my entire life," Georgia said. "Lady Beatrice and I practically grew up together."

"Oh, well, of course. I meant today in particular," the countess said. "I was going to invite you to our summer ball."

"That sounds lovely," Georgia said. "I'd love to go."

"How wonderful, I'll be sure to send a formal letter, of course, and oh, look who's here. It's my youngest son, Lucas, fresh from the bocce game. We call him Luke around the house, of course."

"Of course you do," Georgia said. Lucas Greenheart looked precisely like a Luke. Unlike Alfie, he was less flaxen-haired and darker. His eyes were the shade of gray that prompted people to say things like, "What color are your smoldering eyes?"

And then Lucas would probably say something like, "My eyes? Oh, nobody ever looks at my eyes."

"Duchess Goldenheart," he said, falling to one knee, startling Georgia out of her reverie. For an instant, she feared he would fish a ring out of his pocket right on the spot. Instead, he stood up.

"It is a pleasure to meet you, Mr. Luke," she said quickly, then turned to Lady Constance. "Forgive me, Your Grace, I must catch up before they start making the speeches, but I look forward to your summer ball."

Georgia turned to Luke, "I do hope you will be at the summer ball, Mr. Luke."

"Most assuredly," he said, darting a glance at his mother.

The countess twitched a smile and gestured for him to do something.

Lucas turned back to Georgia, gazed at her for another moment with his smoldering grey eyes, before saying, "Your Grace, I will be anywhere you want me to be, anytime you want me."

"Thank you?" Georgia said, unsure.

She hurried off. As she went, though, a man she didn't even know forgot all about decorum and said hello in passing, and waved his arm to catch her attention. Georgia dodged to the side and kept walking.

"Everyone is going crazy," she announced, catching up to Mr. Blue and Lady Clara. "Who are these people? I thought Vexbury and Grandhall were full of cows, but obviously, they're growing something else there, too."

"It's the article," Mr. Blue said, laughing. "You're famous now. One quick peek at the Book of Peers, and they all must have learned who you are, your status, and the rules surrounding your peerage."

"It would appear so," Georgia mumbled. "I think Lord Wickham is about to give his speech. We should go over and listen, don't you think?"

They made their way over to Bea, who was standing with her sisters and mother.

Lord Wickham moved to the center of the green with Mr. Hampton at his side.

Bea turned to her as she approached. "I swear, Georgia, if you wind up engaged before today ends, I shall never stop patting myself on the back."

"I take it you saw the Countesses," Georgia said.

"Wickham invited them specifically," Bea said. "He has it in mind to leverage whatever connection you make at this party. I told you he could make money off anything, didn't I?"

"You did, but I find his tactics vulgar. I'm not some cow to be auctioned off at his command."

"Georgia," Bea gasped.

"Apologies, Bea, but you have to admit it is rather tacky of him."

Lord Wickham held his arms up and called for quiet. "Friends," he said

"Is your brother-in-law well?" she asked in a whisper. "I know he shaved that hideous beard, but it looks like he's lost a stone."

"Bonnie and Mother put him on a diet of greens and unsalted chicken," Bea whispered back. "His physician said he had to cut out all delicious food or he would die. At first, he was cranky about it, but now his gout is gone, and he's like a different person."

"Yes, a different person trying to marry me off," Georgia said under her breath. Beside her, Mr. Blue chuckled softly.

"Friends, welcome to the Irvingdale annual social. What a wonderful day we have ahead. It's made all the better by the announcement we are about to make," Wickham said. The crowd milled, with some clapping politely. "As it happens, it's about our own dear Beatrice. You see, she is about to be married."

The crowd cheered and Bea beamed. "Georgia, this isn't how it's done, and horrid Wickham is completely throwing bathwater, but somehow I'm still so delighted. How is that possible?" she whispered.

Georgia was about to answer but Mr. Hampton caught her eye. Like an enormous glacier, he crashed to the ground in front of everyone.

"Father," Ollie cried.

Mr. Blue stepped in and turned Mr. Hampton over. "He's dead," the wizard said, checking his pulse. Next to the older man, Mr. Bailey, the footman, collapsed in tears. Ollie and Manx stood to one side, each wearing a blank look of—what must've been—shock.

Lord Wickham had already stepped away, directing one of the Irvingdale staff to call the constables.

Lady Clara swooped in to inspect the body beside Mr. Blue. "Puffy neck," she said quietly. "Note the discoloration. His fingernails are cracked up, too."

"He never looked healthy," Mr. Blue said. "It must be poison." He pointed out another swollen area around Mr. Hampton's lips, which went black in front of their eyes.

Mr. Bailey stood up, weeping. He looked at the Hampton boys and said, "You did this."

"What?" Manx said. "Bailey, come away. You're a mess."

"Not you," Mr. Bailey said. "You did this." He pointed at Ollie.

Ollie Hampton stepped back, his eyes growing wet as he shook his head. "Bailey?"

"You killed him. You finally got him," the footman said, stepping forward.

"Ollie, what is he going on about?" Manx asked.

"That night, I saw it," Mr. Bailey said, moving faster. Ollie Hampton stumbled backward as the footman crashed into him. "You killed Mr. Hampton. It was you."

"Get off me, you lunatic," Ollie cried, shoving Mr. Bailey to the ground. "You're sacked, Bailey. Get away with you." He pushed through the startled crowd.

"Ollie!" Manx called out. "Wait." He chased after his brother, leaving them all standing there in shock.

"Don't let them go," Mr. Blue said.

Georgia pushed through the crowd in pursuit. The twins had a head start, but she could sprint. Actually, Georgia could move at speeds no one expected.

The crowd blurred past. Behind her, she heard Bea calling out for the Hampton twins, too. Ollie ran fast, weeping as he went.

Manx was right behind. "Ollie, wait," he shouted.

They charged out to the carriage lane where the horses were waiting.

Georgia was right behind him when Ollie ran head-on into the rigs. "Ollie!" Manx landed next to his brother.

Georgia caught up to find the horrible sight of Ollie Hampton twisted on the cobblestones with his brain matter spread across the landing in an ever-growing pool of blood. Manx was next to him, rocking back and forth in silence.

CHAPTER 13: HENDON.

The ride took six days across the country, thanks to the weather. Four of the nights on the road were perfectly civilized. Somehow, Mr. Blue booked ahead in suitable hotels, and the roads were reasonably clear. On the final night, they were caught in a snowstorm and had to sleep in the cramped coach. Fortunately, everyone took it with humor. Mr. Blue slept in the front compartment, next to Mr. Cafferty, the driver. At the same time, Georgia shared the second cabin with Lady Clara Gaye and their ladies maids, Millie, and a Volusian girl named Charity. Georgia worried about Bea. Not for the last time, she wondered if they shouldn't have left her behind. If she were here, they could keep an eye on her. Georgia hated the idea that her friend might be left alone after the tragedy at the Irvingdale social.

Georgia shook her head.

Bea's mother and sisters would care for her. She would be fine.

The coach rolled into Hendon as the snow began to fall.

Georgia gazed out the window, yearning for a warm bath. She was accustomed to the spring of the southland, so this was both exciting and annoying. Fortunately, her traveling companions turned out to be good company.

Mr. Blue and Lady Clara Gaye were ensconced in the coach, comfortably preoccupied reading books.

Mr. Blue looked up as they crossed into the village. "Not much further to the hotel," he said. "I looked on a map. Pere Castle is about a mile north of town. We should be there within the hour."

Lady Clara stretched in her seat. "Excellent," she said. "I don't know about you, but the first thing I'm going to do is order a bowl of spicy potato soup, and then I will need to find the nearest bath."

Mr. Blue chuckled, nodding.

Georgia smiled and looked through the window. Hendon was a riverside village, and she could see the masts of water-craft to the north.

"Is it always like this?" she asked. "It's so quiet."

"The snow muffles everything in the Volusian northland. You are accustomed to the city. Oradale is always bustling, and let's face it, there's never any snow down there."

The coach rolled on as the snow continued coming down. Georgia looked up at the gray-blue sky. "A storm is coming," she whispered.

Mr. Blue nodded. "We will get to the hotel before it hits."

Lady Clara sat up and looked out her window. "Do you feel that?" she asked. "There is something wrong with this place."

"Wrong?" Georgia asked.

"You are the witch of Volusia. If anyone can feel it, it is you," Mr. Blue said, pulling the cord to stop the coach. "Shall we look around before we go to the hotel?"

"I think we should, Mr. Blue. Lady Georgia?" Lady Clara asked.

Georgia pulled her sword and scabbard out of the sideboard. "Lead the way," she said. "Millie, you and

Charity stay here."

Millie nodded quickly, her eyes wide. Charity, the other ladies maid, sat quietly.

Mr. Blue opened the door before Mr. Cafferty could get there. "Mr. Blue, I'm sorry," the man said. "I had to calm the horses."

"I know you did," Mr. Blue said. "Mr. Cafferty, did you lock their bridles down?"

"Well, yes, sir. I can unlock them easily enough, though."

"Mr. Cafferty, get inside the coach and lock the door. If the horses panic, stay where you are and do not come out, not even if they injure themselves. Do you understand? Wait for us to return and keep an eye on the girls." Mr. Cafferty did as ordered.

Georgia drew the magic blade, which glowed faintly. The air was windy, brittle with the cold, and the light was falling rapidly. She looked around the road, blinking rapidly. They were in the village square with no one else on the street.

"No lights in the windows," Mr. Blue said, looking around.

"No fire in a hearth," Lady Clara responded, pulling her coat shut. She pointed to the nearby chimney tops to prove her point.

Behind them, the horses snorted in fear. Georgia stalked around them, blade at the ready. Across the square, a hunched figure moved quickly from building to building, scurrying in the shadows. Georgia sprinted forward in pursuit.

"Georgia, be careful," Mr. Blue shouted.

She caught up with the figure, who squeaked in fear and slipped.

"Please," the woman said, her eyes wild. "Please spare my life."

"Who are you?" Georgia asked. She noticed the glow of the magic sword ebbing.

"Mrs. Clutchey. I'm Mrs. Clutchey," she stammered. "I'm a librarian."

Mr. Blue ran up with Lady Clara. "Where is everyone?" he asked the woman. "Why do we not see lights in the windows?"

"We hide at night," Mrs. Clutchey said. "The wolves… they come in packs in the dark and break into the homes with lights. I should have been home an hour ago, but fell behind and had to finish stacking the books."

"How far do you live?" Lady Clara asked.

"Just a few blocks, my lady," Mrs. Clutchey said.

"We shall drop you off at home," Georgia said. She held up the magic sword, which was no longer glowing. She looked at Mr. Blue and Lady Clara. "Whatever was here is gone now, but I'd hate to leave her alone."

"Oh, thank you, mistress," Mrs. Clutchey said. "Thank you."

Mr. Cafferty and the maids were relieved when they returned.

"We'll need to make a quick stop on the way," Mr. Blue said. "I will ride up front with you, Mr. Cafferty. The way is not safe, and we should keep an eye on one another."

"Excellent, sir," Mr. Cafferty said, climbing into the front compartment. Five minutes later, they dropped Mrs. Clatchey off at her modest home. Georgia watched as the older woman went inside, throwing the door shut with the curtains closed. The windows in a few other dwellings slipped open for a moment and then quickly closed again.

"They really are hiding," Lady Clara said quietly. "In the morning, we should send a message to the Earl of Simsley. He will want to know about this."

"What if he does know about it?" Georgia asked.

"Then he needs to do something," Lady Clara answered.

Snow fell harder as the coach rolled up the road, north to the hotel. Trees lined the way, making it difficult to see anything beyond a few feet. The rest of the landscape lay in darkness.

In the distance, Georgia spotted faint lights.

The coach arrived at a vast gatehouse adjoining a walled-in property. The sign on the gate read 'Castle Pere Resort.' Two guards emerged, waving, and opened the gate. The coach continued up the lane through the trees, and the guards hurried back to their gatehouse. She turned back to see the ancient castle rising through the trees. Several modern designs were recently added to the structure. Lanterns were strung across several balconies, and the front lobby was quite bright. A handful of people in coats wandered the snow-covered gardens in front, laughing and sipping hot drinks.

They pulled in, and a footman opened the coach door with a sweeping bow.

Georgia stepped out first, breathing in the crisp air.

"I'll get us checked in," Mr. Blue said. "Once we all have a moment to clean up and get settled, perhaps we can meet downstairs for dinner?"

"Sounds good," Georgia said.

"Perfect," Lady Clara said, following them in.

Minutes later, they were each given keys, and Georgia went up to a suite of beautiful rooms. Her bags were delivered as she walked in, and a hotel maid was already drawing a hot bath. She let Millie deal with the other woman and went directly in to change and relax.

After a quick bath, Millie had a new outfit ready—a lovely soft white wool walking coat ensemble with blue ermine trim. Millie finished it off with a soft white ermine cap.

"I've never even seen this outfit," Georgia said. "You've outdone yourself."

"Thank you, my lady. Sir Lionel is a good teacher," Millie said.

Georgia had almost forgotten Millie was checking in with her designer regularly. Clearly, they were hatching all sorts of exciting ideas.

"You are a good student," Georgia said. "I'll be back in a couple of hours. You must be just as tired as the rest of us after that ride."

"I'm fine, but thank you," Millie said.

"Nonsense, I'll take care of myself tonight. You should enjoy your evening. Is there a bar for the servants in the hotel?"

Millie couldn't help but laugh. "I'm sure there is not." Of course, Millie would likely be staying all night. It wouldn't be proper for her to be seen wandering the hotel while her mistress was, too. If it weren't for the snow and packs of roving wolves, she might have gone to a pub in town.

Georgia had a feeling her ladies maid would be in their suite of rooms for the night.

"Well, don't spend the night cleaning, Millie. You can catch up on that tomorrow."

"I promise, my lady," Millie said.

Georgia crossed the hall to Lady Clara's suite and knocked. Charity opened it and allowed Georgia in.

"That was a good bath," Clara said as Charity fit her into a stylish black hat and heavy fur coat. "The north is my home, and when I see the snow, I see the footprints of every witch of Volusia who came before me."

"What a lovely thought," Georgia said.

"Yes, but again… there's nothing like a hot bath to warm the bones," Lady Clara said. "Now, we need some spicy potato soup to round off our arrival."

"Good Volusian fare," Georgia said. "Count me in."

Mr. Blue was waiting downstairs, having changed to a bright azure coat and felt hat. He led them to a door marked 'Humble Dining Hall'. From there, they entered a long room where painted portraits hung on wood-paneled walls, and through a screened passage. Festive lanterns hung everywhere. Halfway down the hall were massive fireplaces with elaborate mantles covered in coats of arms held by caryatid pillars. Each fire was the size of a room and burned massive logs. At the far end was a long table where the lord of the manor must have sat in front of a great window. Lights illuminated the snow outside, now falling in full force.

A quartet assembled on a landing above the entrance of the screen and started with an upbeat tune as the dinner crowd filtered in. There were maybe a dozen other guests in the hotel dining room.

"How marvelous," Georgia breathed. A footman led them to a table near one of the fireplaces where a charming young woman poured glasses of cucumber water.

"Palate cleanser," Lady Clara explained. "We're about to have a traditional Volusian meal."

A butler went up to the Lord's Table and cleared his throat. "Ladies and Lords, gentlefolk and nobles, welcome to Pere Castle," he announced. "I am Mr. Humble, your friend and tireless assistant for the evening. Do you know why it is so great to have a job here in the cold Volusian northland? When the days get short, you only have to work a 30-minute workweek." A few people clapped and laughed.

Georgia leaned over to Lady Clara. "What is that fellow doing?"

"He's going to tell us a few jokes to start the evening," Lady Clara said, smiling. "It's an old tradition. The hotel is quite modern, so it's a bit of a surprise. I suppose that's the point, though—the old and the new together in the north."

"What did the northern constable say to the suspect? Where were you on the night of September to March?" More laughter. The musical quartet joined in with a little flat note at the end of each joke.

The waitress returned with a tray of champagne and three menus. The meal was pre-fixed baked hens, potato soup, and seasonal vegetables.

"What did the northern girl say to the southern girl?

Nothing. She gave her the cold shoulder."

"You are ridiculous," a man called out from a nearby table, laughing. "Pull yourself together, sir." Somehow, it was all meant in good humor.

Lady Clara leaned over to Georgia and Mr. Blue. "Fair warning, hecklers are common in the north. In fact, they are sometimes necessary to keep everyone awake."

Mr. Humble bowed to the man and continued his monologue for another few minutes. When he was done, the quartet above provided a pleasant backdrop without being too musically invasive. Georgia enjoyed the soup, the lame jokes, the music, and the company of her friends.

She tried not to worry about the wolves outside.

After dinner, they migrated to another grand room to play cards and socialize. The card room was vaulted and featured more rose lanterns and a fireplace.

"Warm and jolly," Georgia said, looking around.

Mr. Humble sauntered in, shaking hands and bowing to various guests. "Hello, everyone," he said, turning to Mr. Blue. "Introductions are in order, methinks. Everyone, this is Mr. Blue. He is a wizard from the Southlands. Along with him is the stunning Lady Georgia, whom I believe is a duchess?"

He bowed to Georgia outrageously low and then fell on his face, as if drunk. Several guests laughed and clapped. "Nice to meet you, Mr. Humble," she said, smiling. Such behavior would never happen back home.

Before Georgia could introduce Lady Clara, Mr. Humble leaped to his feet.

He cried, "The witch of Volusia graces us with her presence."

Lady Clara curtseyed and smiled.

Mr. Humble expanded his introduction, turning to another group of guests. The first was a tall, older white-haired gentleman in black tie and tails. He looked a bit out of place in the northern lodge but also very elegant. "May I introduce Sir Gregory Middleton."

Sir Gregory nodded to the room and then bowed formally to Georgia.

She smiled and nodded.

Next to Sir Gregory was a younger fellow, but they looked related. "Also, Mr. Gerard Middleton, youngest son of Sir Gregory." The younger Middleton wasn't dressed in formal tie and tails but was well-clad for the cold. Mr. Humble turned to their other companion, a tall woman with jet black hair who bundled in a lovely blue satin double-coat. "And of course here is Lady Martha Clutterbuck, daughter of the great poet Lord Martin Clutterbuck."

Lady Martha curtseyed formally to Georgia, saying, "Good evening, Lady Georgia, and all here tonight."

She smiled brilliantly, although there was something haunted in Lady Martha's eyes.

"My friend, Lady Beatrice, would be so jealous right now," Georgia said. "She loved your father's work, Lady Martha."

"What a wonderful thing to say," Lady Martha answered, smiling.

Mr. Humble moved over to the other table of guests, where four young gentlemen sat, all dressed in heavy black coats and wool hats.

"Allow me to introduce Mr. Bennet Gower, Mr. Seymour Bridgman, Mr. Douglas Jackman, and Mr. Warren Wynch—all hailing from the great city of Oradale, and here for the delights of the season."

The four young men bowed to Georgia and then nodded to everyone else in the room.

"What are the delights of the season?" Lady Martha asked the group of young men. "Skiing and drinking warm cider, I take it?"

"Oh, my lady," Mr. Gower said, "I suppose there is some of that, yes. Alas, we are not here for a holiday."

"We are enjoying the cider, though," Mr. Jackman said, grinning. "I see you have no drink in hand. Perhaps we can convince you to imbibe with us?"

Lady Martha laughed. "Thank you. I believe I will." She winked at her companions and went over to their table. Sir Gregory Middleton shook his head, chuckling. His son looked pained, though, but then turned to Georgia. He smiled at her as his father watched and then looked down. The younger Middleton was waiting to see if she would address him.

"Hello," Georgia said. "Are you enjoying the northlands, Mr. Middleton?"

"Yes, I am, Duchess. We are not here for a holiday though," Mr. Middleton, the younger said, quickly. "My father and Lady Martha are looking for an investment. I am along for the ride."

"And to carry luggage," Sir Gregory said, poking his son's shoulder.

"That part is quite true," Mr. Middleton said, grinning. He looked at his father, who smiled back. "Duchess, are you here for a holiday?"

"Not really," Georgia said. "We are here on business of another sort. I would hate to bore you with the details, however."

"A duchess is traveling with a witch and a wizard. I suspect nothing is boring about you, my lady," Mr. Middleton said.

"Don't be too cheeky, son," Sir Gregory said. "Forgive us, my lady. We have only recently returned to the Realms. My dear son has no practical experience with nobility."

"It's quite all right, Sir Gregory. We are all friends tonight," Georgia said with a smile, "And I am not your typical duchess."

"Are there typical duchesses?" Lady Clara asked, smirking.

Georgia laughed.

Mr. Blue leaned in. "It's a pleasure to meet you, Sir Gregory. Where were you living before?"

"We were in Dora, sir," Sir Gregory said. "I was an

attaché to the ambassador until last year when he retired. My son grew up in Dora. The people there are a bit less formal."

"It's a lovely island," Mr. Middleton said, "A bit warmer than these northlands. I am enjoying the frost, though. It is an exhilarating change of pace." He patted his coat. "Also, they have deep-fried cheese in the north."

"And now you are here to invest," Mr. Blue said, prompting them for more information.

"Yes," Mr. Middleton said. "We are here to pull the rug out from under the four gents over there." He indicated the group chatting with Lady Martha.

"All in the name of fair business, of course," Sir Gregory said. "We are here to make a bid on the river dock and boatyard. It's all up for sale to the highest bidder."

"The river dock is up for sale?" Lady Clara asked. "Who is the current owner?"

"Some holding company down south," Mr. Middleton said. "Father, what was their name again?"

"Hampton Madison," Sir Gregory said. "They put it up a few days ago. It's a rush sale. Tomorrow there will be an auction on their assets. From what I understand, they are consolidating their holdings in the south. The primary owner died, and his son is intent on simplifying."

Georgia looked at Mr. Blue and Lady Clara, but neither betrayed any surprise.

"Well, good luck with it," Georgia said, raising a glass. "To business ventures gone well."

"A toast to business," Sir Gregory said, also raising his glass. He looked at Georgia. "So, may I ask, what brings you to the northlands?"

"We are actually on royal business," Lady Clara said quickly. "I wish I could tell you more."

Sir Gregory nodded immediately. "Oh, of course, I understand completely. In that case, let us discuss other things, yes? Or perhaps we could play cards."

The night passed jovially.

Lady Martha and the four rival gentlemen joined them for a round of cards and drinks before retiring amicably.

Georgia returned to her suite and found Millie had gone and unpacked, pressed, and sorted everything. "So much for relaxing after the long ride," she said, shaking her head.

Dawn was cold and dark.

Georgia opened her eyes and listened to the wolves.

Through the window, she could see the snow was falling harder than ever. Dark shapes moved in the distance. She should have closed the curtains before sleep but hadn't thought of it.

"Come near me or anyone I love, and you will regret it," she whispered to the shapes. She went into the brutally cold sitting room to stoke the fire. Pere Castle may have been upgraded, but it was still prone to drafts.

Georgia found a kettle and set it on the hook to warm up.

Millie moved around in the adjacent room. Her maid poked her head out, looking alarmed. "Oh, my lady, please let me do that." Vapors escaped her mouth as she spoke.

"Too late, the kettle's already on," Georgia said. "I'm perfectly capable of making tea, Millie. You have a choice—put on something warm or go back to bed."

"Yes, my lady, of course," Millie said. "I'll just get dressed and be right out."

"Take your time," Georgia said, settling into a fur on the couch. She felt oddly moody. Was she tired? No, it was something else. Something was weighing on her. She shook her head. "Weeks of murder and supernatural monsters, that's what's getting to you." She sighed.

Millie reappeared a moment later, looking completely clean, refreshed, and ready to work. "My lady, can I help you with your coat?"

"I'm fine," Georgia said. "I could use some bacon. Millie, do you ever eat bacon? You know, in your off-time?"

Millie smiled. "Yes, my lady. We have a grand breakfast on the first Saturday of the month as a rule. Mr. Derry said it is a Goldenheart tradition."

"Ah, yes. Uncle Raymond used to take me to those breakfasts when I was a girl. Only a few times, though. He said it was for the staff to enjoy because we already have everything." Uncle Raymond. She stung for a moment, remembering him.

"What a kind soul he must have been." Millie smiled. "My lady, how about I go down to the kitchens and fetch some bacon, eggs, coffee, scones, and see if they have any of the sweet creams you like? Lady Beatrice told me you used to like raspberry jam, and Charity—Lady Clara's maid—mentioned it's a staple in the northlands."

"Bring enough food for an army, Millie. On your way down, would you swing by Mr. Blue and Lady Clara's rooms? Ask if they would like to join me in my room to eat? The northerners don't make sideboard breakfast as we do in the south. I can't imagine it in this cold."

"I don't know what they do, my lady. I will find out." The kettle boiled up, and Millie set the tea more efficiently than Georgia would have. There was no fiddling with spoons or teapot lids. She went right at it as if she had been using that teapot her whole life, then set the milk for Georgia to pour as she preferred. After that, Millie curtseyed and went out of the door.

The howls returned, and she went to the window. The glass pane in the sitting room was blurred with snow, but she saw someone standing in the garden below—a figure in a dark coat. Other shapes moved around it slowly. She watched as it stood there, and then it started walking. The different forms seemed to vanish. The figure moved to one side, and the glass was clear.

"Mr. Humble?"

He walked through the garden and picked up wine glasses from the night before. He turned back to the hotel, spotted her in the second-floor window, and waved. She waved back. He turned away, suddenly seeming quite mundane, and found another glass in the snow.

There was a knock on the door.

Georgia opened it to find Lady Clara with her maid, Charity, in tow. "The protocol in the north is that we eat in our rooms when it snows, and we let the maids join in. It's a little odd for a southerner," Lady Clara said.

"It's preferable," Georgia said. "I'm pretty sure Millie is skipping meals. Now I can make sure she's fed. Come in."

"You are hilarious," Lady Clara said. "Charity, have you ever missed a meal?"

"Of course not, my lady," Charity said. "I eat when you're not looking."

"They eat when we aren't looking," Lady Clara said. "You see? It's the circle of life."

"Sensible," Georgia said.

"More sensible than we are, actually," Lady Clara said, smirking. "How many times have you skipped a meal to impress some silly man?"

"It is as if Bea never got left behind," Georgia answered, laughing.

Lady Clara grinned. "She is wonderful. I tried to sound like her just now. I do hope she is all right after ..."

Georgia shook her head. "Bea is a tough one, yes. That said, I think the death of Ollie Hampton may have been too much for her."

Lady Clara tilted her head. "Do not lose hope. Last night I had a dream that Lady Beatrice will find a truer love than she ever expected."

"You did? Is that a witch thing—dreaming like that?"

Lady Clara shook her head. "Not for me. I rarely have prophetic dreams."

Georgia laughed.

"Seriously," Clara said, "I do have a good feeling with Bea, though. I had it last week, even after we saw the Hamptons implode. Also, Lord William wrote me a note before we left town, asking how he could talk to her again."

"Lord William? Seriously? He needs no excuse. He could simply contact her."

"He's looking for something more nuanced. I have known him since we were children, Georgia. He isn't nuanced by nature. No, he's entirely about the heart, I think. You should add him to a possible list of alternatives for her. Oh, you don't mind if I have opted for the familiar? May I call you Georgia?"

"Only if I may call you Clara," Georgia said, feeling slightly less cranky.

"Perfect," Clara said. "In the meantime, how do we solve this murder mystery? We have come to the end of the north. Wolves surround the hotel. What happens next?"

Georgia shrugged. "I suppose I can always cut our way out of here."

Lady Clara nodded, thinking. "I should tell you, Volusia is my home, and I am truly the witch of these lands. My spirit is here. I was born to protect this place, as surely as anything else. My bones are here, and well after I am young and wandering, I will return to Volusia to protect it. Does that make sense?"

"I have a magic sword and of late feel almost no fear in the face of supernatural evil," Georgia said. "I am more worried about wearing the right hat than about battling against any force that would hurt the innocent. So, yes, I can accept your bones are here, Clara."

"Allies surround you in the light," Lady Clara said. "The Order of the Blue is the first school of magic, founded by the brothers in blue. From there, other cults and schools arose to resist the darkness."

"What is that from?" Georgia asked.

"Pardon me? Oh, sorry, my mind was wandering for a moment. It was something your ancestor, Emeil Onaura, said to one of my ancestors. They wrote it down, as it was wisdom. Say, where is Mr. Blue?" Lady Clara asked. "Don't tell me he's sleeping late."

"I think he is, actually," Georgia said.

Lady Clara turned to Charity. "Would you go see if Mr. Blue is ready for breakfast? Even with the limited staff this morning, Millie will be returning soon."

"Yes, my lady." Charity curtseyed and left.

"We have limited staff?" Georgia asked.

Lady Clara shrugged. "There are a few dinner trays in the hall and a raging snowstorm outside. I suspect some of the hotel staff stayed home."

Charity returned a moment later, followed by Millie with a rolling tray of food. The smell of bacon, tea, and scones filled the room.

Georgia's stomach growled audibly.

Charity looked at Lady Clara. "My lady, the wizard is not in his room, and the door was unlocked."

"Unlocked?" Lady Clara stood up. "Eat up, girls. Lady Georgia and I will return after investigating this unexpected turn of events."

Georgia grabbed a piece of bacon and followed Clara to Mr. Blue's room.

Clara quietly pushed open his door, and they entered. "Something is wrong," she said, quietly. "I feel it in the air."

The room looked normal enough. Mr. Blue's suitcase was to one side, and the drawers packed in an orderly way. The bed looked slept-in as if he had risen early, but the maid hadn't come yet. That didn't seem odd, given the weather and Clara's previous comment about the hotel being short-staffed.

Georgia noticed his walking stick was on the table. "He wouldn't leave without this," she said.

Clara picked up the stick. "A wizard without his staff,"

she said, shaking her head. "We might check the privy, but I have a feeling he won't be there."

"How about you do that while I get my sword," Georgia said. Millie set out her good wool coat, boots for the snow, and a warm fur-lined hat. She drew the magic sword from its sheath to find a faint glow.

Something supernatural was afoot but not close.

Clara returned, holding the wizard's walking stick. "Mr. Blue is not in the privy. I had one of the footmen check."

"We'll need to search for him," Georgia said. "Can you get the footmen?" Millie helped her pull on the coat and then the sheath over her shoulder.

"I'm sure I can," Clara said. She looked at Charity and Millie. "Stay here in case Mr. Blue returns. Keep the door locked, though. If anyone knocks, be certain you know them before you open it. You understand what I am saying, yes?"

"Yes, my lady," Charity said.

Georgia and Clara went back to the hall and began knocking on other doors. "The hotel is almost empty because the skiing season ended weeks ago. The storm is unusual for this time of year," Clara said. "We will likely find all the doors on this story locked." They were on the third floor, which were all suites. The level below had singles. Just in case, they checked everywhere. Only Mr. Blue's suite was unlocked. At the end of the hall, they found the dinner trays stacked in front of two doors. Georgia knocked politely on the first one.

After a moment, Sir Gregory Middleton, clad in a night robe, peeked out. "How do you do?" he asked.

"Sir Gregory, I'm sorry to interrupt your sleep, but I wondered if you had seen Mr. Blue? I'm afraid it is a matter of some importance," Georgia said.

"The wizard? No, I'm afraid I haven't seen him. I mean, I haven't seen anything, I've been quite asleep for— is that the time?" he said, looking to one side. "Is it really eight o'clock?"

"That sounds about right," Georgia answered. For a moment, she thought he was going to shut the door in her face. Instead, he let her in.

"Forgive me, Duchess. We were supposed to be at the river docks by now," he said. "Why didn't my son wake me? Surely, we didn't drink that much last night? Now we've made everyone wait."

"I suspect you won't be able to get to the docks today," Clara said, looking in. "Forgive me, Sir Gregory. I didn't mean to intrude."

"It is odd," he said. "We are in the north, I suppose."

"Is your son across the hall here?" Georgia asked.

"Ah, that is Lady Martha's suite," Sir Gregory said. "My son is down one floor. You don't think they will start the auction without us?"

"I would be surprised to learn they start it all today," Clara said. "There are three feet of snow outside, and it's still coming down. We are having a late-season storm."

"We're all likely stuck in the hotel today," Georgia said, looking down the hall, half expecting Mr. Blue to come sauntering out of nowhere. "Once again, I am sorry to intrude on you, Sir. If you happen to see our friend, will you tell him we are looking for him?"

"Of course, Duchess," Sir Gregory said. "Have a good day." He shut the door.

"Let's knock on Lady Martha's door," Georgia said. "Perhaps she can help."

"I wouldn't bother," Clara said. "Lady Martha is hiding in Sir Gregory's room, I'm afraid. His son will be disappointed. He was hoping to lure her into a marriage."

"She was?"

Clara laughed. "I know what you are thinking: Did I glean her location through witchcraft? No, it's nothing as exciting; I spotted her in the mirror behind Sir Gregory. She was hiding behind the door while he talked to us."

"How scandalous," Georgia said.

Georgia led the way down to the next floor. A lone

hotel maid pushed a cart down the middle of the corridor.

"Pardon me," Georgia said to her. "Have you seen our companion, Mr. Blue? You cannot miss him. He's always dressed in blue."

The maid kept her eyes down and shook her head. "No, my lady, I have not seen him."

"If you do see him, will you tell him we're concerned over his absence?" Clara said.

"Yes, my lady," the maid said quietly.

They walked on. "We should see if Mr. Middleton is in his room. I say, can you tell me which room—" Georgia said. The girl was gone. Her cart was still there, but she vanished. Georgia and Clara walked back, looking to see if she was in a nearby room, but the doors were shut.

"Georgia, look," Clara said, pointing at her back. Georgia looked over her shoulder to see the edge of the magic sword glowing. She drew it immediately, and the corridor lit up. The ground rumbled ominously.

"Stay behind me, Clara," Georgia said, holding the blade at the ready. "Let's see if we can get down to the ground floor." She moved forward slowly, watching as they passed each door. At the end of the corridor, they proceeded to the next landing.

"The front doors are open," Clara whispered. She held up Mr. Blue's walking stick, apparently ready to cudgel anything unpleasant.

"I once saw Mr. Blue draw flames from that walking stick," Georgia whispered. "I don't suppose you could do that?"

"Flames are a wizard's tool," Clara said. "Witches are a bit different. Fortunately, we are standing on Volusian soil. Give me a moment, will you?" She closed her eyes as if concentrating.

Down the hall, Georgia heard something growl. "What new devilry is this?" she whispered. The growl grew louder, closer.

"It is a Hoo Adoon," Clara said, "an ancient spirit of

the underworld."

"Are you serious?" In her hand, the blade grew brighter.

Clara nodded slowly and then pointed down the hall.

At the far end, near the front doors, a dark figure appeared. It crouched on all fours—an enormous black wolf. Shadows rolled over the thing, but its eyes blazed with a terrible white-blue light.

"Frost and darkness together bound by the will of an ancient evil," Clara whispered. "That thing walked the world when only the stars gave light. Georgia, we should leave. This is a power beyond us."

"It's too late to run," Georgia said, gritting her teeth. She watched as the Hoo Adoon moved with unnerving speed angling toward Clara's throat with bared obsidian fangs. In the last instant, Georgia stepped between them and brought the magic sword up in an arc. The blade swept through the beast, exploding with argent fire. The Hoo Adoon shrieked and crashed against a wall. The impact shook the building as the wall shattered to reveal a broom closet.

She kept her body between the beast and Clara.

The creature was on its feet and leaped at her.

Georgia leaned away, arching with the thing as it moved, and brought the blade across its mouth in a flowing stroke. Once again, white fire erupted, tearing a hole in the Hoo Adoon's face. Georgia kicked it hard, sending the creature flying down the hall. It was back on its shadowy legs, with only a slight delay. Still, it was a delay. She took that as an encouraging sign and drove the flaming sword directly into where its brain should be. The Hoo Adoon exploded, sending ice and, oddly, charcoal in all directions.

"Wow," Clara said, crouching low against another wall. "That was incredible. You didn't even blink."

"I am getting used to the supernatural. Alas, I suspect none of the hotel maids are going to think I am a good guest after this." Georgia cleaned her blade as she looked around. The ice was already melting and staining the walls and floor with residue.

"They will have a high opinion if you save their lives," Clara said. "I think I know what is happening here."

"Obviously, it is some sort of magic," Georgia said.

"Yes, but not just any magic," Clara answered. "This is true northern power, but corrupted by evil. Do you remember the tale of the vampire queen?"

"I remember Mr. Blue talking about it when I was in my trance. He talked about my ancestor, Gwendolyn Goldenheart, and her battle against the queen. Good heavens, are we living in a chapter from the *Midnight King*?"

"I don't think so, but it does look like the work of Doria Nanette."

Georgia knew the name. "Wait, Mr. Blue told me about Doria Nanette, a few weeks ago," she said. "An evil spirit from folklore who served the Midnight King, is that right?"

"The very same," Clara said. "Except, this isn't folklore: Doria Nanette is as real as the magic sword in your hand. I have never met her, but a couple of my sisters in the Lunar Circle have, and they say she is terrifying."

"Is she responsible for Mr. Blue's absence?" Georgia asked.

"I do not know," Clara admitted. "It can't be a coincidence, though."

Georgia nodded slowly. "Let's keep looking." They continued down the hall to the main lobby area, which was empty. Snow blew in through the open doors, accompanied by an icy wind that cut through all the layers of Georgia's clothing.

Clara moved behind the main desk. "No sign of blood or anything here," she said. "Hopefully, they fled."

"Let's check the main dining hall," Georgia said.

"Wait," Clara said, strolling to the edge of the snow. Beyond the doors, it felt like a great curtain blotting out all view of the trees across the courtyard. Clara gazed at it. "Mr. Blue is that way." She pointed outside.

Georgia didn't hesitate. Sword in hand, she pushed into the snow. The freezing wind hit immediately, stinging her eyes and nose. Georgia squinted. Behind her, she saw Clara following, although the witch didn't seem to mind the wind.

"Mr. Blue, are you there?" Georgia called out.

"Mr. Blue!" Clara shouted against the wind.

Behind them, the hotel faded as the storm intensified. The wind gusted snow all around and slammed into Georgia, nearly knocking her off her feet. The magic blade blazed like a golden beacon, and wolf-like shapes appeared. Their eyes were the color of blood. Snarling, they leaped from the sides.

Clara gasped, and Georgia spun.

Two wolves circled the witch, snarling, ready to pounce. Georgia moved between them, bringing the blade down on one, and then swept around to the other—cutting both in half. Another beast sailed out of nowhere, slamming into her. Georgia dropped the magic blade as the wolf tried to get at her, its fangs inches from her face. The wolf was not a living creature but rather was some snarling dead thing. Lying in the snow, she looked it in the eye and knew a force beyond was in control. Rage welled, and she punched the wolf away. The thing didn't react as it flew, because it wasn't alive. Instead, the wolf hit the ground and ran at her again.

She recovered the blade. As the wolf came again, Georgia swung around with a great shout and cleaved the undead creature in half and the beast exploded in a spray of ice and charcoal.

Georgia went about to find Clara, who was singing as the ice wolves circled. Everything near the witch slowed, even the snow in the air. Georgia held a hand up to see a snowflake linger in the air. Clara stepped past the beasts.

"Doria Nanette is desperate," the witch said. "Her plan

is failing. She was impatient and acted too quickly."

A figure loomed ahead. Georgia readied herself for another attack when Mr. Blue came into view.

He was in his nightclothes, half-buried in the snow, gazing at nothing.

"Let's take him back," Clara said. "She tried to lure him into the darkness, but we stopped it."

Georgia picked Mr. Blue up. Clara followed, keeping an eye out as they made their way back inside.

Mr. Humble was in the lobby, looking uncharacteristically serious. "You live," he breathed. "Forgive me, my lady. We hid in the basement when the wind and wolves intruded. It is the only way we know to survive the Lady of the Snow."

"The Lady of the Snow," Georgia repeated. "Is that what people call her in these parts?"

Mr. Humble shrugged.

"Why have you not sent a message to the Earl?" Clara asked. "How long has she been menacing you?"

"We always mean to send word to the Earl, but the memory of her seems to fade quickly," Mr. Humble explained. "She sent beasts before. They abduct people and murder others."

"How long has this been happening?" Georgia asked, setting Mr. Blue down in a lobby chair. "We'll need a blanket for him."

"Of course," Mr. Humble said, snapping a finger at one of the footmen. "Henry, blanket, and soup, please. Thank you." The fellow hurried away, only to return a moment later with a huge wool blanket. Mr. Humble looked at Georgia. "The abductions started almost immediately after the hotel opened, just over four years ago. I always tell myself this is the last one, and I'm going to find another job. The next morning comes, and every one of us forgets it even happened."

Clara nodded, "And you only remember when it happens again. It is an old enchantment."

"Failure is your teacher." Mr. Blue startled awake. "No, you have no power here," he said to no one in particular.

"You are safe now, old friend," Clara said in a soothing tone. "We found you outside."

Mr. Blue's teeth chattered as he wrapped the blanket around himself. "You found me outside, eh? Did I say she had no power here? I was wrong about that. Note to the wise: I'm wrong more often than not."

"You know who did this?" Clara asked.

"I suspect we are looking at an ancient spirit," Mr. Blue said. "I cannot be certain, though. Do you have any suggestions, Clara?"

"I think it is Doria Nanette," Clara said, "the winter sorceress of the far north."

"That makes sense in part," Mr. Blue said. "The ice wolves and the remote location would be consistent with what we know of her. I could hear her whispering in my mind, beckoning me to go outside and fall asleep in the storm. What I do not understand is why."

"She's an evil spirit?" Georgia said. "She wants to frighten us. What more reason does she need?"

"Normally, I might agree, *if* she were a mere ghost. No, Doria Nanette predates the Three Realms, and there are tales going back generations about her power, cunning, and desire for more. She wants to control us—all of us." Mr. Blue pulled the blanket tighter around his shoulders.

"Mr. Blue, let's be Cymbre about this. An answer exists even if we don't know all the questions."

Mr. Blue nodded. "The Cymbre way is to seek order and simplicity above all else. The reason is the method, but what is the goal? The question is *why*?" He looked at Georgia.

Georgia pondered the question. "The goal is survival, but the hope is to flourish. Ultimately, the answer depends on the state of mind."

"Based on that, the question is why did Doria Nanette come to this tiny northern part of Volusia instead of somewhere more populated? In the stories, she always comes from the north and goes into the south to trick people, commit murders, and create fear. She makes beasts from the elements," Clara mused. "We must also ask the question: Is her arrival here related to the blood zombies back in the city, or is that a coincidence?"

"I don't understand," Georgia admitted. "She's an evil spirit. Why wouldn't it be her?"

Clara threw her hands up. "None of the histories about her mention anything to do with vampire bats or blood zombies. She is a shapeshifter and illusionist who conjures monsters from snow, water, and earth. She's tricky, but her methods are historically the same."

"More than ever, I doubt this is a coincidence," Mr. Blue said.

"The trail of clues led us here, and we find her."

"Precisely. Also, there is nothing in the stories to say Doria Nanette couldn't create a blood zombie if she wanted to. For all we know, there were stories about her and blood zombies, but we've never heard them."

"Much that was known is now lost," Clara murmured. "Agreed."

"It seems like her impact would be limited in this place," Georgia said. "We're on the edge of the world, aren't we? What could she possibly gain by being here?"

"No one has seen her in hundreds of years," Mr. Blue added. "What if she didn't come here to affect, but rather to recover?"

"There is a story about her from about two centuries ago. I remember something about how she was driven away by a Magestrix wizard named Loris Brimley. Is that right?"

"It's in a book of legends called *The Findorian Saga*," Mr. Blue said. "I don't think I ever read it, but it was fairly popular a few years ago. There was a reprinting done, and for a while, people were reading it. If we can find a copy, perhaps we can find a clue?"

Georgia grinned. "Let's go to the Hendon Library. Maybe Mrs. Clutchey has a copy."

"Excellent idea," Mr. Blue said.

"Forgive me. What library are you going to?" Mr. Humble asked. He had been standing there the whole time. "I ask because, well, there is no Hendon Library. The nearest one is at Simsley Hall, about sixty miles away. I can have the coach brought around as soon as the snowstorm clears up."

"There's a library in the village," Georgia said, unsure. "We met Mrs. Clutchey, the librarian herself, only yesterday. She was out after dark and—"

"I assure you, Hendon has no library," Mr. Humble cut her off. "The only businesses in the town are the hotel, the little café, and the docks. I have never heard of a Mrs. Clutchey, and I have lived here all my life."

"We met her yesterday," Georgia said, shaking her head. "She's a little old lady. I talked to her myself."

"I think we just found Doria Nanette," Clara said quietly.

Georgia stepped out of the coach, wearing a long white wool coat and blue satin bonnet tied with white silk ribbon.

Everywhere she looked, the ground was mud, and the snow was gone.

Behind her, Mr. Blue and Lady Clara emerged, ready for anything. Clara was cinched into a sharp black wool cloak with a matching, wide-brimmed hat. Mr. Blue was in his usual all-blue ensemble.

Georgia looked at Mrs. Clutchey's modest little house and then at her friends.

"We should probably knock on the door," Clara said.

Georgia drew the magic sword, which glowed.

Mr. Blue knocked on the door with his walking stick.

The door opened for them.

"Hello?" Mr. Blue called out. "Is anyone home?"

He looked at Georgia and Clara and then turned to go inside.

"I'll go first," Georgia said. "If there's trouble, I'll handle it."

"Spoken like a true Goldenheart," Clara said. "Be careful. She uses illusion all the time."

Georgia nodded.

The front hall was all pale pink wallpaper, with knickknacks on little shelves. Georgia scanned them as she entered, wondering if perhaps they were mistaken. Was Doria Nanette a fan of hummels? She passed a small mirror on the wall next to a filigreed hat rack. In the mirror, her reflection was bathed in blood, and the pink walls were strewn with entrails.

"Okay," she whispered, "maybe not such a crazy theory after all." In her hand, the sword crackled with small flames.

The hall opened to a little sitting room, where the scent of cinnamon, ginger, and scones filled the air. At the center was a comfy chair with a huge basket of yarn to one side. Settled in the chair was Mrs. Clutchey.

"What a shame," the old lady said, "I was hoping for more time."

"You were hoping for time to do what exactly?" Georgia asked, not sure how to proceed. Should she leap at the older woman and start hacking her to pieces?

Behind her, Mr. Blue and Lady Clara entered the room.

"Hello, Mr. Blue," the old woman said. "Hello, Lady Clara Gaye."

"Hello, Doria Nanette," Clara answered, her voice quivering slightly. "I was also going to ask what you were hoping for time to do."

"I fooled you for a long time, Witch of Volusia," Doria Nanette said, impishly. "I've been living right under your nose for years, but you never sensed me."

"You are thousands of years older and one of the greatest sorcerers in history," Mr. Blue said. "It would be surprising if any of us sensed you. I am still unsure of how we found you at all."

Doria Nanette set her tea down. "I suspect it was my fault, Wizard. When I decided to move to the next part of the plan, I must have chosen the wrong agent to deliver the blood zombie infection to your city."

"So you are the source of this," Georgia said. "We weren't sure, but you freely admitted it."

Doria Nanette held out her hand, showing off a gold ring with a black opal that glittered malevolently. "I found Mehira's Ring," she said grinning. "Is it not beautiful?" The opal seemed to hum along with the magic blade. Georgia could hear them singing together. There were words to the song of the sword and ring... but they were not in harmony.

"Wait, Mehira, the *mythical* vampire queen?"

Doria Nanette laughed. "I love how you emphasize the word 'mythical,' Lady Georgia. Yes, the vampire queen had an ancient ring of magic. It was forged in the very flame that made your sword, Duchess. But this bauble was made by very different hands. I found the ring in the ruins of her old castle in the Rust Mountains. I took it, and it whispered lore in my ear. I listened to the whisper and learned one of the nine words of power. Typically, my schemes are all illusion and the conjuration of snow monsters. Still, I decided to try a new tactic, this time."

"You learned the *word of un-life*," Clara whispered.

"I did, child. Worse still, I spoke it, and the old powers answered," Doria Nanette said. "Despite that, I was impatient. It is, and always has been, my great failing. I should have waited and continued to consolidate my hold on the northlands before venturing down to Oradale. I knew the risks, of course. The great city is crawling with detectives and prestidigitators who think themselves the last line against the darkness. I grew overconfident and thought my time had finally come, but there you were, dear." Doria Nanette gazed at Georgia. "The last Goldenheart. I failed to consider how powerful you would be, Lady Georgia. Your cousin was relatively weak. I thought for certain I could get past you."

Georgia stiffened. "You knew William?"

"Of course, I knew him. I observed him. He wasn't like you or your uncle. He had no inner-reserve and failed to see the value of his friends. Isn't that right, Mr. Blue?"

Mr. Blue shook his head, but not in disagreement. "Lord William was a complicated fellow."

"That is wizard-speak for 'he was a jerk,'" Doria Nanette said, chuckling. She stood up as shadows pooled around her feet. "Unfortunately, we must end this lovely conversation. It was such a pleasure to meet you all in person, but I was only talking long enough to gather the storm outside. Now I am going to kill you. After that, I will destroy the Three Realms and cast a long shadow over the world. From my darkness, the monsters will return. I will sing and the Midnight King will hear me beyond the void." Doria Nanette raised her arms, and a wall of force rolled out.

The house came apart around them and Georgia hurled straight into a blizzard. She landed hard on the frozen lawn, rolling in the mud and snow. In the sudden blast, she lost her grip on the magic blade.

Mr. Blue and Lady Clara were gone. Faint howls and screams were all around. Wolf shapes ran to and fro. Georgia scrambled to her feet, searching for the sword.

Doria Nanette strode from what remained of the house, wrapped in an elegant gown of living shadow. It crawled across her, whispering and cackling. No longer was she a little old woman but grew to over seven feet. Doria's eyes blazed with an infernal light, her skin turned blue, and her hair glittered with icicles. Calling out, her voice thundered the sky as lightning gathered in her fingers and danced around Mehira's Ring. Laughing, she threw lightning at Georgia.

Georgia screamed as her coat caught fire, and she had to rip it off. She realized some of her hair singed, which was sort of even more frightening. Flustered, Georgia cast around, looking for the magic sword.

Doria Nanette didn't give her time to regroup. The sorceress swept her other arm around, and a vast wind slammed into Georgia. She was lifted from the ground and tossed across the street. She landed in someone's living room in a spray of glass, snow, and blood. The residents were long gone. Blinking rapidly, she flitted on the edge of consciousness. Doria Nanette chased her across the street, planning to finish the job when azure fire flared around her shoulders. The ancient sorceress turned to face Mr. Blue.

"Begone, Doria Nanette," he cried out. "You are a foul demon of darkness and have no place in this world."

"I have been in this world longer than anyone can remember, wizard," Doria Nanette answered.

Georgia tried to get up, but her head swam. She tasted metal, and darkness flooded her eyelids. Faintly, she heard Mr. Blue call out again, followed by more cruel laughter and the howl of wolves.

Cruel laughter.

She was in her old room at Wending Way, looking in a mirror.

Old Nan was fixing her hair and singing a song. What was that song?

> *Golden sky, this we see,*
> *Clouds are fleet, this we know,*
> *All the days, the world goes by,*
> *Nimloden stands, all alone.*

It was snowing that day, too. She could see the blizzard through the window. Blue fire rolled across the windowpane, and faintly there were howls, but she took no notice. Mr. Derry had the mail in his hand, and she was reading her acceptance letter to the Cymbre School.

"I must tell Uncle Raymond," she had cried, hugging Old Nan and even Mr. Derry, who laughed in surprise. Old Nan kissed her forehead, and Georgia realized the older woman had red hair as it fell in her eyes.

"Wake up, little one," Old Nan whispered in her ear. "Wake up."

"The Master is in his library, Miss Georgia," Mr. Derry had said. "Let's go see him."

Leaving Mr. Derry and Old Nan behind, Georgia ran downstairs with the letter. Uncle Raymond was in his room, as always. Georgia could hear him talking to someone through the door. Faintly, she heard him say, "Are you quite sure it is Mehira's Ring?"

Another man's voice, someone familiar, said, "Yes. The ring is an artifact of immense power. To control it, she had to bind it with spells and a considerable share of her own will. Take it from her hand, and her spells will unravel. She will be weakened for a time and be vulnerable."

"How can I simply take it from her hand?"

"You know what you will have to do."

Usually, she would wait for Mr. Derry to announce her, but this was important. She threw the door open and went in. "Uncle, I got in!" she had cried, surprising him and his visitor. The visitor was a curious fellow—dressed all in blue tie and tails with a gold flower pin on his lapel that matched the gold of his spectacles. She knew him somehow.

"Georgia, that's wonderful. I knew you could do it," Uncle Raymond had said, smiling brilliantly. "This is my friend Mr. Blue."

"Nice to meet you," Mr. Blue said, shaking her hand.

Georgia was confused. "Wait, how can you be here?" she asked.

"Much that was once known is lost," Mr. Blue answered.

Old Nan was singing once again. Georgia turned to look at her, but she wasn't old anymore. Old Nan was young, her hair a vibrant red, and she had a quick smile for everyone.

> *Golden Georgia, time is now,*
> *Life is short, this we learn,*
> *No more days, the world burns out,*
> *Nimloden stands, all alone.*

Georgia snapped awake in the ruined living room with the wind and snow howling outside. Faintly, she heard Mr. Blue shout something, followed by a dull explosion—and then wicked laughter. She stood up unsteadily and then ran into the gale.

Ahead, a huge figure loomed.

Doria Nanette held Mr. Blue by his neck in her hand. Around her, wolves made of ice and charcoal snarled.

Georgia didn't have time to think. She sprang over the ring of wolves, spinning in the air to gain momentum, and brought her heel crashing to the side of Doria Nanette's head. She struck with such force the sorceress was startled and fell over.

Mr. Blue slumped to the ground.

Georgia rolled to her feet, snatched him up, and ran for it.

Behind her, the wolves shrieked, the sky rolled, and lightning exploded. The ground buckled, and she stumbled. A second tremor sent her and Mr. Blue to the ground. Behind them, the shadow of Doria Nanette grew in the raging wind, while the glittering blue eyes of the ice wolves encircled them.

Georgia caught the first one, latched on to its head, and slammed the creature into the ground. The wolf snapped at her, tearing the cloth of her sleeve.

The air was full of blue fire. Mr. Blue was on his feet, looking disoriented but determined. Flames whipped around harmlessly around Georgia, but the wolf squealed and pulled away.

Georgia didn't wait. Grabbing Mr. Blue's hand, she pulled the wizard away, and they ran through the darkness.

"I have you, Goldenheart. Do not run like a coward. Face me and perish. You are the last of your kind. Let the days of darkness begin on a happy note." Doria Nanette cackled.

Lightning flashed all around Georgia's feet. She caught glimpses of shattered homes and the ruined road. They were still on the street in front of Doria Nanette's house.

Lady Clara stood next to a tree, waving frantically. "Georgia, come here," she said, pointing at the ground. At Clara's feet was the magic sword.

With ice wolves snapping at her heels, Georgia closed the gap and snatched the blade up. Instant rage welled, and the blade blossomed with flame. Clara grabbed Mr. Blue, who was toppling over and pulled him behind the tree. Georgia spun and split open the head of an ice wolf with one arcing stroke, and went on to fight the next one.

Whirling, Georgia slashed through the beasts one after the other.

"No. You cannot win. You cannot," Doria Nanette cried, appearing.

Georgia charged at the sorceress, but Doria sent another wave of force, which slammed her to the ground. Georgia kept her grip on the blade and rose to her feet.

Doria Nanette howled, sounding much like one of her ice wolves, and raised her arm. Fell shadow rolled up to Mehira's Ring. Pure power began to coalesce.

With a shout, Georgia flew, bringing the blade high and then down on Doria Nanette's wrist. The sword cut her hand off clean in an explosion of wildfire. The sorceress screamed, falling backward as the shadows consumed her on the spot. "No. You cannot win. You cannot," she shrieked before vanishing.

The wind stopped. Slowly, the snow ceased.
Light returned.

Georgia strolled through the lobby in a stunning white cotton coat with elegant lacing on the collar and sleeves, refreshed and clean. Spring had finally come to the northlands, and she looked around with satisfaction.

Millie helped one of the hotel footmen with the luggage as the sun shone brightly through the windows.

Mr. Blue and Lady Clara were waiting at the front desk with Mr. Humble. "Thank you so much, Duchess Goldenheart. You saved all of our lives this week," the host said, bowing low. Behind him, most of the hotel's staff assembled, and they too bowed.

"We heard from the Earl of Simsley today. He's sending troops to secure the region around the village, along with doctors and nurses to help the locals," Lady Clara said.

"Excellent," Georgia said. "What about the dock going on sale?"

"The Earl has halted the sale until we can get back to the city and make sure that wasn't another scheme of Doria Nanette," Mr. Blue said. "Sir Gregory wasn't happy to hear he had traveled all this way for nothing, but he saw the ice wolves, so he accepted the ruling."

"I'm going to talk to Lady Emily about it, too," Georgia said. "I know she had nothing to do with her husband's business, but it seems like she should know what happened here and how it could affect her fortunes. That reminds me, we still have the murder of her husband to resolve fully."

"Indeed," Mr. Blue agreed. "Even though Doria Nanette was likely behind it somehow, we still haven't figured out how or why."

"I had a thought about that. We might be able to find

another clue as long as we are up here," Georgia said, smiling. "You remember when we were at the Hampton Madison dry docks and found the magic circle?"

"Of course, how could I forget?"

"Remember the Bill of Lading we saw? Sir Alexander signed it, but he misspelled his name. We later saw the same error on his death certificate."

Mr. Blue agreed. "You want to see who signed the adjoining Bill of Lading here at the docks where the ship launched."

Half an hour later, Georgia stood in the dock office looking at the signature and her suspicions were confirmed.

She looked at Mr. Blue and Lady Clara and said, "I think when we get back home, we need to have another dinner party."

"I think we should," Mr. Blue said. "A big one."

CHAPTER 14: YET ANOTHER PARTY.

Georgia's gown tonight was an off-white satin number with intricate edges. The finishing touch was a pearl tiara, and woven through her hair were tiny white rosebuds.

"You look perfect," Bea said across the room. She was sipping tea as she waited.

In light of the evening, Millie had gotten to her first.

Bea's gown was a splendid high-waist lilac skirt contrasted with a remarkably simple white satin blouse. She accented her dress with a lovely pearl necklace and a lilac shawl.

"You're right, of course," Georgia said as Millie placed her scabbard gently across her shoulder. Georgia glanced through the window to see another carriage pulling up outside. "Oh, Lady Emily has arrived."

When they were ready, she led the way to the library, where the real party was starting. Many of the guests were already there: Lady Emily was her usual statuesque self, still in mourning black. She carried it off with great panache, though, opting for a long silk gown that dragged behind a veil.

Chatting with Lady Emily was Mr. Blue, looking elegant in white tie and black tails with only a discreet blue rose-mallow pinned to his lapel. Naturally, he kept his wizard's walking stick in hand. The evening wasn't going to be entirely about drinking and dining, after all.

Lady Clara stood across the room, regal in a black silk dress with white buttons. She wore an up-do, with pearls decorating her hair like stars. She lifted a glass in greeting and then turned back to her chatting companion Manx Hampton.

Manx was perfectly clad in white tie and black tails.

A moment later, Mr. Turner and Mrs. Smythe arrived together. Mrs. Smythe opted to wear no adornment on her head. No doubt, this was because of the startling engagement ring on her hand, which she showed off to anyone who cared to notice.

Mr. Turner, sharp in black tie and tails, was delighted with himself.

Bea ran over and hugged Mrs. Smythe. "Congratulations to you both," Georgia said. "Is this a whirlwind romance?"

"It is," Mr. Turner said, grinning. "After our adventure in the morgue, I couldn't get my mind off Miranda. We went for tea a week later, and I proposed while we waited to be seated."

"How romantic," Bea said.

Georgia was fairly certain that if a man proposed to Bea while waiting for a seat, she would never speak to him again. Mrs. Smythe was on her second marriage, though. A certain level of expediency implied greater sincerity. The happy couple wasn't alone, either. Behind them, Chief Inspector Morris walked in, clad in perfectly acceptable attire. He nodded at Mr. Turner, smiling. Mr. Turner smiled back as Mrs. Smythe kissed her soon-to-be uncle on the cheek.

Georgia was glad to see they mended their family rift.

Mr. Bailey paused with a drink tray at Georgia's side.

Taking a flute of champagne, she asked him, "John, how are you getting on here?" In Georgia's house, Mr. Bailey would have to go back to his first name. Footmen in her service didn't get the butler's honorary of 'Mr.' She had worried Mr. Bailey would insist on keeping it from his last job, but when she made the offer, he accepted without question.

"Quite well, my lady, I cannot thank you enough," he said. "I'm so grateful to you, and I must admit, my room upstairs is like a palace."

"It all worked out then," she said, smiling.

Manx Hampton spotted the footman and did a double-take. "Mr. Bailey," he said, blinking rapidly, "I am quite surprised to find you here."

"Oh, the duchess was so kind as to offer me a position in her house, sir," John replied. "Please, call me John, sir."

"John. Yes, of course," Manx stammered.

"As it happened, I needed to expand my staff a bit," Georgia said. "Mr. Derry and Millie determined together that an additional parlor maid and footman were needed to round off the house. We haven't found a good maid yet, but I quickly realized I already knew an unemployed footman, so we offered it to John. I assume you approve, Manx? You gave him such a lovely letter of recommendation."

"Certainly," he said quickly. "We were quite sorry to see, er, John go."

Georgia was reasonably sure that was not the truth, but she smiled and tilted her head.

Two more guests—Lady Johanna Price and her husband, Sir John Price—arrived. Lady Johanna was elegant in a full blue satin gown with a daring neckline. Her husband was impeccable in a white tie and black tails, and he smiled broadly.

"Welcome to our little get-together," Georgia said as they entered. "I think you know most of the other guests already, Lady Johanna."

"Yes," Lady Johanna said, looking around with some surprise at the room. She nodded to Lady Emily, who half-smiled back. They weren't precisely cold in their movements, but there was a certain formality. "Allow me to formally introduce my husband, Sir John Price."

"Well met, Sir John," Georgia said. "I must tell you I am a tremendous fan of your bakeries. We based tonight's dessert on one of your classic recipes. I hope you will not judge it too harshly."

Sir John blinked rapidly, obviously surprised, but also delighted. "Duchess, you honor me tremendously."

"Excellent," Georgia said. "Come in and have a drink. Before we all go into dinner, we're having cocktails and will embark on some mischief."

"Mischief? How exciting," Lady Johanna said as John brought them two flutes of champagne.

"I've never heard anyone describe their dinner party with the word 'mischief' before," Sir John said.

"Ah yes, our last two guests," Georgia said as Mr. and Mrs. Duckworth arrived. Mrs. Duckworth was wrapped once again in her green dress from years before.

Mr. Duckworth was already drunk and had another stain on his collar.

Georgia decided it was best to let the pair be their authentic selves and nodded to Francis and Mr. Derry. They shut the doors to the library, leaving Georgia alone with her guests and John, the new footman.

"Perfect," she said. "Everyone has a drink? John is over there if you need it freshened. Now that we are all here, I thought we would get right to it. Originally, I was going to have Mr. Blue handle this part since he is the real detective."

"The real detective?" Lady Johanna asked.

"Well, Mr. Blue is a trained detective," Georgia said. "I am still learning the craft. I would defer to him, but he insisted I do the honors tonight."

"It is your house, after all," Mr. Blue said, standing next to Lady Clara.

They were both smiling.

"As most of you guessed, tonight's dinner party will be

more than that," Georgia said. "Hopefully, it will still be fun, of course. Now let's discuss the murders."

"Oh, dear," Lady Johanna and Mrs. Smythe said in unison.

"I'll begin," Georgia said. "For me, this all started two months ago at the Hampton House party. That was the day before I was to go up the mountain with Mr. Blue and begin my formal role as Knight-Protector of the Three Realms from Dragons. It was at that party where I met many of you and witnessed the tragic death of Sir Alexander Madison."

From the corner of her eye, Georgia saw Lady Emily twitch and rub at her eyes. She felt terrible about that, but it was necessary. She continued, "Our first thought was poison, even though there were problems with the theory. Sir Alexander was affected too quickly for arsenic or polonium. Still, his symptoms were in keeping with one of those agents as a murder weapon. We began our search from that point of view."

She gazed at everyone in the room. Not surprisingly, they were all wide-eyed and pale, except for Bea, Mr. Blue, and Lady Clara. They were watching the expressions of the others, too. A few in the room were listening in mere curiosity, as they should be.

"We enlisted the aid of Lady Clara Gaye, the Witch of Volusia, because her coven knows more about poison than almost anyone," Georgia said. "She confirmed there was no poison in the cocktail glasses we retrieved from the scene."

"Sir Alexander wasn't poisoned?" Mrs. Duckworth asked, blinking rapidly. "Wait. Can you start over?"

"I cannot start over," Georgia said. "Fear not, Mrs. Duckworth, it will all make sense eventually. You see, the real weapon of murder was something far less mundane than poison. Lady Clara's sisters found traces of bat's blood in a glass, and Mr. Blue commented it sounded more like a magic potion."

"Oh, good heavens," Sir John Price said, shaking his head. "We've arrived there already, have we? I had no idea this invitation was for a night of live theatre." He stood, preparing to take his wife and leave.

"I suggest you stay put, Sir John," Mr. Blue said quietly. "We have only just begun, and you will find more of interest as we go."

"You cannot leave, Sir John," Georgia said. "I invoke my ducal privilege. You must stay until I release you from my home."

"My word," Sir John said, sitting down again. Lady Johanna quietly took his hand in hers and smiled to reassure him.

Georgia continued, "We were ready to embrace the whole magic potion idea later. You see, a creature of shadow visited my home and tried to kill my staff and me. Fortunately, I was able to dispatch the thing with the help of this." She drew the magic blade, and it glowed with a pale yellow light. Everyone gasped, of course, because it's not every day you get to see a magic sword being magical. "Normally, this blade stays cool and never shines with light. Tonight is different, though. It only glows in proximity to supernatural evil."

"This is absurd," Manx Hampton said, wiping a tear from his eye. "I can't believe you are forcing me to revisit the worst tragedy of my life."

"In the end, it will all be worth it," Georgia said. "As it happened, we solved the bat's blood question fairly quickly—one of the guests at the party was wearing a lipstick that had it in the formula. It is more common than one might think these days. Whoever drank from that glass got it in there, and the witches caught it later. Still, it did lead us away for a moment."

"How trivial," Sir John Price said. "Lipstick?"

"I couldn't agree more. Lipstick is very trivial," Georgia said. "It was unrelated, but you are only objecting because you were not involved, Sir John. Your day-to-day has nothing to do with the murder. Understandably you're hoping to spare your wife the ugliness of it all. When your father-in-law was murdered, that certainly was another matter."

"What?" Lady Johanna jumped in her seat. "Father wasn't murdered. He died of natural causes."

"He was dying, but it wasn't natural," Lady Clara said. "He was going to move ahead with his lawsuit against Hampton Madison, but that couldn't be allowed to happen. If he proceeded, the authorities would send someone to inspect the warehouse as evidence during discovery. They would have found the blood zombies. The real killer knew this, so he acted."

Georgia watched as everyone in the room fell quiet.

Finally, Manx Hampton stood up. "I'm leaving," he said. "You have no right to cause me this pain. I do not care about your ducal privilege."

"But you are the killer," Georgia said. "You cannot leave, Manx…or should I say 'Matison.'"

Manx Hampton stopped walking and looked at her. "How do you know that name?"

"It took us a while to put it together. You were forging Sir Alexander's name on documents—your first name is only one letter different from his last name. Your father named you that way to honor his old friend. The urge to spell it correctly, well, correctly for you that is, would be strong. Something Mrs. Smythe said when we met popped into my mind recently. Her maiden name before her first husband was Smith, and she said she had difficulty adjusting to Smythe. At one point, your brother mentioned once that you called him 'Ollie' because you couldn't pronounce his name as a child. He even said the nickname stuck. At the time, it didn't occur to me, but he must have suffered the same problem with you. We pieced together the truth while in Hendon.

"Two years ago, just before you sailed on the *Gladys* down the East River with the vampire bat onboard, you signed the Bill of Lading at the source with your real name—because you were legitimately signing a document."

"How desperate and absurd you are. That does not make me a murderer," Manx said, shaking his head. "I will not stay here and be accused of this. Duchess or not, you have no proof and no right to keep me in your house. Next, I suppose you are going to tell the police I am a vampire."

"Technically, you are a Revenant—a person in partial transition to a state of un-death learning dark magic. However, you no longer have a teacher. Doria Nanette is defeated," Georgia said. She held up Mehira's Ring so everyone could see it. Manx stopped in his tracks and stared. "We know how she corrupted you and the path you walked. We even know why you killed your father, Manx. He was a traditional man and was never going to make you his heir. He was always going to will it all to Ollie, wasn't he? Ollie was born first, so that meant he would get the lion's share. It didn't matter that you were twins. He wasn't going to split the fortune. Even though Ollie was born, what, twelve minutes before you? What I don't quite understand: Why kill Sir Alexander. He was out of the picture."

Manx's face twisted as he stared hungrily at the ring of power. Finally, he tore his eyes away and glared at Georgia. "Father was a fool, and Ollie was an even bigger one," he spat.

For a moment, she thought he would storm out, which would get him nowhere. Beyond the front door, Chief Inspector Morris had half a dozen men waiting. Georgia also had the magic sword, not to mention Mr. Blue and Lady Clara. Manx wasn't leaving. Perhaps he realized it too, as his features softened.

"Tell me what happened," Georgia whispered. "Start at the beginning."

Manx's shoulders slumped. He looked at her and said,

"I went to the north the first time four years ago, and she was there. At the time, I thought she was just some northern girl. We met at that hotel when it opened. Doria Nanette didn't look like—like the way she looks. Does that make sense?"

"Yes," Mr. Blue said.

"She was beautiful, and we had a wonderful time. I was doing my father's business. He wanted that infernal dock at the mouth of the East River. I went up there and had it built, and then I began the building of the other docks along the way. Father wanted to consolidate an easy line of trade on the river, and I made it happen for him. People know you can find a Hampton Madison dock in any town on the river. It worked. When I finished, he told me one day I would make a fine employee for Ollie."

Georgia shook her head. "You killed Ollie, too."

"I stopped his heart as he ran," Manx said. "I can do that with this. That is how I killed Sir Alexander, too." He held his hand up, showing off the gold ring with the black opal. It looked like a less impressive version of Mehira's Ring.

Lady Emily gasped.

"Why did you kill Sir Alexander?" Georgia asked.

Manx looked insane. "He knew something was happening. The men on the docks mentioned him coming around the week before. He was asking about the warehouse and the *Gladys*. When I saw him at the party, I decided to act. I also knew his death would embarrass Father and his stupid friends. It was our party, not his. Instead of just celebrating, he had to turn it into Ollie's night. I told you, Lady Georgia, everyone loved Ollie's light."

"I remember you said that," Georgia said. "You were the dark, and he was the light." In this case, he meant that literally. From the corner of her eye, Georgia saw Bea weeping quietly.

It was Lady Emily who spoke next. "Alexander missed

the work," she said, glaring at Manx. "He wasn't on to your disgusting secret. He was bored. In a month or two, he would have gone back to retirement and would have been fine."

"I realize that now," Manx said, looking almost ashamed. "I should have let him live."

"You should have let all of them live," Lady Clara said. "You should never have taken up with Doria Nanette."

Manx laughed. "She had me from the beginning, Lady Clara. There's no going back." He pulled the ring from his finger. "I suppose this is worthless now. You have the ring of power, and Doria is gone. You killed her."

"She lives, but in a diminished state," Mr. Blue said, taking the ring from Manx. "We may see her again one day, in about a hundred years."

The constables came and took Manx Hampton away, much to the relief of everyone. Lady Emily departed a few minutes later. She had no stomach for the party after that. Lady Johanna and Sir John Price also left quietly.

Once they were all gone, Georgia turned back to her remaining guests. The Duckworths were already on their third round of champagne, so she decided to catch up.

"I have no idea how we are going to charge Mr. Manx Hampton," Chief Inspector Morris said. "I suspect there are no laws about vampire lords or whatever he was."

"You won't need to charge him," Mr. Blue said. "He cursed himself when he became linked to Doria Nanette. As awful as it sounds, I will be surprised if he lives past the morning, now that he has given up his ring, and the truth is before us."

CHAPTER 15: LOOSE ENDS.

"Bea, it's been six months," Georgia said, exasperated. "There hasn't been one single vampire bat, revenant, ghost, or other creature from the abyss during that time. Everything seems to be fine."

"Thanks," Bea said, curling up on the library sofa in a frumpy house dress, apron, and not even a bit of blush on her cheeks. Her tea was piping hot, and at her side was a copy of *The Cymbre Guide to Teaching*. "I'm perfectly fine right where I am. No more husbands. No more infernal brother-in-law telling me where I can go and what I can do. No more whatever. It's a teaching life for this Cymbre girl."

Georgia rolled her eyes. "Fine, Mr. Blue is going to the Earl of Cadwin's Delicate Rose Ball with me. If it is an enticement, we expect to see Lady Emily Madison there. You know she's been running the family business, now that every Hampton is dead. She is doing a wonderful job with it."

"Have fun, Georgia. See you when you get back."

Georgia shook her head. She found Millie at the top of the stairs admiring the large stained glass window. In the waning light, gold and lilac hues made a paradise of the hall separating the men from the women's servant quarters.

"Millie, I suppose it's time," Georgia said. "Miss Beatrice will not be joining, so we might as well head out early."

"Yes, my lady," Millie said, picking up the magic sword in its scabbard and following her downstairs.

John, the new footman, was in the hall. "My lady, you have a visitor: Viscount Lord William Reade and company."

Georgia glanced at the front hall, where Lord William was chatting amiably with Mr. Blue—and Bea's brother-in-law, Lord Wickham. Georgia blinked rapidly. Bea's mother was stepping out of the carriage behind them, followed by all four of Bea's sisters. "Oh dear," Georgia breathed. She turned to Millie. "Change of plan. Millie, get Miss Bea out of the library. Take her through the back and get upstairs. Make her presentable and radiant. She's about to have company. I think today is about to be the best day of her life."

"Yes, my lady," Millie said with a grin, breaking into a run down the adjoining hall.

"John, fetch Mr. Derry. I know I gave him the night off, but he's probably just sitting in his room anyway. After that, get the kitchen staff on their feet and put them into formal serving clothes," Georgia said to the footman. "I'll be down in a moment with instructions."

"Yes, my lady." John went through another door to the basement.

Georgia checked herself in a mirror and then strolled out to the foyer. "Hello everyone," she said, smiling. "This is a lovely surprise."

"I'm so sorry to intrude without notice, Duchess Goldenheart," Lord William Reade said. "I hoped I might speak with Miss Beatrice on a matter of importance." Nervously, he smiled and shuffled from foot to foot.

"You are always welcome in this house, Viscount,"

Georgia said. They nodded formally. She turned to Wickham and tilted her head slightly. "Lord Wickham." She hadn't spoken to Wickham since the Irvingdale social. His clumsy attempt to find her a suitor was still too near.

"Duchess Goldenheart," Lord Wickham said, also tilting. Nothing in his demeanor even hinted that he might have realized he crossed a line. Alas, this was not the time to bring it up.

Mr. Derry appeared behind her and whispered, "The library is now open, my lady. Francis and I will serve drinks. We are preparing the dining room."

Georgia turned back to the group, saying, "Mr. Derry will take you into the library. Make yourselves comfortable. Bea will be down in just a moment. I will be there shortly, as well." She watched as the men went in, followed by Lady Briana Irvingdale, and finally Bea's four sisters Bernadette, Bridget, Barbara, and Bonnie. The group was so quiet it bordered on alarming. Once they were in the library, Georgia dashed down the stairs to the kitchen where Mrs. Cotton was at the center of a growing storm. To one side, Eunice was setting cookies and cakes on a tray. To the other side was another girl, whom Georgia had never met. The girl was in a black maid uniform with an odd little cap. She worked for someone else's house.

Mrs. Cotton turned to her. "My lady, we are nearly there with the appetizers and the last of the goose. I'm just bulking it into a gallimaufry, served with asparagus, potatoes, and a light green salad. We have scallops roasting on the side. Oh, we borrowed a few helpers from Lady Compston down the road. I hope you don't mind. Her man told us it would be no problem, as Lady Compston is at her country house. We'll keep them down here and behind closed doors while the regular staff attends to the guests."

"Good thinking, Mrs. Cotton," Georgia said, "I'll leave you to it." She didn't wait for a response and hurried upstairs into the library. Mr. Blue was chatting with Lord

William and Lord Wickham near the fireplace. Across the room, Lady Briana and Bea's sisters all sat quietly in a row from oldest to youngest.

The ladies started to stand as Georgia entered, but she waved them to stay seated. "Does everyone have a cocktail?" she asked. "Are we comfortable?"

"I suspect Mother would have preferred something less spontaneous," Bonnie whispered.

"Lord Wickham is wasting no time on this," Bernadette said.

"Nor should he," Georgia approved.

Bea appeared in the doorway in a sleek black cotton Spencer jacket with a high white waist skirt and mutton sleeves. Her collar arched with a smart button front. Bea's hair was in a black lace ribbon, and her face had just enough blush to look like she had been out in the garden until now. Millie was a master. Bea entered the room slowly, wide-eyed, and curtseyed low. "Hello," she said, "what a lovely surprise."

Lady Irvingdale and all four sisters discreetly dabbed at their eyes. Georgia smiled at them reassuringly and then turned back. Mr. Blue, she noted, also appeared to catch something in his eye and turned away for a moment.

Lord William Reade almost tripped over himself. "Miss Beatrice," he breathed. "I wanted to talk to you. I—I am not one for this sort of... no, that's wrong."

Lord Wickham, of all people, cleared his throat and said, "Bea, you should take a seat. Lord William, start over."

Bea sat next to her mother. Lord William coughed and smiled. He turned to Bea. "Miss Bea, ever since we met at the ball, months ago, I have relived our conversation. It was so easy talking to you about every subject. I felt like I was talking to an equal. I know how that sounds. But it is true. By now, you must know the scheme the Dowager-Countess Hermione concocted on our behalf with my great aunt. At the time, I was content to let it be only that—a fantasy—two old ladies remembering the long-lost Dale family or whatever. But I kept thinking about you and how much I enjoyed simply talking to you. Your mind was what struck me at first. Later, when my great aunt told me she did prefer the idea of a descendent of the Dales— well, I didn't quite know what to think of that. And then you and that Hampton fellow made your plan. I decided to let it be. I know the difference between us. It would always be there."

Bea blinked rapidly.

"I'm sorry," Lord William said, looking down. "I am much better at negotiating trade deals with foreign powers than I am speaking to proper ladies about matters of the heart. It is—it is a problem. Bea, I am in love with you. We only met once, but that is the way it is. I cannot help it. I cannot stop thinking about you, and I don't care what people say. I knew it the moment we met., but with the way society works, I felt I had no options. I love the way you know everything and nothing at all, and yet you are the most charming person I ever met. I could spend the rest of my days waking up next to you and just hearing whatever trivia you learned that week—whether it's about farm equipment, obscure business practices in the dress industry, or even why it always seems to be raining in Cadwin."

"Occluded fronts," Bea said.

"I beg your pardon?" Lord William asked, smiling.

Bea looked around, blinking rapidly. "Well, I mean, Cadwin is located at the delta of the great River Palas, and also at the end of the southern Jetstream off the coast. The convergence of natural forces doubles the duration of the rainy season every year."

"This is precisely what I am talking about," Lord William said. Bea's mother and sisters all made a low noise. Georgia had to lean against a table. Even Lord Wickham looked like he might have to sit down. Lord William looked at Bea again. "Miss Beatrice Irvingdale, I ask you now with no hope other than our happiness: will you marry me?" He pulled a simple gold band from his pocket.

"Yes," Bea said, tears running down her face, "yes, William, I will marry you." She held out her hand, he put the ring on her finger—and they kissed.

It was all a blur afterward. Everyone was hugging, and Georgia even embraced Wickham. Mr. Derry alerted her that dinner was ready, and she eventually guided them into the dining room to enjoy a very odd last-minute dinner of goose and scallops. When it was all done, and the men went to smoke in the other room, Georgia looked at Bea. "Any more clouds to worry about?" she asked.

"It was all just a whiff of cumulus," Bea said. "You were right, Georgia."

FINI (POUR L'INSTANT)

APPENDIX:
CHARACTERS, PLACES, AND THINGS

Lady Georgia Goldenheart–Duchess of the House of Goldenheart, Knight-Protector of the Three Realms from Dragons and bearer of the magic sword Anamagal.

Anamagal—the magic sword of the Goldenhearts, its formal name is Anamagal the Sun Blade of the East.

Miss Beatrice Irvingdale—one of Georgia's best friends, and fifth daughter of the 8th Baronet of Irvingdale.

Mr. Blue–wizard, leader of the Order of the Blue Wizards.

Lady Clara Gaye—the witch of Volusia, member of the Lunar Circle.

IRVINGDALES

Lady Breanna Irvingdale, Countess-Dowager—Bea's mother

Lord John Wickham, 9th Baronet of Irvingdale—Bea's brother-in-law, and head of the family.

Lady Bernadette Wickham—Bea's older sister, married to John Wickham.

Mrs. Bridgett Elliot—Bea's older sister, married to Sir Roger Elliot.

Mrs. Bonnie Bertram—Bea's older sister, married to Sir Michael Bertram.

Mrs. Barbara Crawford—Bea's older sister, married to Sir Henry Crawford.

GOLDENHEART HOUSE

Mr. Derry—the elderly butler.
Francis—the pristine footman.
Millie—the notable ladies maid.
Mr. Ellsworth—the sulking gardener.
Eunice—the maid who cleans everything else.
Mrs. Cotton—the harried but gifted cook.

OTHER CHARACTERS and PERSONS OF NOTE

Mr. Hampton—patriarch of the Hampton family.

Matison 'Manx' Hampton—one of the twin sons of Mr. Hampton.

Colin 'Ollie' Hampton—the other twin son of Mr. Hampton.

Sir Alexander Madison—former business partner of Mr. Hampton.

Lady Emily Madison—widow of Sir Alexander Madison.

Mrs. Miranda Smythe—wealthy widow suspected to be a writer for the *Weekly Men's Journal* under the pseudonym of Mr. Adina.

Mr. Tom Turner—went to school with Ollie.

Mr. and Mrs. Duckworth—a couple who live down the street from the Hamptons.

Lord Christopher Hart—the teenaged Earl of Cadwin.

Mr. Clanahan—Lady Emily's solicitor.

Mr. Stackhouse—Lady Georgia's solicitor.

Miss Blue—a wizard who works with Mr. Blue.

(another) Mr. Blue—the doorman at the Order of the Blue.

Chief Inspector Morris—constable and Mr. Turner's uncle.

Sir Aubrey Algernon—former merchant competitor who lost his warehouse to Hampton Madison. Lady Johanna Price—daughter of Sir Aubrey, and noted restauranteur.

Sir John Price—husband of Lady Johanna, and owner of the Price Bakery chain.

Lord William Reade—Viscount of Simsley in Volusia, and a handsome roguish nobleman.

Lady Lucinda Kilgore—daughter of a baronet in Volusia.

Lady Carlotta Landsmere—daughter of a baronet in Volusia.

Sir Richard Bourne—a knight from Volusia.

Lady Hermione Nisbett—Dowager Countess of the House of Nisbett.

Lady Osibeth Crighton—Countess of Vexbury.

Sir Alfie Crighton—nephew to Lady Osibeth.

Lady Constance Greenheart—Countess of Grandhall.

Mr. Lucas 'Luke' Greenheart—Lady Counscience's youngest son.

Gaffey—foreman of the dry docks at Hampton Gilmore.

Irma—a woman who works in the manifest office at Hampton Madison.

MONSTERS

Alpon—a type of vampire bat that looks like a human figure with leathery wings shrouded in shadow.

Nimloden—the name of the Tree of the Mountain.

Lady Gwendolyn Goldenheart—ancestor who lived in 3904c.e.

Mehira—legendary queen of vampires.

Hoo Adoon—ancient spirit of the underworld that looks a wolf made of ice and darkness.

Doria Nanette—an ancient spirit of darkness.

ANCIENT ROYALS

Prince Glendon Oakes—ancient prince of Findor.

Prince Dalton Rose—ancient prince of Palas.

Prince Damon Mather—ancient prince of Volusia.

King Tobias Hart—the first king of the Three Realms.

Queen Antonia Hart—the first queen of the Three Realms.

KNIGHTLY ORDERS

Order of the Eagle—the highest ranking order of generals and admirals.

Order of the Buck—nobles of military family and training.

Order of the Horse—honorary knights (Sir and Dame) granted to non-military.

Knight-Protector—one of the highest knightly titles in the Three Realms. Anyone with this title is automatically considered a general or admiral, should the times require it.

VOLUSIA

Pere Castle—haunted hotel in Hendon village.

Mrs. Clutchey—the librarian in Hendon.

Charity—Lady Clara's ladies maid.

Mr. Humble—comedian at Pere Castle Resort.

Sir Gregory Middleton—former ambassador to Dora. Georgia met him at Pere Castle when he was planning to buy the docks from Hampton Madison.

Mr. Gerard Middleton—son of Sir Gregory Middleton.

Lady Martha Clutterbuck—daughter of the great poet Lord Martin Clutterbuck.

Mr. Bennet Gower—businessman from Oradale.

Mr. Seymour Bridgman—businessman from Oradale.

Mr. Douglas Jackman—businessman from Oradale.

Mr. Warren Wynch—businessman from Oradale.

ABOUT THE AUTHOR

I am a writer and illustrator.

I have written and illustrated several works other people found very clever and later told me how they felt. It was both gratifying and a relief. I am, and always have been a huge fantasy, mystery, and regency era fiction fan. My favorite authors are JRR Tolkien, Jane Austen, and Agatha Christie. I also have about forty other favorite authors, but opted not to include them in this list for the sake of brevity.

If you enjoyed this novel and want to see more of the Duchess Georgia Goldenheart and her friends, please visit my website and sign up for my newsletter. I promise not to spam you.

MPATRICKDUGGAN.NET

THANK YOU

Thank you so very much to all of the people who
helped me complete this work of fiction, either with
advice, reassurance, artwork, or patience:

Alan Pierce
Joseph Naftali
Monique Snyman
S.L. Shelton
Nicole Jones-Dion
Rachel Fain
Katy Duggan
Sheila Noonen
Lisa Harris
Italia Gandolfo
Liana Gardner
Mikki Noble
Bob and Joyce Pierce
John and Virginia Duggan

OTHER BOOKS BY M. PATRICK DUGGAN

Myths & Monsters Grown-Up Coloring Book 1
Myths & Monsters Grown-Up Coloring Book 2
Myths & Monsters Grown-Up Coloring Book 3
Myths & Monsters Story Idea Book
Moon Princesses & Space Monsters Coloring Book
Mandalas & Punctuation Marks Coloring Book

What Lurks in Foster's Grove – Adventure Module

Foodang, comic book series
NUOS, comic book series

COVER ARTIST

Mikki Noble – Paracoze Designs –
paracozedesigns.com

Paracoze Designs began in February 2020, but Mikki likes to say the thought of starting her own design company had been brewing for over a decade, as she'd always been into graphic design--even going to college to study Web and Graphic Design.

Mikki is an author herself, so she knows what authors go through and she's here to help. It's her dream to help make your book the best possible design it can be.

EDITOR

Monique Snyman – moniquesnyman.com

Monique Snyman's mind is a confusing bedlam of glitter and death, where candy-coated gore is found in abundance and homicidal unicorns thrive. Sorting out the mess in her head is particularly irksome before she's ingested a specific amount of coffee, which is equal to half the recommended intake of water for humans per day. When she's not playing referee to her imaginary friends or trying to overdose on caffeine, she's doing something with words—be it writing, reading, or fixing all the words.

Monique Snyman lives in Pretoria, South Africa, with her husband and an adorable Chihuahua. She's the author of MUTI NATION, a horror novel set in South Africa, and the Bram Stoker Award® nominated novel, THE NIGHT WEAVER, which is the first installment in a dark fantasy series for young adults.